What was it about this guy that had her acting so out of character, so insanely weird?

She wasn't the kind of person who lied to herself—and she wasn't about to start now. She was hot for Chancellor, homeless or otherwise. The man made her pulse race and she couldn't even put a name to what else occurred to her physically. She just knew she felt flushed all over whenever he was around. No one—but no one—had ever made her feel this out of control.

Laylah's parents, semiretired television news correspondents Jack and Selma Versailles, would think their youngest child had totally lost her mind. Brandon, her entertainment-correspondent brother, would rib her unmercifully if he ever found out about the man she secretly admired. And her uppity, well-to-do sixty-seven and sixty-nine-year-old aunts Cora and Gertrude, both celebrity newspaper columnists, might be stunned to learn that their niece was hopelessly infatuated with a homeless man....

Books by Linda Hudson-Smith

Kimani Romance

Forsaking All Others
Indiscriminate Attraction

LINDA HUDSON-SMITH

turned to writing as a healing and creative outlet in 2000, after illness forced her to leave a successful marketing and public relations career. Dedicated to inspiring readers to overcome adversity against all odds, she now has twenty published novels to her credit, spanning an array of genres that include romance, contemporary and inspirational/ Christian fiction. Linda has traveled the world as an enthusiastic witness to other cultures and lifestyles, which has helped her craft stories set in a variety of exotic and romantic locations.

For the past seven years, Hudson-Smith has served as the national spokesperson for the Lupus Foundation of America, and has made Lupus awareness one of her top priorities. She travels around the country delivering inspirational messages of hope.

Linda Hudson-Smith was born in Canonsburg, Pennsylvania, and raised in Washington, D.C. She furthered her educational goals by attending Duff's Business Institute in Pittsburgh, Pennsylvania. The mother of two sons, Linda shares a residence with her husband, Rudy, in League City, Texas. To find out more about this extraordinary author go to her Web site, www.lindahudsonsmith.com.

LINDA HUDSON-SMITH

Indiscriminate Attraction

KIMANI
ROMANCE

KIMANI PRESS™

ISBN-13: 978-0-373-86066-1
ISBN-10:   0-373-86066-8

INDISCRIMINATE ATTRACTION

Copyright © 2008 by Linda Hudson-Smith

www.kimanipress.com

Printed in U.S.A.

Dear Reader,

I sincerely hope you enjoyed reading *Indiscriminate Attraction* from cover to cover. I'm very interested in hearing your comments and thoughts on the romance story featuring Laylah Versailles and Chancellor Kingston, a couple who meet under very unusual circumstances.

If you are interested in receiving a reply, please enclose a self-addressed, stamped envelope with all your correspondence, and mail to: Linda Hudson-Smith, 16516 El Camino Real, Box 174, Houston, TX 77062. Or you can e-mail your comments to LHS4romance@yahoo.com. Please also visit my Web site and sign my guest book at www.lindahudsonsmith.com.

Linda Hudson-Smith

This book is dedicated to all the wonderful
staff members at Dental Etc:

You guys are the very best.
Thanks for all your unyielding support.

Mitchel Mai, D.D.S.

Veronica Morales

Trini Pham

Hope Salcedo

I want to acknowledge each and every one of you for your
love, support and dedication. Thanks to all of you who helped
to make my first annual Book Club Luncheon a huge success.
It was such a pleasure hosting each book-club member.

Kumosa Book Club
Cover2Cover Book Club
Coffee, Tea & Read Book Club
Turning Pages Book Club
One Really Awesome Woman Book Club
Thomasine C. Smith—Palatka, Florida
Mable B. Mosley—Palatka, Florida
Ronald and Sheila Wright
Mitchel Mai, DDS
Ralph Tharp, M.D.
The 3-Gs Grace, Georgia and Geraldine—
    my Winnsboro connections
Sydney and Gwen Mulkey
Donna Hill—Donna Hill Promotions
Misherald Brown—Donna Hill Promotions
Rosemary Poole
Kristina Smith
Leroy Hamilton—Photos by Hamilton
Mattie Watson—Little Rock AFB Exchange

Chapter 1

As Laylah looked up at the large clock on the back wall of the *L.A. Press* newspaper office, where she worked as a top-notch feature-story reporter, her light gray eyes expressed shock. Totally lost in her deadline story, she had also lost track of time and everything else. Since she had less than an hour to get her assignment in, she really had to step it up. This was a very important feature she couldn't dare to fudge on, not that she ever would. Laylah was a very conscientious reporter.

Ashley Roberson, a seven-year-old child, had been missing for over a week now. Thus far, not one clue had turned up. Byron Gates, the lead detective, had told Laylah he'd rarely worked on a case where there wasn't at least something to go on. "Nothing about this story makes any sense to me," he'd said at the end of the interview.

Ashley allegedly had been abducted from her own bedroom in the wee hours of the morning. The timing was just speculation on Renee Matthews's part, since the single mother hadn't discovered the child missing until 7:00 a.m., when she'd gone to the child's bedroom to get her ready for the summer day-care program. Then Renee had dialed 911.

This sad and interesting story had intrigued her from the onset. Laylah always took great pride in her job at *L.A. Press*—she was known for writing her features in painstaking detail and with loads of passion. Once she was given an assignment, she went right to work on it, lending it her undivided attention until it was in actual print. Numerous awards had already been bestowed upon her for excellence in journalism and for her strong commitment to community service.

Laylah also penned various articles for several nationwide magazines; she positively lived and breathed her craft. The "All Around Town" column she wrote was a favorite to many.

"Laylah," Joe Angleton called out from across the room, "March needs to see you in his office right away." Joe chuckled lowly, knowing how their personalities clashed. Sparks flew whenever they were in the same room.

March Riverton was the boss, yet he wasn't nearly as knowledgeable about running the newspaper office as Laylah. Not only did she know her job inside and out, she was able to execute everyone else's duties with relative ease, including March's.

"Ugh!" Laylah had no desire to butt heads with her boss yet again, especially not when she had more important things to take care of. March always seemed to know when she was a bit behind on her assignments, never failing to call her into his office at the most crucial, inopportune times. Most of what he'd call her in for was pure nonsense.

If anyone would ask Laylah why March was so hard on her, she'd be inclined to tell them she believed he had a romantic interest in her. While he was a very attractive man—tall, slim and velvety dark—she wasn't the least bit attracted to him. In her opinion, no chemistry whatsoever existed between them. His sense of humor was about as dry as a bale of hay—and his cockiness was anything but a turn-on for her.

March had once been employed as a senior editor for a San Francisco–based newspaper. Shortly after he'd landed the heralded position of editor in chief with *L.A. Press*, he'd made his intentions toward Laylah known. When his initial flirtatious hints had gone totally ignored by her, it seemed to her that he'd made a conscious decision to annoy her instead of continuing to try to charm his way into her heart.

The entire staff thought he was a serious pain in the rear. Well, she thought, there is one exception. Amelia Markham thought March was the cat's meow, the light in lightning. She was often horrible to Laylah because she also knew March had a *romantic jones* for Laylah.

The intercom line on Laylah's desk phone suddenly buzzed, signaling an internal call. "Yes, March." Intuitively, she had known it was him calling to personally make his demands known. He loved to rub her the wrong way, as often as possible.

"Did Joe not give you my message?" March inquired in a sarcastic tone.

"You know he did. Can you give me a few more minutes to wrap things up?"

"*Right now* works best for me, Miss Versailles. Step on it." He had spoken in a tone that wouldn't have brooked an argument from anyone other than her.

Laylah all but slammed down the receiver. Before closing the software program she was working in, she saved her last entries. Since she hoped to get right back to the job at hand, she didn't bother to turn off her computer.

She looked youthful and fresh, dressed in white denim jeans

and a cute red and white polka-dot sleeveless blouse that fit her slightly curvaceous figure to a T. After getting to her feet, she smoothed her hands down the thighs of her jeans, as if she thought the gesture would press out the slight wrinkles caused by sitting.

As she passed by Joe's desk, she rolled her eyes to the back of her head to show him just how annoyed she was with March's untimely disruption. Her co-worker was a great guy, sweet as he could be, and they had a great relationship.

Thirty-seven-year-old Joe stood just shy of six feet tall, possessing one of those hard bodies most men worked doubly hard to achieve. Fair complected, with bourbon-colored eyes, he was a dazzling light that brightened up everyone's day. He wasn't without a mischievous streak, but Joe was as harmless as a newborn baby.

As Joe was a very spiritual man, numerous staff members sought him out when they were down on their luck. He was always good for an uplifting word of prayer and also a guiding hand. He was the type of man who'd help anyone in need, the type who never met any strangers.

Without bothering to knock on the door, Laylah entered March's office. Seeing his feet propped up on the desk only annoyed her more, causing a bit of red to infuse her rich, honey-brown complexion. *He is such an arrogant, macho-male animal.* Nodding in his direction, Laylah took the chair in front of the large desk.

"Good morning to you, too," he snapped in a gruff tone. "How are the plans coming for Patricia Blakeley's retirement dinner?"

No, he didn't call me in here for that! Laylah seethed inwardly. As mad as she was with March, her expression belied how truly upset she was over his insensitivity toward her situation. She was only behind on her deadline because of all the other assignments he'd piled up on her. Many of them were his own. "Everything to do with the retirement party I turned over to Constance Waller, so you'll have to ask her."

"Excuse me? When I give you an assignment, it's inappropriate for you to delegate it. Therefore, you need to get the information I'm after. STAT."

As Laylah got to her feet, she held her temper in check. "As you wish, sir." Knowing March hated it whenever she went formal on him, she celebrated inwardly at the frustrated look on his face.

March snorted. "I expect you to report back to me within the next half hour."

Tired of constantly going toe-to-toe with March, Laylah had begun to seriously consider the generous job offer she'd recently received from *L.A. Press*'s top rivaling newspaper, the *California Herald*. The salary they'd offered her was off the chain. The only major drawback was the commute. She lived only a short distance away from where she currently worked and the *California Herald* was much farther.

Besides the long commute, Laylah had her eye trained on March's job. As sure as she was breathing, she didn't expect him to make it much longer in his current position at *L.A. Press*. He just didn't have what it took to run a newspaper this size. There were too many serious complaints about his lack of ability. Several had reached corporate level.

She immediately went to Constance's office, hoping she had the information March needed so she could get back to work. Since when did a retirement party become more important than a feature story, especially when it involved a missing seven-year-old child? If Laylah dared to ask March that very question, he would declare war on her.

Constance welcomed Laylah into her office with a tooth-paste-white smile and a slight nod of her head. "What can I do you for, sweet girl?"

Laylah laughed at the backward way Constance had posed the question. "The retirement party for Patricia. Can you give me an update?"

"I'd be happy to. Have a seat while I get everything together." Constance opened the file drawer connected to her desk and instantly came up with the correct folder.

Laylah took a moment to peruse the file. Instead of taking it with her, she wrote down all the pertinent information. When she was finished, she looked up at Constance and smiled. "You're a woman after my own heart. You keep very detailed records." Laylah got to her feet. "I hate to run, but the boss wants this STAT. It's his time of the month again."

Constance laughed. "Either that or he hasn't been laid in a while."

"That's probably more like it," Laylah said, chuckling softly.

"All he has to do to remedy the situation is take Amelia up on her obvious body language. She'd be only too happy to turn out the brother. The girl is on fire for him."

"You're too bad. I'm out." Laylah wasn't going to touch that comment.

Laylah set the manila folder on the right-hand corner of March's desk. "All the information you're after is inside here, sir," she said, pointing at the file. She then turned and walked away, gritting her teeth out of sheer frustration.

"Not so fast, young lady," he said. "I need you to go over with me what's in this folder. You seem to be in an awful hurry."

Laylah turned sharply on her heel and looked dead into March's eyes. "I don't know about you, but I have very important work to do. All you have to do is open the folder and read what's inside. You *can* read, can't you?"

March's eyes narrowed to tiny slits, hoping Laylah read the danger sign there. It would serve her well to check her tongue. "I can read, but I'd rather you read it to me."

Exasperated was an understatement for what Laylah felt. She had two choices: she could stay and read the contents of the file to him or she could go back to her desk and finish her feature story. Selecting the last option would more than likely get her fired.

Taking the least controversial way out, Laylah opted to sit back down, praying for an abundance of patience. Slowly, almost methodically, she picked up the folder and opened it. She then read to March the date, time and location of Patricia Blakeley's retirement dinner, the projected number of guests who had already RSVP'd, the regrets and the numbers of those who hadn't responded one way or the other.

The meal choices and prices per person were run down for March, as well as the company information on the DJ and his fees. Last but not least, Laylah gave March the list of gifts suggested for the retiree. "No final decision on a gift has been made."

"What's the total projected budget for all this?" March queried Laylah.

After turning the folder around so March could see the top sheet, she pointed at the last set of numbers. "Those are the bottom-line figures."

March whistled. "That's a lot of money to spend on someone unworthy. Well, I guess it's a small price to pay to finally be rid of her. Patricia is a constant thorn in my side. The woman has too much darn mouth. I hope I never hear her speak again."

Laylah understood all too well why March had made such ignorant statements. Patricia was one of the employees who had made several complaints against him. She made no secret regarding the way she felt about him, telling anyone who'd listen that March was an inadequate administrator, one that should've never been hired.

Laylah agreed with Patricia wholeheartedly.

"Now that you have everything you've requested, may I please return to work?"

March looked down his wide nose at Laylah. "By all means. Thank you."

The polite way in which March had last spoken had Laylah wondering if she'd heard him correctly. Even when he tried to be nice he still annoyed her, just as his condescending look had done. "You're welcome." Hoping she could get out of March's office without any further communication with him, Laylah rushed to the exit.

March cleared his throat. "Hope you meet your deadline. Being late won't look good for your record, especially on your next evaluation."

If I have my way, you'll never do another evaluation at this newspaper.

After Laylah returned to her desk, she sat down and began pounding away at the computer keys. Staying focused was a must if she was to meet her deadline. There had been enough disruptions already—and now she had to put her nose to the grindstone.

Less than an hour later, Laylah skidded into the printing area, where she handed over her feature story to Sean Lackland, the senior copy editor.

As Laylah cleaned off the vacant tables inside the shelter, Second Chances, she smiled beautifully at several other volunteers who had just sat down to eat. Her lovely gray eyes dazzled in the same way her effervescent personality did. She was always sweet and polite to everyone who came into the shelter. Folks loved her because she was so genuine. Though small in stature, she had a huge heart overflowing with love.

As a volunteer at the homeless shelter, her second gig, her duties pretty much ran the gamut. If she wasn't serving meals, she could be found cleaning various areas of the shelter, stocking shelves with food and other items, or passing out new or used clean clothing. From time to time she helped Pastor Ross Grinage with the bookkeeping and any other duties he needed her to perform. She also wrote the shelter's monthly newsletter. The patrons actually enjoyed reading her writings.

Laylah had very little personal time and she liked it that way. Keeping busy kept her from being too lonely. Since she hadn't been involved in a serious relationship in quite some time, she was actually fearful of getting into another romantic saga.

Benjamin Irvine, the shelter's founder and CEO, walked up to Laylah and gave her a warm hug. "How's my favorite girl?"

She smiled wearily. "A little tired, but still blessed."

She noticed that Benjamin had just gotten his wavy white hair cut and neatly edged. In her opinion, he was a nice-looking man, a very personable one. Standing around six feet, he towered over Laylah's frame. The man was sort of an exercise freak, working out six days a week. He was single and was currently looking for the right woman to enhance his life.

"How long will you be working this evening?"

Laylah hunched her shoulders. "As long as I'm needed. Is it my imagination or are the numbers of the homeless increasing? I've seen so many new faces this month."

Benjamin sighed hard. "Unfortunately, this particular population is growing by leaps and bounds. What's really frightening is that many of the newer ones who've wandered in here lately were once high-salaried professionals. It makes me wonder."

"I know." Laylah nodded. "Just the other day I talked to a guy who's an engineer. The company he worked for folded unexpectedly, leaving him without a job. When he could no longer pay his house note, he began living on the streets. People don't realize we're all just a paycheck away from homelessness. I try to stay very mindful of that."

"I know what you mean. Putting a little money aside for emergency situations is something many of us fail to do." Benjamin scratched his head. "Well, I guess we'd better get back to work. It's close to the dinner hour and the outside lines for meals and a bed are already forming."

Benjamin went on his way and Laylah resumed her duties.

Laylah still had a lot to do before the doors were open for meal service and bed assignments. Those seeking shelter were only allowed to stay on one night at a time. The patrons had to line up and then sign up each day. The hardest part of the process for Laylah was when someone was turned away once they ran out of beds. There were referral places they could send folks to, but other agencies had the same procedures in place. No matter how she viewed things, it was still rough emotionally for everyone.

Once Laylah put away the cleaning products, she slipped into the bathroom, where she thoroughly washed and dried off her hands. After changing into a clean smock that covered the upper portion of her body, she headed for the kitchen. Meal service would begin in about five or ten minutes. Once the doors were open, the place could get busy as a beehive until everyone was served and later assigned a bed for the night.

All smiles, Laylah began filling sectional plastic plates with food and handing them out to those in line. Everything was running smoothly, which wasn't always the case. It could get pretty noisy inside the dining room and many times hot arguments ensued, the majority of them born out of sheer frustration and a low tolerance.

Benjamin was normally great at quieting things down. However, he had failed to restore calm a few times that she could recall with crystal clarity. The police were called in on those rare occasions, but no one had ever been arrested. More than anything, most of the patrons were just happy to have something to eat and a place to lay their heads.

The next guy in line had Laylah doing a double take. His dark hazel eyes were strangely alluring. Although he appeared somewhat disheveled, his clothing was cleaner than most. The slightly shaven appearance he wore actually looked good on him. His dark, curly hair was a bit long, lacking any sort of style, but it wasn't dirty and straggly. From what she could actually see of his physique, he appeared to be in darn good shape.

Laylah suddenly felt the weirdest sensation right in the pit of her stomach, a totally unfamiliar one. Why'd she suddenly feel like she'd met this guy before?

The moment she realized she was blatantly summing up a homeless guy, she felt so embarrassed. The color of her humiliation was noticeably reflected in her cheeks.

"Thank you," he said in a deep voice after she handed him a plate of food.

The man's deep tone had surprised her, turning her on in the process. That she was attracted to his sexy voice also embarrassed her. "You're welcome." As the man moved on through the line, her eyes followed him, as if she had no control over them.

"Lady, can I please get served? We don't have forever here."

At the intolerant sound of the loud male voice, the color in Laylah's cheeks deepened. She couldn't help wondering if he sensed she'd lusted after the man served before him. God forbid, she thought, too embarrassed to make eye contact with the older man as she handed over the plate. Glad that the little shameful ordeal was over, she vowed to keep her mind *on* serving food versus being *of* service to some sexy stranger.

Thirty minutes later, as the line began to thin out, Laylah knew they'd already served more meals than they had the previous night. By stacking plates in groups of twenty-five, she was able to keep track of how many patrons were served. Paper cups could be accounted for in the very same manner even though people often used more than one.

With no one else standing in line, Laylah once again retrieved her cleaning tools. Her daily routine was to clean each table once it became empty, rather than cleaning them all at the end of meal service. As soon as the dining room was put back in order, she'd join Benjamin up at the front area of the shelter to assign beds.

Second Chances could accommodate up to thirty-two people a night.

Because Laylah had gotten herself involved in an interesting conversation with Bud Wilkes, one of the shelter's regulars, she was a tad late getting up front to help out Benjamin. All new patrons had to fill out a personal-information form, which she thought was ridiculously silly, especially since it requested an address and phone number.

If the homeless had addresses and phones, they wouldn't be seeking out shelters.

There were four guys filling out information forms, including the one Laylah had been somewhat intrigued with. She was very interested in reading what he'd put down, hoping the information might give her a few clues about him. *What had led up to the patron becoming homeless?* It was one of the most important questions on the form.

Stealing covert glances at the man she was slightly smitten with made Laylah feel awkward, but she couldn't seem to keep her eyes off him. There was something familiar about him, but she couldn't pinpoint it. She had the craziest notion that he had been quite a success story before his downfall into homelessness. She even thought his situation might be an excellent story to write, though she didn't know any of his circumstances.

As far as Laylah was concerned, every person, homeless or otherwise, had an interesting story to pen. She couldn't recall all the provocative stories she'd written on people who had once led a normal existence, yet had had a very powerful story to share with others.

As Laylah quickly assessed the situation, her heart broke. There were only three beds left, but the line was still quite long. Unfortunately, it was part of her task to turn the others away. She hated to be the bearer of bad tidings. Saying she was sorry for turning someone away just wasn't enough, but there was nothing else to tell. The long, sad faces always tore at her heartstrings. In the first few months of volunteering at the shelter she had cried all the way home. She still hadn't quite come to terms with all her emotions.

While she passed out a list of other shelters, she felt as though someone was staring hard at her. As she turned around, her eyes locked with the ones that had intrigued her earlier. His dark hazel gaze pierced her soul, making her wish she could've met him under different circumstances. What was it about this guy that had her heart beating so hard and fast? Why was it so easy for her to imagine him dressed to the nines and looking every bit the corporate raider? Why did he have such sexy, expressive eyes?

Once she handed the newcomer a list, she had a hard time hiding how sorry she felt for turning him away, especially since he had been the very next person in line.

He briefly touched Laylah's hand as she turned to walk away. Her obvious emotional state had rocked his soul. "This job's really tough on you, isn't it?"

Surprised by his question, Laylah lowered her lashes, nodding. "Very hard."

"You seem to take it personally when turning someone away. I just need you to know I understand. I don't take it personally." He eyed her with genuine concern.

"Thank you for that. It means a lot to me. By the way, my name is Laylah," she said, pointing at her name tag.

"You're welcome. And I'm Chancellor. Everyone calls me Chance," he remarked, extending his large, smooth-looking hand to her, his fingernails clean as a whistle.

Chancellor's grip was firm and warm, causing Laylah to feel as if she were sweating internally. His voice was a real turn-on, but she wished it wasn't. What she experienced with him was nothing short of insane—and he still seemed so familiar.

Chancellor looked down at the list. "Think I'll have any luck at one of these other places? It's getting late."

The question was a difficult one. She didn't want to lie to him. The truth was that people lined up at the same time every day at most of the shelters; the chances of him getting a bed this late were nil and none. "I wish I could tell you yes, but I can't."

A disturbing look suddenly clouded Chancellor's eyes. "Why do you people pass out this list if you already know the outcome? It then becomes a wild-goose chase."

"Good question. I've asked the same one myself dozens of times. I don't make the rules. I just volunteer here."

"Why do you do it?"

Laylah looked perplexed. "Do what?"

"Volunteer your time in such a cheerless place?"

The smile Laylah flashed Chancellor was soft and sweet. "I

love helping out others. If I can put a simple smile on one person's face, or just pass on a few kind words to someone, it makes me feel so good inside. I derive a lot of pleasure from this job."

"I don't see how you get pleasure out of working here, unless you enjoy seeing others suffering. If nothing else, I'm sure this nonpaying job is a thankless one."

"I can see how you might feel that way." Laylah shook her head from side to side. "But I'm not looking for gratitude. I simply want to be of service to the people in my community and to others who are in need. I really love people."

"Why not volunteer at the Red Cross or at a local hospital? Why here?"

"Why are you asking all these questions? Why do you care, anyway?"

"I'm curious to know why a beautiful, vibrant young woman wants to be around so much pain and suffering. There has to be a darn good reason why you do this."

"And I'm curious to know why you give a darn one way or the other."

The dark look on Laylah's face told Chancellor he had deeply offended her. That hadn't been his intent. He had merely wanted to know why she wanted to spend her free time in a godforsaken place like this one. Had someone in her family become homeless? Was she possibly doing this out of some sort of guilt complex? He'd really like to know.

Knowing she should bring this conversation to an end, Laylah nervously shuffled her feet. "I really have to get back to work now. Wish I could find you a place to stay tonight, but I can't. Try to get here earlier tomorrow. People start lining up at least two hours before we assign beds. The regulars all know the ropes."

"For what? So you can hand me another list and send me

packing?" For whatever reason, Chancellor wanted to keep Laylah talking, wanted more time in her company. He also had to wonder if she was truly an angel of mercy. He somehow thought she was. She was certainly as beautiful as what he'd always imagined an angel to look like.

A light suddenly came on in Laylah's eyes. "Can you please wait a minute, Chance? I'll be right back. Don't go anywhere."

Wondering why she wanted him to wait for her, Chancellor looked after her dazedly as she skidded down the hall and quickly disappeared around a corner. His gaze dropped to the floor as he wished he was anywhere but inside a homeless shelter. Upon closing his eyes for a brief word of prayer, he heard heels clicking against the concrete floor. He cut his supplication short and then looked up to await her arrival.

Discreetly, Laylah pressed several neatly folded bills into Chancellor's hand. "Go get yourself a room. There's a very nice motel, Sweet Dreams Inn, about three short blocks from here. The place is very clean and well tended to. Tell Mr. Arlie Jones I sent you. My full name is Laylah Versailles. Arlie is a dear friend of mine. He's good people."

Chancellor was positively amazed by Laylah's altruistic spirit. He felt ashamed to take the money, but he figured she'd be offended if he did otherwise. He got the feeling she didn't make a habit of handing out cash, otherwise she'd probably be broke by now. Out of all the folks who came to the shelter, why had she decided to help him? Knowing full well that he'd pay her back every red cent, he slipped the money in his pocket. This was one kind gesture he'd never forget. It was very special. "Thanks. I'll be going now."

"Be safe, Chance. Hope you get here in time tomorrow to score a bed."

Laylah couldn't take her eyes off Chancellor's retreating

back. His stride was confident. This man was somebody important. Though she couldn't explain why she felt that way, she was darn near sure of it. Something devastating must have occurred in his life recently, but what? What had sent him out into the mean streets of Los Angeles to look for a place to lay his weary head? And why was she so darn interested in him?

Laylah couldn't stop thinking about Chancellor as she fulfilled the last of her duties. Once Laylah gathered her belongings, she gave her cheerful farewells to the night crew and then hurried from the building. Chancellor was still heavy on her mind as she reached her car and got inside.

Chapter 2

Arlie Jones gave Laylah a warm hug and a brilliant smile. "Happy to see you, but what brings you down here so late in the evening?"

"I referred your motel to a homeless guy and I came by to see if he checked in. Unfortunately, I don't know his surname." She then provided Arlie with a first name.

Arlie shook his head in the negative. "No one by that name has checked in here this evening. All but two of my rooms are occupied. If you'd like, I'll try to save one for the guy just in case he shows up."

Hoping she hadn't given away her money in vain, Laylah couldn't hide her bitter disappointment. What if Chancellor was a drinker or drug user? If so, she'd supplied him with enough money to score himself a few highs. "I have to go now, Arlie. I hope Chance shows up before you run out of rooms. I really thought he needed somewhere to stay."

"He does," said a slightly familiar voice. "That's why I'm

here." Chancellor made direct eye contact with Arlie. "If you're Mr. Arlie Jones, I'm supposed to tell you Laylah Versailles sent me over here to rent a room for the night." Chancellor moved over to the counter and extended his hand to Arlie. "Am I in luck?"

"You surely are," Arlie responded with enthusiasm, handing Chancellor a clipboard with a registration form attached to it. "Just fill out this baby and we'll get you all squared away. All I really need is a name."

Laylah was embarrassed to no end. It was one thing for her to stop by the motel to check on Chancellor, but it was another matter altogether to get caught red-handed at it. The things she'd already done regarding him were so unusual. He had to think she had lost all her marbles. If he didn't think so, she certainly did. As well as purely insane, her behavior was also dangerous. She was actually inside the office of a motel to track down a virtual stranger, a homeless one at that.

How sick was that?

Arlie appeared amused as he looked back and forth between Laylah and the disheveled man she had come there to inquire about. If he didn't know better, he'd think his little friend was infatuated with the man she had earlier referred to as Chance. He thought it was very strange indeed, since she'd also told him the guy was homeless. One thing Arlie was certain of was Laylah's embarrassment. Her deeply reddened cheeks were a dead giveaway.

Feeling skittish, Laylah backed up toward the front door. "Glad you made it here safely, Chance. I have to go now. I hope you get a good night's rest. Good night, Arlie."

Raising his hand in a farewell gesture, Arlie smiled sympathetically at Laylah, wishing he could say something to make her feel better. She looked so down. If nothing else, she should feel really good about helping out others. She was known around the community for trying to make life easier for folks. However, he thought there might be something else going on with her regarding this man. A more personal interest, perhaps.

Laylah hit the car's remote button to open the door. Just before she got into the driver's seat, she heard her name drifting softly on the air. Chancellor had called out to her—the last thing she needed right now, especially since she had only made a total fool of herself. She was embarrassed enough already, yet she waited on him to reach her.

Chancellor stopped a few inches away from Laylah, careful not to step into her personal space. "I want to thank you again. Your generosity means a lot to me. If you have any odd jobs you'd like me to do or any errands you need run, please let me know. It'd make me feel better if I can pay you back somehow. I'll be around for a while."

"Payback is not necessary. However, if I hear of any decent jobs, I'll try to let you know." She laughed softly. "I guess the only way I can do that is when you stop by the shelter. Just remember what I said about getting there early to land a bed."

"I won't forget it, Laylah. Take care and drive safely."

She quickly turned around and called out, asking him to wait a minute. As Chancellor faced her, he smiled beautifully. Laylah's breath caught at the sight of healthy white teeth and pink gums. Why was his smile so familiar? His good dental hygiene was further evidence that he may have recently gotten down on his luck.

Laylah smiled back. "How are you at gardening? I have some yard work you could do at my place. I haven't had the opportunity to hire a permanent gardener yet. Interested in the job?"

"Definitely! When do you want me to come by?"

"How's tomorrow morning? Early, say, around seven?"

"Works for me, Laylah," he said, sounding nearly out of breath.

Loving the way Chancellor had breathlessly said her name, Laylah wrote her address down on the back of one of the shelter's business cards. Without further comment, she got into her car and fired the engine, waving to him as she drove off.

Chancellor Kingston was pleased that Laylah had been right about the motel. It was very clean and well tended. The bed was comfortable but nothing to write home about. He often missed his extremely comfortable digs, but this was his lifestyle now. Drifting from pillar to post wasn't as easy as he had imagined.

Chancellor's twin brother, Chandler, had made drifting sound glamorous when it was anything but. Tears came to his eyes as he thought about his twin, who he hadn't seen in a couple of months. He'd give anything to find Chandler. He wouldn't allow himself to even think that some harm may have come to him. If his brother was still in southern California, he'd locate him. He had to find him. Chandler was all the meaningful family Chancellor had left in the world and he just couldn't imagine spending the rest of his life without his very best friend at his side.

The ageless photographs were more than compelling, darn near tangible. The greatest memories of their lives were all through the pages of the photo album he'd pulled out. Tears were hard to hold back. The pain in his heart was searing.

Chancellor and Chandler Kingston had accomplished so much in their thirty years of life. One had rarely been seen without the other. When had so many things changed…and so drastically? If he took the time to do so, Chancellor was sure he could chronicle all the weird changes, since they hadn't been very subtle ones.

As Chancellor forced his thoughts to a brighter spot, the effervescent Laylah, he couldn't help smiling. He had never met anyone quite like her. As beautiful as she was, it wasn't just her outward appearance he was so darn attracted to. This woman had a pure, selfless heart. She didn't know him from Adam, yet she had had a desire to help him out.

The fact that Laylah hadn't asked him a lot of personal questions was astounding to him. He wasn't used to being so readily accepted for who he was. Not in this world or the fictitious world he'd just arrived from. Living as a homeless person was so new to him, as was his meeting with a perfect angel of mercy. Laylah was every bit that.

After he stretched out on the bed, he looked up at the cracking ceiling, wondering how he had gotten from there to here. Where would his journey take him next? How far would he have to travel down this rocky path before he got the answers?

He had no clue about the future, which was unusual for someone who had always had a solid plan for his life. However, he was pretty certain about one thing. Knowing he'd see the lovely Laylah tomorrow helped him close his eyes and relax just enough to give his soul a break from all the terrible sorrow he felt.

Dressed in jade-green silk pajamas trimmed with pink satin piping, Laylah was stretched out across her king-size brass bed watching the ten o'clock news, dismayed that there still hadn't been any clues or the least bit of news about little Ashley.

It was so disheartening for her to think of that precious little girl somewhere out there in the world desperately wanting to be at home with her loving mommy. Since everyone around the country was also praying for Ashley, she was filled with the hope that she'd soon be found. Prayer worked, lots of it worked even better.

Once the news was over, she surfed through the channels.

When she didn't find anything interesting to view, she turned off the television. Rarely did she go to sleep this early, but her body felt completely worn down after putting in serious hours at both her jobs. She wasn't complaining. Working long hours kept her from being too lonely and helped to keep her mind off the fact she hadn't a decent relationship in a long while.

Laylah wanted nothing more than to find Mr. Right and settle down in a nice cozy home, one a bit bigger than her current town house, and then eventually start a family. All the men she'd met over the past year had been totally into self. These guys could've cared less about her, let alone about her dreams and future aspirations.

When had guys stopped opening doors for women? Not to mention their refusal to occasionally spring for dinner and a movie. She had met some real pieces of work in the dating world. Some of these modern-day men seemed to be looking for a woman to take care of them and to enhance their lifestyle through monetary and material gifts.

Many of the guys Laylah had gone out with had been kind of disrespectful in general. Pulling out a chair for her to be seated in had rarely occurred. Most of her dates had been blind ones arranged by mutual friends. Never again would she go on a blind date. The last one had turned out to be a date straight from hell.

Maybe it was her, Laylah thought as she pulled the white and deep lavender comforter under her chin. Perhaps she simply didn't fit the bill as Miss Right.

As the alarm clock crowed annoyingly, right at 6:00 a.m., Laylah moaned and groaned with displeasure. A couple more hours of sleep would work wonders for her fatigued body, but it was an impossible desire. Her schedule was full. Another hour of rest might have been doable had she not invited Chancellor over to tend her tiny yard.

All she had to do was hit the shower since she'd laid out her clothes the night before. Dragging her tail out of bed was done in dramatic fashion. After trudging into the bathroom, she turned the water on full blast and stepped inside the clear glass cubicle. Once she'd thoroughly washed her body, she reached for the thick white towel to dry off.

The doorbell rang at six-thirty, just as Laylah poured a cup of hot coffee. How the visitor had gotten through the gates was her first concern. If it was Chancellor, she realized she hadn't told him about the security measures. After setting her mug down on the kitchen table, she ran toward the front of the house. A look into the safety window gave her a full view of Chancellor. He appeared to have cleaned up a bit, but his baggy jeans didn't fit his powerful physique and his jacket wasn't pressed.

Did she let him inside her private space or what? Laylah then realized she hadn't thought everything through. Well, for sure, she couldn't leave him outside. Praying she was doing the right thing, she put on a bright smile before opening up. "Good morning. Gee, you're more than prompt. You're about a half hour early."

Smiling gently, Chancellor nodded. "I'd much rather be early than late."

"I'm an advocate of promptness myself. Do you drink coffee?"

A look of surprise briefly flashed in Chancellor's eyes. Her offer had shocked him. "I do, but are you sure you're okay with that?"

"If I let you in, you're not going to kill me, are you?" If only she knew how to hold her tongue. While Laylah had always had the nerve to speak her mind, she wished she hadn't done so in this instance. Even if she had been joking, the comment was inappropriate.

"I'm not a dangerous person. You don't know that for sure, so maybe I should just get to the gardening. Perhaps you can hand me a cup of java outside the back door."

Laylah sucked her teeth. "That's not happening. Come on in. Please."

Feeling the awkwardness of the moment, Chancellor seemed reluctant to cross the threshold. This entire situation made him nervous despite that he'd never bring any harm to her. Only he knew that for sure. He in fact planned to warn her not to ever do something like this again. If she were to let the wrong type of person into her home, it might prove hazardous to her health. A male neighbor had let him in the walking gate.

Still regretful over her offhand comment, Laylah extended her hand to him. "It's okay. Really, it is. Please come inside."

Not wanting to hurt her feelings in any way, Chancellor took her hand for a brief moment. He then came inside. At her suggestion, he followed her back to the kitchen, where she gestured for him to take a seat at the table. Upon noticing where her mug had been placed, he sat on the opposite end.

He liked the feel of her warm, cozy kitchen. It was a cheerful place and was a comfortably accommodating size. Equipped with stainless-steel appliances, everything was shiny and bright. A stainless-steel bowl of sunny lemons and fresh limes served as a centerpiece for the round maple table and accompanying six chairs.

After filling another mug with steaming hot coffee, Laylah carried it to the table and handed it over to Chancellor. She then pulled out a chair and plopped down onto it. "How'd you do at the motel last night?"

"Good. The room was nice and clean. Thanks for asking."

"You're welcome. Glad you had a good night. Did you get to talk to Arlie?"

"Just for a minute or two. He seems like a nice guy. He also offered me work."

"Doing what?"

"A few odd jobs, nothing major. I just happen to be a great handyman."

"That will certainly work in your favor. How long have you been out there?" She couldn't bring herself to use the "homeless" word to describe his situation, not to his face. In her opinion, the term itself was fraught with desperation.

"Not long. I'd imagine a minute or two is too long for most folks. Stuff happens." Because she had been so nice to him, he wanted to share more of his story with her, but he didn't think the timing was right. He lifted his mug. "You make a great cup of coffee."

Laylah blushed slightly. "Thanks. Would you like some breakfast?"

"No, thank you. I'd just like to get to work before it gets too hot out there."

"I know what you mean. If you want to bring your coffee along, we can step out the back door so I can show you what needs to be done around the place."

Chancellor grabbed his mug. "Mind if I ask for a refill?"

"Not at all. I'd be happy to get it for you." Laylah took the mug and marched right over to the stove and refilled it. She then again summoned Chancellor to follow her.

The small patch of lawn wasn't even half the size Chancellor had expected. There were only a few ornery weeds in the flower beds, nothing overwhelming. Living in a town house offered limited space for a yard and such, but he could see that Laylah had made the most of what she had. All her plants and shrubs were evergreen, giving her greenery year-round. The colorful flowers were perennials rather than annuals.

"I can knock out this job in no time. Where do you keep the mower?"

"In the garage." She pointed at a side door. "I'll open it for you to get the mower out. All my other gardening tools are hung on the walls inside the garage. They'll be easy enough to spot. Knock on the back door when you're finished."

"How much time do I have?"

"An hour and a half before I have to get off to work. Is that okay?"

"That's ample time. There's not that much to do."

"Let me know when you're finished." She turned to go back inside, only to turn back around. "By the way, there's plenty of bottled water and lots of other cold drinks in the fridge inside the garage. Help yourself to whatever you want."

Overwhelmed again by Laylah's generosity, he nodded his understanding. Other than his deceased grandparents and a few folks from their generation, he hadn't run into too many people as kindhearted as her. In the dog-eat-dog world he had lived in, mostly everyone had looked out for number one, hardly ever caring about the needs of others.

Laylah felt hot all over by the time she finally opened the side door. What was it about this guy that had her acting so out of character, so insanely weird? She wasn't the kind of person who lied to herself—and she wasn't about to start now. She was hot for Chancellor, homeless or otherwise. The man made her pulse race and she couldn't even put a name to what else occurred to her physically. She just knew she felt flushed all over whenever he was around. No one but no one had ever made her feel this out of control.

Laylah's parents, semiretired television news correspondents Jack and Selma Versailles, would think their youngest child had totally lost her mind. Brandon, her television entertainment correspondent brother, would rib her unmercifully if he ever found out about the man she secretly admired. And her uppity, well-to-do sixty-seven- and sixty-nine-year-old aunts, Cora and Gertrude, might be stunned to learn that their niece was hopelessly infatuated with a homeless man.

"Tell Cora and Ask Gertrude" was the name of the newspaper column her two spinster aunts wrote, which just happened to be a write-in column to seek advice for the lovelorn. She was already entertaining the idea of anonymously writing in with her dilemma just to see what sagacious advice they'd offer her.

How would someone go about presenting a weird situation like this one to their very own family members? What would she say when questions were asked about Chancellor, like what profession was he in and where did he reside—and what were his future aspirations? Laylah knew this was much too serious a situation for her to continue making light of it. She was too smitten.

"Whoa!" Laylah suddenly began to realize she had gotten way ahead of herself…and way ahead of Chancellor, too. Sure she was wildly attracted to him, but was he even remotely interested in her on a romantic level? If so, she hadn't seen an inkling of such. The man had been nothing but polite and friendly toward her, yet she had been going on and on in her mind about him since the first moment she'd laid eyes on him.

There was nothing at all in Chancellor's demeanor to suggest he was hot for her, so she really needed to cool off. The only way she could find out for sure if he was interested in her romantically was to ask him, which was something she wouldn't dream of doing. She was outspoken, frank and to the point, all right, but she wasn't nearly as bold in speech and in deed as she'd like to be with men. She had already pushed the envelope by inviting him to her home under the guise of him working for her. She had gotten him there easy enough, but how was she to keep him coming back?

Laylah wailed inwardly as she anxiously peered out at Chancellor through the half-open slats in the plantation shutters covering the half window on the back door.

Slick with sweat, Chancellor's muscled arms bulged as he easily pushed the mower around the small yard. His jacket had been discarded and thrown over the back of a lounge chair. Laylah couldn't help wondering what the rest of his anatomy looked like naked. More than that, she had to wonder if she'd ever see him in the buff. No doubt it would be a mind-blowing experience.

Continuing to watch Chancellor's every move, Laylah's mind began to take her places she shouldn't dare let it wander. A moonlight stroll in the nearby park seemed like an ending to a perfect night out on the town; what might occur after the stroll had her libido reacting wildly. Although she could only imagine those strong arms holding her close, she was sure he would treat her to an unforgettably seductive encounter.

The moment Chancellor turned off the lawn mower, Laylah knew she had to get moving. Although she was already dressed for work, she hadn't done anything but watch and lust after him. The coffeepot needed cleaning and the table had to be wiped off. She didn't want him to come inside and see that everything was just as it was before he'd gone outdoors. That would be embarrassing.

Laylah rushed around the room as she did her best to put it back in order before Chancellor knocked to say he was finished in the yard. After dumping the coffee grounds, she lifted the removable basket, carried it over to the sink and gave it a good washing. Sponging off the table with an antibacterial spray cleaner was done quickly.

Hoping Chancellor wouldn't knock before she made it back to the kitchen, Laylah rushed down the hallway and sped into her bedroom, where she rustled through her purse to come up with enough money to pay for his services. She wasn't sure if she should offer him twenty or thirty dollars for the lawn, but she was sure he could use whatever she paid him. She settled on thirty dollars in the next instant, hoping she wasn't over- or underdoing it. The man had to eat, and he'd need another night in the motel.

Just as Laylah skidded into the kitchen Chancellor firmly knocked on the back door. Her heart fluttered wildly as she reached for the knob. Calm down. You need to stop making a fool of yourself in front of him. She hated talking to herself, but she had no one else she could trust with her deep secret. At least no one that wouldn't think she was absolutely stark raving mad. Her best friend, Kelly, would think she had gone daft.

As though she hadn't already observed his every movement, Laylah stepped outside the house. "You did a great job. I'm very pleased."

"Thank you. As I said before, there wasn't much to do. I'm pleased that you're pleased." He pointed at a row of hedges. "Those plants seem to have some sort of infestation. Probably mealy bugs. You might want to treat them. You can pick up something at Home Depot to take care of the problem. If you'd like, I could get it for you. I can then treat the plants whenever it's convenient for you to have me come back."

Without knowing it, Chancellor had just solved Laylah's dilemma of finding a way to keep him coming back to her place. She really did want to get to know him better, almost sure that his personal story was a fascinating one. No matter how crazy it seemed, she was simply attracted to him…and she still didn't know his last name.

Laylah quickly decided that she wasn't going to try to fight her attraction to him. Nothing may come of it, but she wouldn't know one way or the other if she didn't explore the possibilities. "That would be great. Maybe we can go to Home Depot together since I'll have to pay the bill with a credit card."

Chancellor shrugged. "Whatever works best for you. I'm at your disposal."

Thinking Chancellor should be mindful of his loose tongue, Laylah blushed at the very idea of having him at her beck and call. It certainly worked for her. "Thanks for taking care of things. If you're looking for a job, you can keep this one until you get something permanent. You can do it weekly if you're interested." Though she'd been nervous about how to present him with the money, she went ahead and pressed it into his hand.

Chancellor frowned. "I can't take this from you. You already paid for the motel last night. I did the lawn to try to show you my gratitude for your kindness."

Laylah wrinkled her nose. "I wasn't expecting repayment for the motel. That was a gift. This money is for the work you did. I won't have it any other way."

Suspecting that it would be hard to win an argument with Laylah, Chancellor rapidly decided not to go against the grain. Since she had also sounded pretty adamant about her decision, he'd let it go for now, but he had no intention of sponging off her. She'd definitely get it all back. "Thanks again. You're too kind."

"If I were down on my luck, I'd hope that someone would treat me with kindness. Some people in this world just aren't caring enough. Glad I could help you out."

"Glad you offered." He stroked his chin. "Hope you'll take what I'm about to say in the spirit in which I intend it. Never let a stranger into your home. I'm not a killer or rapist, but I could've been both. Promise me you'll never do that again."

"Not if it means I can't let you in when you come back," she boldly flirted.

Chancellor grinned. "You can make me the exception. You're safe with me."

Drats! She wanted to feel anything but safe with him—and in a delicious way. On the other hand, she'd love to find herself snuggled safely into his strong arms. Chancellor looked strong, as if he could make her feel protected in so many wonderful ways.

"I actually believe I'm safe with you. When can we go to Home Depot?"

Chancellor folded his arms against his chest. "When do you want to go?"

"I get off work around three. Is three-fifteen okay with you?"

"Fine."

"I can pick you up at the shelter. Can you meet me there?"

"Three-fifteen. I'll be there."

"How'd you get here today?"

"Bus. By the way, I gained entry through a walking gate, by your neighbor."

Interesting, she thought. "On my way to work, can I give you a ride somewhere?"

"You can just drop me off wherever you're going. I can find my way from there."

"Let me grab my purse. We can go out through the garage." She bit down on her lower lip. "I'm sorry. I didn't give you a chance to wash up. Would you like to do so?"

"I'm fine. I washed my hands off with the garden hose. I'll clean up later on."

"I'll be right back." Deciding she should tread lightly, she made direct eye contact with him. "By the way, what's your last name?"

"Kingston," he responded, smiling, hoping his name didn't ring a bell for her.

"Chancellor Kingston." The prestigious name sounded slightly familiar, Laylah thought as she rushed off to the back of the house, where the master bedroom was located. She quickly grabbed her purse off the bed and shot back up to the front.

"Ready?" she asked him, giving him a hundred-watt smile.

"Ready."

Despite how busy Laylah had been, the day still dragged. She had accomplished quite a lot of work, but she had a lot more to do. The phone calls put through to her desk had been incessant, but she had handled each one with her usual aplomb. The woman was patient beyond belief and was known to have nerves of steel, more so in the face of adversity.

A quick glance at the clock let Laylah know it was time for her to wrap things up if she was to meet Chancellor on time. They'd have to hurry through their shopping at Home Depot so she could get him back to the shelter before the lines began to form. Because she had thought of that scenario before she'd dropped him off earlier, they had changed their meeting time to two o'clock. She had plenty of comp time on the books.

Just as Laylah pushed back her swivel chair from the desk, she caught a glimpse of a figure entering her office door. A slight turn in her seat brought her face-to-face with the formidable-looking March. What now? She had to wonder. As sure as she breathed air, he was there to mess up the end of her day. "You need something?"

"As a matter of fact, I do. You weren't getting ready to leave, were you?"

Laylah knew that he knew, like everyone else in the office knew, that leaving was exactly what she was about to do. Anytime she planned to leave early, she gave as much notice as possible. While she hadn't told March directly, news always traveled fast in these office suites. "What's on your mind?" she asked, refusing to respond to his query.

"I have a phone interview I'd like you to conduct. It's an assignment I planned on handling, but I've been called up to attend a special meeting with city council members."

"What time is the interview scheduled?"

March lifted his hand and looked down at his wristwatch. "In ten minutes."

How could he possibly prepare her for this assignment in such a short time frame? This was just another of his hateful ploys. "Who am I interviewing and on what topic?"

March handed her a sheet of paper with typing on it. "It's all right here."

"Whoopee," she halfway snarled. "Nice to know you always come prepared."

"Always prepared," he said. Without further ado, he turned around and left.

Laylah wished that that was the case. March was the most unprepared man she'd ever met. Calmly, she gathered up her belongings, along with the typed sheet of paper he had handed her. Humming a soft tune, she left the office and headed toward the exit.

March came running out of his office in time to beat Laylah to the employees' exit. "Where do you think you're going? I just gave you an important assignment."

"I know," she said blandly, stepping around him, looking down at her watch. "If you hurry, you won't be late for your special meeting." Thank God for cell phones.

Laylah planned to conduct her interview by cell phone. She was sure March hadn't thought about that. If he had, he would've found another way to try to sabotage her plans. Since she was well seasoned at this sort of thing, it should be a piece of cake for her. Besides that, she had already interviewed this high school principal several times. Seventy-year-old Clara Holliday had just won another prestigious, newsworthy award.

March would more than likely call her on the carpet on Monday morning, accusing her of belligerence, but getting the assignment done was always the best revenge against an idiot boss. She would be ready for his tired behind, just as she always was. He'd never best her because he simply wasn't the best.

Chapter 3

All finished with the Holliday interview, which had gone off as smoothly as a summer breeze, Laylah pulled her car up in front of the shelter instead of parking in the lot, her normal routine. She had made it there right on time. Upon spotting Chancellor, she quickly blew the horn, regretting it the moment lots of heads turned her way. She couldn't help smiling broadly as he made his way over to the car.

Chancellor opened the door and slid into the passenger's seat with ease. He looked over at Laylah and smiled. "How's your day been?"

As Laylah thought about how it had made her day to best March at his evil deeds, laughter trilled in her throat. "Beautiful! And yours?"

"Pretty darn good, considering. You ready for our little shopping trip?"

"I am. I know people who'd give up a limb or two for the chance to go to Home Depot to shop for plant-pest spray."

Chancellor roared with laughter from deep inside his belly. "That's funny."

"I thought so," Laylah remarked, trying hard not to sound too flirty.

Wondering if she was trying to be cute or cocky, Chancellor gave her a wry look. He liked her sense of humor, but he didn't care for artificially overconfident women, hoping she wasn't anything akin to those types. Too much confidence in folks was hard for him to take, period. He had never been arrogant; he thought of himself as both humble and compassionate. "Do you always toot your own horn like that?"

Laylah seemed baffled. "What do you mean?"

"Your comment after I said you were funny was kind of arrogant."

The look in Laylah's eyes was sincerely apologetic. "It wasn't my intent to come off like that. You're the first person who has ever called me arrogant." Well, that's not quite true, she mused, suddenly recalling March saying that about her a time or two. She really didn't like being referred to as such. She was very confident but never haughty. She *had* been pompous with her boss on a few occasions, which she hated to admit.

As Laylah pulled into the parking lot of the Home Depot, she quickly glanced over at Chancellor. "I'm sorry if I offended you in some way."

"You didn't. And I'm not insulted. I think I simply read you wrong."

"I'm happy you've changed your mind about me." She turned off the ignition. "I guess we'd better go inside so I can get you back to the shelter in time."

"Why do you even care whether I land a bed there or not?"

"I just do. I'd like to see everyone get one. It doesn't make me happy to know that our country is the greatest superpower in the world, yet it lacks compassion." Laylah sighed hard. "If you're wondering if I've taken a special interest in you, I have. I'm attracted to you, Chancellor Kingston. I know that may seem ludicrous, but it's true."

"Is an attraction to me ludicrous? Or is it ludicrous to be attracted to a homeless man? Which one is it, Miss Versailles?"

Laylah could easily refuse to answer that question, but she thought it might make her seem shallow. She was anything but superficial. "I guess I could say both. There are people out there who would definitely think it's ludicrous to be romantically attracted to a homeless guy. To be real honest with you, I feel as if I've been acting a little insane over my attraction for you. What do you think of it?"

Chancellor grinned. "I think I like having you attracted to me. Despite you not being homeless, the attraction is mutual. The truth is, I think you're pretty hot. I guess a guy down on his luck shouldn't even be thinking or saying something like that, huh?"

Laylah blushed fiercely, something she'd done a lot of since meeting Chancellor. "I'm truly flattered. Thanks for the return honesty. I appreciate it."

"You're welcome. Now that we both know we're attracted to each other, how do you suggest we handle it?" He was very interested in hearing her response.

Laylah gave a resigned sigh. "Wish I'd asked you that question first."

They both laughed, seemingly content to leave the question unanswered for now.

Feeling less foolish than she had before her confession, Laylah slipped out from under the steering wheel. That Chancellor was just as attracted to her made her feel much better. How they'd go about establishing any type of relationship was any-one's guess. This wasn't an everyday situation. Nor was it an ordinary boy-meets-girl scenario.

Woman meets homeless man and falls head over heels in love. Go figure… That would definitely be one exciting story to write. Laylah laughed inwardly.

Chancellor located the item he needed to treat the plants right away. The formula came in a spray and a powder. When he couldn't make up his mind which one might work best, Laylah made it up for him by tossing both items into her shopping cart.

As they proceeded to the checkout line, Laylah spotted an eye-catching lighting display. Because she had been looking for a new chandelier for the dining area, she began to look at the various ones for sale. She gave a few oohs and aahs before she came upon the perfect one for her formal dining room. "What do you think of this chandelier?" she asked Chancellor. She didn't know why, but his opinion mattered.

Stroking his chin, he pursed his lips. "Beautiful. Are you in the market for one?"

"Have been for quite a while." She chewed on her lower lip, thinking about who she could get to install it for her. A bright smile lit up her eyes as she looked over at Chancellor. "Do your handyman skills include working with lighting fixtures?"

"You're in luck." Chancellor winked at her. "They do. I'm very experienced in electrical work. Looks like I'm getting lots of chances to earn my supper."

That's not all you'll get to earn. She quickly chided her devilish wickedness. "When do you think you can hang it?"

He put his forefinger up to his right temple. "I'll have to check my calendar first."

"Okay. Just let me know when."

Surprised that she hadn't caught his attempt at light sarcasm, Chancellor chuckled. "Whenever you need me to *do it* is when I can get it done."

She could surely run away with his statement. She had a lot he could *do* for her.

Chancellor then thought about the place he had once used for all his lighting needs. "If you can wait a little longer, I'd like to take you to a place specializing in light fixtures. Light Up Your World has every type of lighting you can imagine."

"Hmm, I think I've heard of the company. Pretty swanky place if I recall correctly. I have the weekend off. Are you free to take me sometime tomorrow?"

"I'm free." Without all these heavy burdens he carried around, Chancellor would one day be as free as a bird. One day soon everything would, hopefully, be resolved.

He couldn't wait for the topsy-turvy things in his life to return to right side up. He wished Laylah hadn't revealed her attraction to him, since the timing for him to get personally involved with someone was not the best. If everything was the way it used to be, he'd be happy to sweep her off her feet and carry her off into the sunset. He sensed that she deserved a real live hero to enhance her life, a knight in shining armor.

Right now, Chancellor just couldn't fulfill Laylah's romantic needs. There was too much unsavory stuff on his plate. However, once he got his life back on track—and if she was still available—she had better look out. He planned to be hot on her trail.

Laylah thought it was strange that Chancellor had asked to be dropped off a block away from the shelter, but she had obliged him. As she drove the short distance to her destination, she had a chance to briefly think about some of what had transpired between them. Whether she had intended to or not, she had totally changed the nature of their relationship. For better or worse, she didn't know. She had every intention of finding out.

Only time would tell.

Serving meals to a few dozen patrons had gone off without a hitch. Some evenings at the shelter were much easier than others, but rarely were there any without a single incident. Laylah was so grateful for how smoothly things had run, because she felt extremely tired. A hot bath and a couple of hours of reading would help rejuvenate her. Then she recalled it was Friday night. Open mic was something she loved to indulge in and hardly ever missed attending.

As Laylah was a woman who loved to write poetry, she also enjoyed sharing her creative works with others. Seated in the audience and listening to other poets was also a real blast for her. The majority of the poetry was spoken to music and someone might even hum or trill during the performance.

Bella's Café was cozy, pretty laid-back—and the rules of the establishment cited no particular dress code. Most everyone wore jeans, sweats and other comfortable attire, as well as casual footgear. It was so easy to meet people at the event. Folks acted as if they were all one big happy family, as if they'd known each other their entire lives.

The very old jukebox was a favorite fixture. Hot wings and French fries, personal-pan pizzas and a few other fast-food items could be ordered. The only alcoholic beverage served was wine, but lemonade, iced tea and water were also available for purchasing.

Laylah looked all around the room until she spotted Chancellor. Wondering if she should ask him if he wanted to go to Bella's Café with her was at the forefront of her mind. She actually thought he might enjoy it. It might also help him relax.

Then again, Laylah really didn't know what Chancellor might or might not enjoy. She wanted to find out everything about him, though. Suddenly she was fearful about her chances of really getting to know him. It still bothered her that he'd earlier asked to be let out of the car before reaching their destination. Had he been trying to protect her from rumor and innuendo? That was a possibility. However, it hadn't been necessary.

She truly didn't care what people thought of her. Nor did she care what they said about folks she chose to closely associate herself with. It then dawned on her that that might not be the entire truth. All she had done since meeting Chancellor was worry about how she'd present a homeless man to her family, wondering and worrying about what they might think of it and him. Her expression rapidly turned pensive. Perhaps she needed to reassess what she had honestly believed was her position on the matter.

Regardless of how troubled Laylah was by her recent revelations, she still wanted to ask Chancellor about accompanying her or meeting her at the café. She would love to have him tag along. Her desire alone, to have him in her company, was a good enough reason to invite him. There were no rules or laws against becoming friends or even lovers with the homeless. What *did* she want them to become? Friends? Or possibly lovers?

What was wrong with them becoming both? Laylah smiled gently.

It didn't take Laylah long to decide what she'd wear to Bella's Café. A pair of beige jeans and an autumn-orange low-cut top would make a perfect fit for the evening's festivities. The outfit was as stimulating as the sultry poem she'd picked out to read. "Tonight" was an intimately suggestive poem she'd written out of loneliness.

Thrilled only partly described how she had felt when Chancellor had said he'd love to attend poetry night. However, he'd totally refused her offer to pick him up at the shelter, where he'd been fortunate enough to score a bed. Benjamin had told him if he wanted to do a few odd jobs around there on a regular basis, he could do so. There'd be no monetary payment, but he'd already be in place to get a bed assigned at sign-up time.

She had taken it upon herself to ask Benjamin to use discretion in telling Chancellor about the new and used clothing handed out at the shelter, but only after he had expressed dismay with the attire he'd have to wear to the event. She thought he may as well make good use of all the shelter had to offer. She was sure he needed all the help he could get, so that should make it okay. Laylah didn't know how things had turned out, since she had left before Benjamin had had a chance to say anything to Chancellor.

If Chancellor showed up at Bella's Café wearing other duds, then Laylah would know he had been okay with Benjamin's clothing offer. She knew he'd gotten to her place on the bus. There was a bus that ran right out in front of the café and it ran pretty often. If it had stopped running by the time poetry night was over, she'd just drop him off. That is, if he allowed her to.

Most shelters didn't permit folks to come and go after they had been assigned a bed, but Second Chances was different than most places. The patrons were grown folks and didn't need baby-sitters. However, if they didn't come back there to sleep that same night, they'd be penalized. Someone else could've slept in the unused bed. Because of that, the violator of the rule couldn't sign up for another bed for five consecutive nights.

So far no one had run afoul of the very fair rule; at least as far as Laylah knew.

While Laylah nervously drummed her fingernails on the café table, she kept a vigilant eye on the front entry. She was due to go up onstage and recite her poem in a few minutes, but Chancellor hadn't showed up yet. He had seemed sincere enough when he'd told her he'd come down to Bella's later on just to support her.

Maybe Chancellor had been offended if Benjamin had indeed offered him other clothing to wear. He was smart enough to figure out she may've had something to do with it. Not wanting to tamper with his dignity, she prayed that it wasn't the case.

Laylah had really been looking forward to him being there, more than he'd ever know. In the next instant, her name was called out by the emcee. She looked up at the stage and then back at the front entry before she quietly slid out of her seat. Slowly, hiding her bitter disappointment, she began what seemed like a never-ending walk.

Once up onstage, Laylah spoke to the band leader and the emcee, Michael Brady.

Michael stepped up to the microphone and removed it from its stand. "Laylah is hardly a stranger to Bella's Café. She has delighted us numerous times. Let's give our lovely sister a warm round of applause. She's going to excite us with a poem entitled 'Tonight,' penned by her own creative hand. Laylah Versailles!"

Smiling, Michael handed Laylah the microphone. He then gave her a warm hug before stepping aside to allow her to take center stage.

Laylah greeted everyone in an enthusiastic manner, smiling sweetly, cheered on by the houseful of poetry buffs. She took one last glance at the front entry and then at the table she'd just vacated. It was still empty, as empty as she now felt inside.

"'Tonight,'" Laylah breathed softly, looking out at the crowd.

"Tonight I'm going to fulfill your needs and all your wildest fantasies. My darling, just close your beautiful brown eyes, think only of me, while my hot hands work their sensual magic on your entire anatomy.

Tonight it's every part of your delicious body I fully intend to taste, as the ride to ecstasy is accomplished at a deliciously slow and easy pace. Relax and imagine me all dressed up in the beauty of your nakedness.

Tonight I'm going to make it fantastic for you, so turn up on your side. If the sensations are more than you can bear, just ebb and flow with the tide, as I rub this hot, jasmine-scented oil all over your strong back and thighs.

Tonight as you shudder, tingle and squirm under my expert touch, I hear your body talking softly, telling me that it wants me so very much. It's also telling me you've fallen madly into love, as well as deep into lust.

Tonight a single candle turns the shadows on the wall a magical blue. Can you feel my electrifying fingers running rampant all through you? Though your hands haven't even touched me yet, I feel the electricity, too.

Tonight when I'm done, I can't wait for you to return the favor in kind. By your reaction to the butterfly kisses I'm raining down against your spine, I can tell you're ready to surrender, ready for me to completely blow your mind.

Tonight when it's over, I'll be exclusively yours, and you'll be all mine. My darling, raise your head and take a sip of this sweet, aphrodisiac wine. Better yet, let me pour it all over you to taste it from your dark skin so fine.

Tonight is over and now it's time for us to fall into a dream-filled sleep.

The evening's been fulfilling, what's between us has grown so deep.

For some, tonight may be just another insignificant time of the week.

For us, the burning memories of this delicious night are forever ours to keep."

Waiting for the thunderous applause to die down, Laylah bowed at the waist numerous times. Just when she thought it was all over, everyone began standing up, continuing to applaud her. This was her very first standing ovation at Bella's Café.

Unable to believe the avid response, Laylah felt overwhelmed as she stood stock-still. "Thank you for your undivided attention and your kind generosity," she said into the microphone, though she knew no one could hear her. The loud clapping hadn't stopped; her emotional response had just begun. Laylah discreetly wiped away her tears.

Seeming to appear out of nowhere, Chancellor was at the very edge of the stage, holding out his hand for Laylah to take. She didn't know how long he'd been there or how much of her poem he'd heard; she was just beside herself with joy at seeing him. If he could hear her heartbeat, then he already knew it sounded like a runaway freight train. But she didn't care if he heard it. All she cared about was that he'd kept his word.

There were several men who hadn't kept their word to Laylah. And it felt darn good to have one man who'd had enough integrity to keep his. He hadn't said when he'd get there; he'd just said he'd be there to support her. And so he was.

Laylah gently laid her delicate hand inside his. "Glad you could make it."

"Wouldn't have missed it for the world. You were great. Loved the poem."

So, he had heard her, she thought, happy he'd gotten there in time.

Chancellor gave her hand a gentle squeeze as he led her to the back of the café, where she pointed out the dimly lit table she'd occupied before her performance. Once they were comfortably seated, he pulled out a thin wad of cash and showed it to her. "I got enough work today to be able to buy you a drink. Name your poison."

Laylah would have ordered a ginger ale, but she somehow felt he might see through her desire to keep the check fees to a minimum. "White wine, please."

Grinning broadly, Chancellor summoned the waitress.

Tracee, a waitress Laylah knew well, crossed the room to take their order.

"Two white wines, please," he said to Tracee. "One with a twist of lime."

"How did you know I like to drink my wine with a slice of citrus?" she asked.

Chancellor shrugged. "I didn't. I just happen to take mine the same way."

Laylah threw her head back and laughed. "I'm sure we'll probably discover we have a lot more in common than taking our wine with lime."

Chancellor winked at her, smiling suggestively. "I think you might be right."

Tracee came back with their drink order and quickly took off again.

Laylah was hungry, but she hadn't ordered any food because she didn't want Chancellor to feel he had to pay for it. It would do her no good to wish she had eaten dinner before coming to the café. She hardly ever ate before performing. A host of butterflies normally resided in her stomach to keep her somewhat nauseated. Once she got offstage, though, she always immediately ordered a personal-pan pizza.

As though someone had read Laylah's mind, Tracee showed back up at the table with two personal-pan pizzas and a basket of hot wings. Before Laylah could ask about the food, the waitress pointed out a man seated at the bar. His back was turned to them. "Compliments of that gentleman, Laylah. He said to tell you he thoroughly enjoyed your hot poem. He thinks you're a great poet. He also said you're hot, too," she whispered.

"I guess I'll have to thank him myself. Thank you for the food delivery, Tracee."

"You're welcome, girlfriend. Talk to you later. By the way, the poem *was* the bomb! Everyone in the house seemed to enjoy it. All the lovers in the house surely did."

Laylah glowed all over. "Thanks again. Your nice comments are appreciated."

"You are so welcome." Without further comment, Tracee rushed off.

Laylah found it interesting that Chancellor hadn't bothered to turn around to take a look at the man Tracee had pointed out to her. She believed a lot of men would've done so in an instant. They may have also felt threatened by a man sending a gift of food to their date, but she didn't see this as such. It hadn't seemed to bother Chancellor in the least.

Laylah was intrigued. His attitude was that of a very confident man.

Her attention was drawn to her generous benefactor as he slipped off the bar stool. When he turned around, her jaw dropped. Seeing March wasn't a very pleasant experience. She had to wonder what he was doing there, since she'd never seen him in the café before tonight. No doubt it would be very interesting around the workplace on Monday. He would see to it. Laylah was certain of that.

March probably would try to keep Laylah from living this down, but he had no idea what she could or couldn't live with. She wasn't ashamed of her poetry or any of her other creative writings. She wouldn't let him make her feel shame. If he thought he could break her down or embarrass her, the brother was in for one rude awakening.

Laylah pushed the basket of wings to the center of the table. "Would you like to help me eat some of the food? I'm sure one of these pizzas was ordered for you."

"I doubt that. But since I'm a little hungry, I don't mind helping you out. How often do you come here?" He took a slice of pizza and put it on one of the small plates the waitress had delivered along with the food.

"Practically every Friday night. The only time I don't come to the poetry session is when I have to put in overtime at the office. This is a great place to hang out."

"I like it here. It's not loud and noisy like most clubs. The atmosphere is pretty laid-back. How long have you been writing poetry?"

Laylah rolled her eyes back. "Since I was a teenager, maybe even earlier than that. I love to write. I'm also a journalist. I work as a reporter for the *L.A. Press*."

Chancellor hid his displeasure in her profession. He didn't like reporters. His experiences with them hadn't been very good ones. Arrogant, pushy, beyond nosy and downright rude was how he saw the majority of them. He had dealt mostly with the dreaded paparazzi, whom he felt were largely responsible for some of his more serious woes. The band of renegades had given his family a lot of grief over the years.

No matter what he personally thought of the unethical journalists he'd once encountered on a regular basis, he vowed not to let his bad feelings about them spill over onto Laylah, not without just cause. Why she was so interested in him had suddenly taken on new meaning. He quickly decided he needed to be wary of her just in case she had ulterior motives. Chancellor wished this kind of damper hadn't been put on their evening. Perhaps he should make his exit right now, as opposed to much later.

Laylah restlessly flipped through the television cable channels until she came upon *Sarafina,* starring Whoopi Goldberg. The movie was set against antiapartheid riots. She had seen parts of the film before, but never in its entirety, and decided to watch it.

As much as Laylah wanted to watch the movie to hopefully take her mind off Chancellor, she couldn't seem to concentrate. She didn't know why things had suddenly gone wrong for them down at the café, but they had gotten terribly out of whack. He had begun to withdraw into himself right after she'd mentioned what she did for a living.

The communication between her and Chancellor had quickly become stifled and he had suddenly seemed overly guarded. Although he had said he'd help her out with eating the food, he hadn't touched a bite more of anything once he had consumed the first slice of pizza. Minutes later he had said that he really had to go, adamantly refusing her offer of a ride back to the shelter.

What had transpired at the café had Laylah terribly worried, not to mention downright puzzled. Chancellor's behavior had been odd and unexplainable. At this point, she didn't know if she'd ever see him again. Just the thought of that happening had her feeling fearful and disheartened. She could get over her attraction to him if she had to, but that's not at all what she wanted. If nothing else, she wanted his friendship.

She wanted him in her life—and she wanted him to stay there for a very long time. She hoped what had happened was just a freaky instance and that he'd come back around. They'd been so frank when admitting their attraction to each other. Now she just didn't know what the future held for them.

Just in case he did decide to stick around, Laylah thought it might be in the best interest of their friendship to come up with a list of fun but inexpensive things for her and Chancellor to do together. She loved touring museums and visiting different parks all around the city. She also loved outdoor picnics and long drives outside the metropolis.

Although some entertainment venues had small entry fees, Laylah had loads of free passes she'd been given as gifts to thank her for her various community services. In fact, she had all sorts of freebie tickets to one venue or another. Tickets to sporting events were sent to her frequently. She also had quite a few free-meal coupons she'd acquired in pretty much the same way.

At any rate, Laylah knew she and Chancellor had to take their relationship extremely slow. He was reluctant to get involved with her even though he hadn't said any such thing. It was just something she had sensed in him early on, more so this evening.

Because he couldn't afford to pay for elaborate dates, she felt she had to be careful not to make him feel she required that of him in order to be happy. Spending money on her wasn't something she had ever required of any man. She was very easy to please. Spending quality time and indulging in effective communication with her romantic interest was what she desired most out of her relationships.

Chancellor had been tossing and turning on the cramped cot ever since he'd first lain down. Thinking about what had happened at the café with Laylah still had him on edge. He not only felt sad about running out on her like that, he also felt horribly guilty. Reporters of any kind just made him downright nervous. Their intrusive presence in his life had left a lot to be desired. He couldn't help wishing she hadn't mentioned her profession.

At any rate, it more than likely would have been mentioned sooner or later.

Chancellor sensed that Laylah desperately wanted to know all about his life, and how he'd gotten where he was, but he had figured out she was probably too polite to ask. Her not asking what she wanted to know about him was what worried him the most.

If Laylah didn't feel comfortable asking him about his personal and professional life, she just might take it upon herself to snoop around in his private business to find out on her own. That's what reporters often resorted to in getting their information. He recalled her point-blank inquiry of his surname.

The Kingston name was very well-known in the business world and was also well connected with elite social circles. Chancellor's grandparents had worn their prestigious name with pride and honor.

To up and disappear on Laylah or continue to stick around was a difficult decision for Chancellor to make. The fact that he was so personally interested in her made it doubly hard on him. He already knew she was different from any other woman he'd ever dated. This woman knew exactly who she was, with her "take me as I am or just leave me alone" attitude. Laylah wasn't about to change herself to fit into anyone's mold.

Money and prestige obviously didn't mean a darn thing to Laylah, not when she could consider getting romantically involved with a homeless man. She had made no bones whatsoever about her wild attraction to him. Her confession had been rather refreshing. Her down-to-earth and unassuming demeanor was a real turn-on for him.

A part of Chancellor wanted to stick around to enjoy the excitement Laylah brought to his life. Another part of him was telling him to hightail it out of Dodge before all hell broke loose. Judging by her actions, he wouldn't be surprised if she already knew who he was. If she didn't already know, once Laylah found out about the Kingston family background, it would more than likely be over for them anyway.

Chapter 4

No longer interested in eating her breakfast, Laylah absently stirred her soggy cereal over and over again. Wondering if Chancellor was going to show up to take her to the lighting-fixture place had her wishing once again that things hadn't turned out so badly last night. He had left in such a hurry that she had lost the opportunity to confirm with him their shopping outing. She knew he had her address, but she couldn't recall if she'd also written down her phone number.

If Chancellor couldn't call Laylah, he'd just have to show up if it was his intent.

Laylah twirled around and around in front of the full-length cheval mirror, checking out how well the cute white shorts defined her firm, perfectly round derriere. A stretchy, sleeveless top in mint green, boasting a scooped neck, was a great fit, fully outlining her perky twin mounds. Pleased with her breezy-summer-day appearance, she smiled, her eyes filled with love and satisfaction over her mirrored reflection.

Just as Laylah sat down to tackle an easy style for her long hair, the doorbell rang. The first person who had popped into her mind was Chancellor. Perhaps he'd had a change of heart. She sure hoped so. As much as she wished she didn't, she missed having him around something awful. Maybe her day would turn out to be okay after all, she thought, dashing out of the room and rushing up the hallway.

It was obvious to her that Chancellor had received nice, neatly pressed, clean clothing from Benjamin. He had on light-colored lightweight slacks, perhaps Dockers, and a gently used, royal-blue Izod polo. The designer shirt was a surprise, but wealthy people donated all the time. The white tennis shoes on his feet looked fairly new.

Laylah couldn't be sure, but it looked as if Chancellor had gotten a haircut. He had beautiful wavy hair, a rich sable brown. He was also clean shaven, but she had liked the slightly shaven look. After getting an eyeful of his clean-cut appearance, she finally opened the door wide. "Come on in. I wasn't sure if you'd make it or not."

"I always keep my word, kiddo. Ready to hit the place I told you about?" If only she knew how close he'd come to not making it there, he thought. His deep desire to see her had won out over his numerous arguments for not getting himself involved with her.

Beyond excited over the shopping trip with Chancellor, Laylah nodded. "Light Up Your World awaits us."

Chancellor was impressed and extremely pleased that Laylah had remembered the name of the lighting establishment. "That's the place." He momentarily looked uncomfortable. "Would it be too much trouble for me to use the bathroom?"

Laylah pointed out the full guest bathroom. "Right in there." She took a seat on the bottom step of the winding staircase to wait for Chancellor to come out of the bathroom. She was thrilled that he had decided to show up for their prearranged outing. When she thought about the picture of a lighting fixture she'd torn out of a home style catalog, she jumped up to retrieve it from her bedroom.

As Laylah dashed to the back of the house, she heard Chancellor come out into the hallway. "I'll be back in a second," she yelled out. "Make yourself right at home."

Chancellor had only gotten a brief glimpse of Laylah's home on his first visit. He liked the colors of her decor. Soft greens and light beiges were warming, especially when complemented by darker shades of the same hues. Sky-blue throw pillows tossed against the beige-and-white sectional sofa lent the room a burst of brightness. Stark-white plantation shutters also made a nice contrast, as did the smoked-glass and burnished-brass coffee and end tables. The room was very comfortable and homey.

From where Chancellor stood he could see into the formal dining room. He took a few steps closer so he could get a glimpse of where the old chandelier was and to see how it looked. Dark hardwoods had been her choice for the formal dining room suite. Eight matching chairs and a buffet completed the set. In the center of the table was a beautiful six-candle centerpiece. An Asian rug covered the center portion of the hardwood flooring.

He was familiar with the kitchen but he hadn't yet seen the upstairs rooms.

Just as Chancellor had told Laylah, the store was filled with all sorts of amazing lighting fixtures. She had never seen so many chandeliers under one roof. Moving from style to style, she closely examined the brilliant chandeliers she was absolutely taken with.

As Laylah came upon a dazzling fixture, one perfectly fit for her dining room decor, the sparkle in her eyes darn near matched its shimmering crystals. While there were countless chandeliers for her to choose from, she had already fallen in love with this particular teardrop style. She was actually able to envision it in her house. "This is the one," she told him. "It's perfect."

Chancellor was totally surprised by how quickly she had made up her mind. He had thought it would have taken her a lot longer to choose, especially with so many options to pick from. He'd never met a woman who didn't like to continue shopping until they dropped, even after they'd already picked out their choice. The girl obviously knew her own mind, knew exactly what she wanted. Once again, he was extremely impressed.

Laylah bit into her juicy BLT, happy they'd taken time out for lunch. Chancellor had ordered a corn-beef sandwich on rye and a side salad. The shopping trip was over, but she hoped they'd hang out together for a while longer. Even if they didn't do anything else, he was coming back to her place to put up the chandelier. She had offered to pay for their lunch at Friday's, but he had said he'd take care of it. She couldn't accept that, so he had agreed to her suggestion of Dutch treat.

His mention of finally getting steady work had pleased her, but she wouldn't let him spend his hard-earned money on her, not when he didn't have a permanent place to lay his head.

"Where will you be working?"

Chancellor chuckled. "Home Depot. Grabbed hold of an employment application when we were there for the plant spray. When I took it back to the store, they'd just received an interview cancellation so they interviewed me instead. I got the job."

"Congratulations! Permanent?"

"Part-time, with the possibility of lots of overtime. I've never worked a blue-collar job before. Should be very interesting."

Laylah saw Chancellor's comment as an opening to the dozens of questions she wanted to ask him. She wanted to know exactly who he was and what kind of stuff he was made of. He was obviously a tough nut to crack if he could make it while living from pillar to post. Still, she felt she shouldn't pry into his private life, wanting Chancellor to open up to her of his own accord. Laylah only expected that to happen after they had really gotten to know each other. They were still pretty much strangers. If she had her way, they wouldn't be strangers too much longer.

"When do you start working?"

"As soon as I can get a physical. They require that, as well as drug testing."

Laylah looked concerned, wondering how he was going to get the money to pay for the required physical and drug test. *Should she offer to help him out?*

"The company pays for both things," he said, as if he'd read her mind. "They're supposed to contact me once the doctor's appointment is set."

Laylah now wondered how anyone was supposed to contact him. If he didn't have a permanent place to live, he didn't have a telephone number, nor had she seen him with a cell phone. "Under your present situation, how will they make contact with you?"

"I gave them Joshua Clark's number. He's one of my best friends."

If he had best friends, then why was he living in shelters? This Joshua Clark didn't sound like a very good friend in her opinion, at least not by her definition of the word.

Perhaps Chancellor had too much pride to go to his friends with his grave situation. She could easily understand that, but from what he had said, Joshua knew his friend was out there looking for a job. Shouldn't that have given him a clue, especially if he had held a white-collar job in the past?

Chancellor's remarks had made her think of her best friend, Kelly McCloud. Kelly was coming to L.A. next weekend, but Laylah hadn't made up her mind if she'd tell her about Chancellor or not. She thought that maybe she should wait to see if anything romantic developed between them.

Chancellor looked down at his watch, only to realize he must have lost it at the shelter. Panic struck him, but it only lasted a brief moment. He hoped his jewelry had been turned in, but he wasn't holding out much hope. The solid-gold watch was given to him by his late grandfather, so it held significant sentimental value. It would also bring in a good chunk of change at the pawnshop if it fell into the wrong hands. "Speaking of Joshua, I need to find a pay phone right away." He looked around the restaurant to see if he could locate a sign indicating such.

Laylah dug into her bag, pulled out her cell phone and handed it to Chancellor. He looked reluctant to take it at first. Then he reached for it, mouthing his thanks. Once he reached Joshua, he turned sideways in the chair and stuck a finger in one of his ears.

While Laylah studied his handsome profile, she wondered all sorts of things about him. Was he a good kisser? A good lover? Was he a passionate man? Did he like to sleep in the nude or did he wear pajamas to bed? What had been his job in the white-collar world? Did he have siblings? If so, how many? Were his parents still alive? Had he ever been married? Did he believe in God? It did look as if he'd said a quiet prayer a minute or so ago. Maybe that meant he might believe in a power greater than himself.

Since Laylah had only seen him with a good-size duffel bag, she'd often wondered exactly what was inside of it. Probably everything he owned in the world, she surmised, her heart going out to him and others in the same sad situation. She was thrilled that he'd landed a job, proud of him for trying. A lot of people gave up way too easily.

She didn't think Chancellor seemed the least bit concerned about passing a physical or a drug test. Of course, he wouldn't have shown that in front of her if he was worried. She didn't know that much about him, but she sensed that he was a very good man, a respectable and honorable one. He was also proud. His homeless situation did very little to dispel the character of this man. She hoped her intuition was right on.

Grinning, Chancellor handed the phone back to Laylah. "I see the doctor Monday morning, bright and early. Someone from the personnel office called and left the message about a half hour ago. Josh just told them I'd be there instead of saying I'd call back. I'm happy about how he handled it." He suddenly looked upset.

She instantly picked up on his swift mood swing. "What's wrong?"

"Just thinking about the watch I lost at the shelter. It belonged to my deceased grandfather. It means a heck of a lot to me, sentimental wise." It must've rolled off his wrist because he always slept in it. His wrists had gotten thinner due to his recent weight loss. His appetite hadn't been the best lately, not to mention what all the worrying had done to tamper with his once very healthy eating habits.

Laylah put the cell phone up to her ear and called the shelter. When Benjamin's voice came on the line, she inquired about the watch. "Thanks, Ben. Talk to you later."

Reaching across the table, Laylah put her hand over Chancellor's. "Ben's holding the watch for you. One of the cleanup crew turned it in. Ben knew it was yours from the inscription on the back. It was found right by the cot you'd slept on; just another clue that it was yours." She actually saw the worry drain right out of his eyes.

"Thank you, Laylah. Thanks for calling Ben to ask about it.

The watch means a lot to me." He then closed his eyes for a brief moment, as if he was praying again.

Chancellor then leaned down and opened his duffel bag. After pulling out a large brown envelope, he reached inside and drew out a picture and handed it to her. "Have you ever seen this man at the shelter?" The photograph was of his twin brother, Chandler.

Laylah's breath caught. Then she laughed. "I believe I have seen him. He just happens to be sitting right across from me. What, didn't you think I'd recognize you?"

Chancellor had to smile. Her misinterpretation was an honest one. He'd never told her he had a twin brother, let alone a missing brother, one that he was desperately trying to locate. "That's not me. We're twins. Please take a real good look at the picture and see if you might be able to pick out the slight differences in us."

The mole at the right corner of Chandler's mouth was exactly how the Kingston family had been able to tell them apart as babies. He was curious to see if she would pick up on any of the other minuscule differences. Chandler's eyes were also lighter than Chancellor's and his sable hair was slightly curlier as opposed to Chancellor's waves.

As Laylah studied the picture, she took a spin back in time. For whatever reason, her mind had taken her to the first month of spring. She did recall seeing someone who looked like the guy in the picture, but she wasn't exactly positive it was him, nor could she remember the exact circumstances.

However, there was something about the guy that seemed so familiar to Laylah, in the same way Chancellor seemed memorable to her. She closed her eyes to try to conjure up an image of the man in the picture. A second later a rush of adrenaline suddenly shot right through her, causing her to tremble. She did remember him.

In fact, Laylah still had the memento the man had left behind to thank her for being so kind to him. As she opened her eyes, continuing to stare at the picture, things slowly began to become clear in her mind. He was why Chancellor seemed so familiar.

This man, who Laylah had never known the name of, had left a long-stemmed crystal rose for her at the shelter, an expensive little trinket in her opinion. The sweet note he'd also left had been written in his own handwriting, or so she had assumed. She could show the note to Chancellor to see if he recognized the handwriting.

As Laylah relayed her story to Chancellor, she saw the look of hope arise in his eyes. How his sparkling hazel eyes revealed his thoughts was so interesting to her, since the emotions in the eyes of the man in question had also been easy for her to read.

"Why'd you really show me the picture?"

"My brother has been missing awhile now." Chancellor gulped hard. "I need to find him. I'm scared something has happened to him. Some twins are able to feel each other's pain and sorrow. I feel his pain in spades. While I think he's still alive, I'm afraid if I don't find him he may not be that way much longer. He's homeless."

Nothing could've prepared Laylah for the tangle of emotions surging through her. Her heart went out to Chancellor in the same way it had gone out to Chandler, who had also been kind and gentle. Even as kind and soft-spoken as Chandler had been, Laylah had sensed that he was deeply troubled. She had also wondered if he suffered from mental illness. Theirs had been a strange and memorable encounter, though a very brief one.

"Please, I need to know if you can remember anything more about Chandler."

Laylah shook her head. "Just that you remind me so much of him. I'm sorry. The only thing I can suggest is to go back to my place so you can read the note he left for me at the shelter. Would you recognize your brother's handwriting?"

"Of course I would. Besides being brothers, we attended the same college and later worked and played together. We lived in the same house with our grandparents until we became adults. We eventually built our own home and moved in together. To sum it up, we were once inseparable. Then all hell broke loose. That, I'm not ready to explain."

The agony Chancellor was in was visible. He suffered emotionally, a lot. Laylah wished she knew what to do for him. Other than showing him the note, she didn't have a clue how to help lift his burden. She guessed that he'd already told her more than he had intended to. The look that had settled in his eyes was one of deep regret and pain.

Even though he'd barely touched his food, Chancellor summoned the waitress to ask for the check. When Laylah asked that the bill be handed to her, the look he gave her told her not to even try it. The waitress must have interpreted the look, too, because she handed the tab right to him.

So much for them going Dutch, Laylah thought quietly.

After Chancellor got to his feet, he reached his hand out for Laylah to take. "Let's go. I'm really anxious to see your note. Sorry to cut our lunch short."

Laylah looked down at his uneaten food. "Don't you want to take it with you?"

Frustrated now, Chancellor shoved his fingers through his hair. "Yeah, I probably should. I have some nerve wasting food when there are people who go hungry day in and day out." He stared hard at her. "That's what you're thinking, isn't it?"

The frigid anger in Chancellor's voice had set Laylah's teeth on edge. She was sorry that he felt aggravated, but he wasn't getting away with taking it out on her. "I don't appreciate you talking to me like that. I'm not responsible for any of your issues."

Stunned at her challenging remarks, Chancellor pursed his lips. "I know that…and I'm really sorry for directing my anger at you. Can you please forgive me?"

Laylah splayed her fingers over his heart. "I can. Please don't do it again. I have feelings, and I just don't like anyone talking down to me like that."

Chancellor kissed her forehead. "Neither do I. Once again, I'm sorry."

Laylah pulled the car right into the garage, making sure there was plenty of room for Chancellor to get out on the passenger side.

Once she opened the door leading into the house, she punched in the code to turn off the alarm system. Knowing he didn't want to waste any time on meaningless chitchat, she had him follow her upstairs to where one of three bedrooms served as an office.

Chancellor took a seat on a leather reclining chair while Laylah rummaged through the closet. All the boxes she had neatly stored there were labeled. It took her only a couple of minutes to locate the five boxes holding her precious mementos. She still had every birthday card her parents had ever given her. Her mom had started the tradition by keeping cards from the first to the eighteenth birthday of both her kids. Laylah had picked up from there.

A few seconds later Laylah came up with the greeting card from Chandler. She read his sweet message again before handing it to Chancellor. Taking a seat in the leather chair situated in front of her desk, she waited for him to open up to her.

You have been so kind to me. My life has truly been enhanced because of your presence. Please stay as sweet and humble as you are now. Don't ever change. Blessings, C.K., Chancellor had read, failing to keep his roiling emotions intact.

As Chancellor's tears cascaded down his cheeks, Laylah had a strong urge to run over to him and take him into her comforting arms. Instead, she lowered her lashes and prayed for him and his brother to soon be reunited. Now she knew what C.K. stood for.

With his hands trembling uncontrollably, Chancellor struggled hard to fold the card and place it back in the envelope. Before making eye contact with Laylah, he used the back of his hand to wipe away his tears. "Thank you. It's Chandler's handwriting."

Laylah couldn't help herself as she fled across the room and knelt down in front of Chancellor. Gripping both his hands, she laid her chin on this thigh and looked up at him. "I feel your pain. That may not make any sense to you, but it's true. I feel you."

"I know. I feel you, too, deep down inside. You're a very compassionate woman. Thank you so much for being kind to Chandler. People haven't always been kind to us."

Before Laylah could take her next breath, Chancellor had her up off the floor, settling her firmly onto his lap. His mouth took possession of hers, kissing her gently at first and then wildly, deeply. Her heart trembled as she fervently kissed him back, giving in to the electrifying sensations ripping right through her at breakneck speed.

As their tongues were introduced, they both felt the unadulterated passion. She knew how easy it would be for her to lose herself in him, so she had to fight hard to hold back. This man had her on fire and she knew he was just as hot for her. His manhood was erect, standing at full attention. He wanted her as much as she wanted him—and that thrilled her to no end.

She didn't see him as a homeless man or a man who was down on his luck. All she saw him as was a flesh-and-blood man, one who had physical needs matching her own. Their flesh was equally in dire need of physical release. Before things got any more out of hand, Laylah darn near leaped to her feet. The look in her eyes told Chancellor how sorry she was.

Chancellor looked all around the brightly decorated bedroom he had fallen asleep in. It was definitely all feminine fluff. The furniture was all white, including the rocking chair stationed in front of a window. The yellow-and-white comforter was sunny bright.

He and Laylah had gotten lost in talking up a storm. Knowing he wasn't going to get a bed for the night, because of how late it had gotten, she'd insisted on him staying in one of her guest bedrooms. He had enough money to go back to the previous motel, but she hadn't been in the mood to hear any of his solutions.

If Chancellor *had* left, he had somehow felt he would've possibly hurt Laylah emotionally, especially after they'd shared their first taste of passion. The wonderful feel of holding her in his arms had kept him warm and cozy all through the night. It had been hard for him not to creep into her bedroom and slide into bed with her. It wouldn't have been all about sex, either. Holding her body close to his would've satisfied him just as much.

Since it was Sunday morning, Chancellor wasn't in any hurry to hit the bricks. Besides that, he had already landed a halfway decent job; only for the time being. There were so many things about himself that he had to share with Laylah—and he planned to do so in the very near future. He just needed a little more time to pull it all together. Right now his top priority was locating his brother. Once that was accomplished, he felt he could go back to living his life the way he was used to. He missed his old life quite a bit.

He sat straight up in bed when he heard the light knock on

the door. Laylah, no doubt, he thought, since he was in her home. He quickly reached for his pants. Before he could slip them on, she was inside the room, causing him to pull the covers up.

Laylah had a breakfast tray in hand. "Good morning, sleepy-head. Up for a mug of this delicious hot brew?" She set the wooden tray across his lap. "I scrambled the eggs the way I thought you might like them. How'd I do?"

Chancellor stuck his fork into the fluffy eggs. "Soft, just the way I like them." He took a forkful of food and popped it into his mouth. "Mmm, it's good. You're a great cook." He then tasted the sausage and took a bite of buttery toast. "I think I'll keep you around," he mumbled, his mouth still full. "Something tells me you're a keeper."

Laylah let loose with a stream of sparkling laughter. She liked seeing him happy. His smile was nice and warm this morning. His lying nude beneath the comforter had her mind conjuring up all kinds of erotic images of them together. She knew he was naked because his pants were on the bed and his folded boxers were on the chair. If she didn't get out of this room, he might have to fight her off.

Chancellor refilled his fork with eggs and held it up to Laylah's mouth. When her ripe, juicy lips curved around the utensil, he wished they were meshing against his own. He couldn't help recalling how soft and sweet her lips tasted. Her deliciously scented skin was also as soft and pliable as her full mouth. His manhood suddenly responded to his torrid thoughts of her. If she didn't get out of this room, he didn't know what might happen next. He wanted her in the worst way, but she wasn't his to have.

Laylah got to her feet. "Left a clean towel and washcloth in the hall bathroom for you, also a brand-new toothbrush for you to use. No rush for you to get up. I'll be working in my office for a while. I have some important things to catch up on. Just set the tray on the nightstand when you're finished. I'll take care of it later," she said shakily.

"Laylah," he whispered softly, "you're shaking." He lifted the tray and set it on the nightstand. He then reached his arms out to her. "Come here. Just let me hold you until the trembling stops." He felt her reluctance. "It's okay. I just want to hold you."

Totally ignoring her common sense, Laylah inched her way over to the bed, glad she had slipped into jeans and a T-shirt. Being fully clothed should help out a lot. The thin nightgown she had worn to bed would've caught fire the instant he touched her. His hands had felt white-hot on her flesh last evening. If she kept playing with the scorching fire in his desire, she could expect to get burned. With that delectable thought in mind, Laylah slid onto the bed and lowered her head onto his broad chest.

Hearing his rhythmic heartbeat was soothing to her entire being. She felt relaxed, safe and content. With their eyes closed, either of them hardly moved a muscle as they lay quietly in each other's arms. His bare chest was so tempting to her, but she managed to refrain from taking a hardened nipple into her mouth and sucking gently. Instead, she blindly let her fingers glide back and forth over the muscular flesh. Her touch was slight; he felt it down to his core, his own trembling hard to ignore.

As he stroked her silky-soft hair, Chance felt at peace for the first time in a long while. His fears were gone for the moment, but he was smart enough to know this was just a temporary fix. That she was able to comfort him at all made him feel good. He was a lost man, a man who was steadily losing his purpose in life. Could Laylah make the difference in him? Needing her as desperately as he did was surprising. Chancellor wasn't used to being needy. It wasn't that bad of a feeling, he admitted to himself.

Lifting Laylah's head until their eyes connected, he kissed her mouth gently. "Are you ready for this?"

Laylah looked puzzled. "For what?"

"Getting involved with me on a romantic level? It's okay to be scared, 'cause I'm fearful as hell. Everything isn't as it appears, but you'll have to trust me until I can tell you exactly how it is. There's too much at stake to reveal more. Can you trust me?"

"I think so. I know I want to. And I'm not scared of you in the way you may think. The only thing that scares me is that I might give you my love, only to have you up and disappear on me. Can you tell me that that won't happen?"

"There are no guarantees in life. Love hurts. I don't think it should ever cause pain, but it does. Love can wreak a lot of havoc upon the heart."

Her eyes widened. "Are your speaking from experience?"

Emotional pain struck hard at his resolve. "Lots of it. More than I can say."

"Who was she and did you love her a lot?"

Chancellor warred with his emotions. "I never got a chance to love her a lot, yet I did, with all my heart and soul. Never got the chance to show her my love, period."

"That makes no sense. Did you love someone who didn't love you back?"

"You could say that. She was incapable of love. Still is."

"Who are you talking about?"

"My mother." He said the maternal word as if he were spitting it off his tongue, as if it left a bad taste in his mouth.

Shocked by his response, Laylah gasped. What could she say to that heart leveler? By the sorrowful look on Chancellor's face, she felt she needed to say something. "I'm sorry. Maybe I shouldn't be saying anything. The truth is I don't know what to say."

Chancellor brought Laylah's head back to rest on his chest. "There's nothing to say. My mother ran out on my brother and I. She simply didn't want us."

"Why?"

His hands trembled as he began stroking her hair again. "Wish I knew. I've heard a few theories, but I'm not ready to get into any of that. They suck. Believe it or not, it's still painful after all these years."

Her eyes sympathized with his plight. "I can only imagine."

"So, do you understand why I asked the questions I did about us getting involved?"

She nodded. "I understand perfectly." Her eyelashes fluttered uncontrollably. "Do you want to love someone?"

"*Someone?* No, I don't think someone will do. Do I want to love you? Yes, I want to love you. I don't want to love just for the sake of loving. I want to love so deeply, so completely that I won't know where I begin and my soul mate ends. I want love to consume me day and night, to wrap me up in its sweet arms forever. I just don't want it to be a fatal-attraction-type love, nor do I want either party to feel smothered by it."

Laylah thought Chancellor sounded desperate to give his love and to receive it. That was a bit scary but also exciting. She had never been consumed by love, yet it sounded like an awesome experience. More pitiful than that, she'd never even been loved, period. Not by a man. Her family couldn't love her more, but she had yet to experience the kind of love Chancellor desired. *Could she give him that type of love?*

Chapter 5

Laylah couldn't believe what March had just done. Reading everyone the provocative poem she'd recited at Bella's was so uncalled for. It may have backfired on him since everyone had clapped and cheered after he'd finished reading it. Still, her cheeks had turned red, but only because of how he'd chosen to display her work. Many of her co-workers knew she wrote poetry and many of them had also attended poetry night for one or more of her performances. To have him read it out loud to everyone in the office had made her feel kind of creepy despite the fervent clapping and loud cheering.

When the crowd began to disband, heading back to their work spaces, March walked over to Laylah, smiling devilishly. "How did I do with the reading?"

She rolled her eyes. "Please just go away."

"You brought this on yourself."

"Brought what on?"

"You don't recall asking me if could read? I wanted to show

you how well I can read. Now you seem all upset about it. How do I go about pleasing you?"

"You don't! There's nothing you can do to please me." She paused. "I take that back. There *is* something you can do."

"Name it."

"Get off my case. Stay out of my life. Leave me alone. Can you do any one of those things? If so, it'll definitely please me." With that said, she stormed off, leaving March glaring hard at her retreating back.

Inside her private office Laylah threw her purse under the desk and slammed her other items down on the L-shaped portion of the workstation. After turning on the computer, she sat there in stony silence. Her thoughts eventually took her back to the time she had spent with Chancellor. He had stayed at her home the entire day and most of the evening. She didn't know two people of the opposite sex could talk so much. Once again, they had lost track of time while chatting about so many things. While she had learned a lot more about him, she knew there was so much more he had yet to share with her.

Laylah decided to do what she'd been thinking of for quite some time. After opening the Microsoft Word program, she began typing a letter.

Dear Cora and Gertrude:

I am writing to you for advice on an extremely interesting but sticky situation I've recently gotten myself into. I am hopelessly attracted to a homeless man. He's not at all what you might envision. In fact, he's pretty clean-cut. I've never seen him looking dirty and scraggly. He's also handsome, witty, charming and quite intelligent. Right now he's just down on his luck, but he's a very conscientious person, one who is doing all he can to get back on his feet. He has recently landed a part-time job and I assume he'll look for a place to live once he's saved enough money. I love being with this nice man and I love the way he makes me feel. He's very special. I think I'm falling in love with him. Please write back to me and tell me what you think of this situation. I really need some sound advice and the answer to a few questions. Is it wrong for me to love someone who just happens to be displaced right now? Should I judge him by his financial status and his living situation or is it okay for me to love him for the kindhearted human I believe he is?

Laylah saved the letter before logging on to the Internet. Once she went to the Yahoo! site to her numerous e-mail accounts, under many screen names, she chose one of the names she used and then typed in one of the e-mail addresses her aunts used to receive letters from those seeking advice. They wouldn't recognize the address she was using because she'd never used it to correspond with family. Once she wrote a short e-mail, she attached the letter she'd saved on her hard drive and then hit Send.

Laylah couldn't wait to see what advice her aunts would give her. She once again wondered if their guidance would be different from what they'd say to a stranger, as opposed to what they'd tell their niece if she had sat down with them face-to-face.

Upon checking her voice mail, Laylah's ears perked up when she heard one of her sources mention Ashley Roberson. Because she hadn't listened to the news all weekend, which was terribly unusual for her, she hadn't heard that the child's estranged father, Dirk Roberson, had somehow been implicated in the disappearance of the little girl. She would have to call her confidential source to get more information. It was still pretty early in the morning, so she thought she'd wait at least until after nine o'clock.

In dire need of her morning caffeine, she got up from her desk and slowly made her way to the break room, hoping she didn't encounter March. The guy was starting to make her sick to the stomach on sight. What he'd done this morning was cruel and thoughtless. That little dirty scheme of his made her more determined to land his job.

Several of her co-workers were in the break room when she entered. She said her polite greetings then proceeded toward the coffeepot. This morning she would take it black, something she rarely did or needed, but she had lain awake until the wee hours of the morning with Chancellor the past two nights.

"Beautiful poem," Tom Kerns said to her. "Is there a way to purchase a copy? I'd like to give one to Marina. She'll love it since she's a die-hard romantic."

At first Laylah suspected Tom of jerking her chain, but the sincere look in his eyes belied that. "I can arrange that. When do you need it?"

"Whenever it's convenient for you. Come to think of it, her birthday is next week. It would make an awesome gift."

Laylah cracked up. "Now I know you don't plan to present her with just a poem, or do you?" Her look grew sober as she waited for his response.

Tom shook his head. "Hardly! She's getting a *girl's best friend* gift, but I think the poem will add a nice, sentimental touch."

"You are serious about this, aren't you?" Laylah inquired, smiling happily.

"Of course I am. I really like your work. Do you have any others similar to it?"

"Dozens of them." Though Laylah hadn't planned to stay in

the break room, she pulled out a chair at the long conference-style table and took a seat. "I'll tell you what. Since it's for Marina's birthday, I'll type up the poem on fancy paper and use a nice font. Then I'll laminate it for you. Is that cool?"

"That sounds great. Can you personalize it, like put her name on it?"

"I can do that."

"One more thing?"

Laylah gave him a pushing-the-envelope look. "What's that?"

"Will you please autograph it before you laminate it? That'll make it special."

Laylah's mouth broke out into a huge grin. "Flattery is also a girl's best friend, especially when delivered in a sincere way. You just made my day, Tom. Thanks. By the way, is the girl's best friend you mentioned fashioned in an engagement ring?"

Tom blushed. "Not yet. Tennis bracelet." As the cheering rang out, he laughed heartily. "How much will all that specialty stuff cost me?"

"Not a thing. Compliments of the one-day-to-become-famous poet. Then you can say you knew me when."

Everyone in the room had a good laugh at that.

"Can you bring in some of your other work for us to see?" Cherise Crane asked. "I might like to purchase a few of your poems to frame and hang in my apartment. Maybe some of us co-workers can help make you famous."

Laylah had the warmest feeling inside. Her colleagues had her heart filled to the brim. She loved her work, but she was biased, of course. Her family often raved about her poetry, too, but she'd never given any thought to doing anything with it outside of reciting it on poetry nights in different venues. She'd just been given food for thought.

"I think you should write a poetry book," Erika Lowe stated.

"I've heard you recite several of your writings. They're all good. We should get a group of friends together and go down to Bella's Friday night. Are you on the program then?"

"I'm on practically every Friday night. There's a big poetry event down at Two Brothers' this Saturday night. I'm performing there also. I'd love to have the support in the newest venue if at all possible. I know most everybody down at Bella's."

"I'll get the message around to everyone in the office," Manny Lopez offered. "I can make a fancy announcement on the computer to hang on the bulletin board."

Laylah frowned. "Please, not everyone. March doesn't need to know about it. He'll only try to embarrass me again like he did earlier."

"He's out of town this coming weekend," Kaye Sparks added. She worked as March's administrative assistant. He made her almost as miserable as he made Laylah, though it wasn't out of any personal interest. The man made most of the staff unhappy.

"Yippee," Laylah yelped, clapping her hands enthusiastically. She got to her feet. "Thanks, guys. You all have made me feel really good this morning. Now I can get back to my desk and have a kick-butt kind of day. See you all later."

"Are you joining us for our regular Monday luncheon date? We chose Panera Bread for today," Tom mentioned.

Laylah gave a firm nod. "See you all at lunch. Twelve-thirty, right?"

"Twelve-thirty," Kaye confirmed. "You can ride with me if you'd like."

"It's a date. Bye, guys."

While Chancellor was seated in the doctor's office, waiting to be seen, he began flipping through *Black Business Digest,* a very popular enterprise-type magazine featuring successful or upcoming young black entrepreneurs. After turning only a few pages, he saw two very familiar smiling faces staring back at him. He knew exactly when the photograph had been taken and also why it had been taken, but he'd forgotten this feature story was due to run in this month's digest. He moaned inwardly.

Before Chancellor had a chance to begin perusing the story, a cute nurse poked her head out the door and called his name. He laid the magazine aside and followed the young lady into the inner offices. He was then led to a fair-size room and told to strip down completely. Both his eyebrows shot up at that not-so-nice request.

The thin paper gown Chancellor was handed by the nurse would hardly cover all of his anatomy, at least not in his opinion. He handled it as if it was a dreaded disease. Because of his height, he was sure it would look like a miniskirt on him. He surely didn't like the back being open to expose all and sundry. None of this pleased him one iota. The huge frown on his face showed his utter dismay.

Just as Chancellor let go of a mild expletive, the nurse popped back into the room.

She handed Chancellor a clear plastic cup. "Before you disrobe, I need you to give us a clean-catch urine sample." She went on to explain how to attain a clean-catch specimen. "The bathroom is right outside this door and to the left. Please leave the sample in the metal bin on the wall for the lab to retrieve."

Chancellor was glad her back was to him when the heat stole into his cheeks, causing them to burn like fire. Having a woman telling him to go urinate in a cup and how to clean himself off before doing it—and then where to leave it—wasn't his idea of a pleasurable moment. He always did hate physical checkups, but he probably wouldn't mind it as much if no females whatsoever were involved in the procedure. That particular thought hadn't cleared his mind when another female shot into the room as if she'd been fired from a cannon. Facing yet another nurse had him wanting to tear out of there and head for the nearest bar to order a whiskey neat.

The lady in the white lab coat extended her hand to him. "Hello. I'm Dr. Reva Lyons." She looked down at the chart. "Well, Mr. Kriegle, I see you're here today for a prostate exam."

Chancellor's mind was still stuck on the doctor being a female. When what she had said finally registered in his brain, his skin turned ashy gray. "Uh…you got…the wrong patient for that," he stammered, quickly giving her his full name.

Dr. Lyons slapped her hands on each side of her face. "Please forgive my error, Mr. Kingston. This has already been one harrowing Monday morning…and it has barely begun. Why *are* you here to see me?"

"A physical, ma'am. Just a plain old employment physical." Chancellor couldn't remember the last time he had had a checkup. He was sure it hadn't happened in the past few years, but he was obviously long overdue for one.

Dr. Lyons chuckled, knowing Mr. Kingston thought he was off the hook for the prostate test. Not only was it a part of the checkup, so was the infamous finger-wave. That should really get his Bunsen burners burning, she thought, laughing inwardly. After telling him she'd be back in to see him shortly, she hurried out of the room, leaving him staring at the urine cup in his trembling hand.

Chancellor couldn't wait for this appointment to be over.

Laylah hung up the phone from speaking to her source about the Roberson daughter-and-father situation. She knew that the father and mother were estranged. Though unmarried, they had been living together from the onset of Renee Matthews's pregnancy. It was believed that the father may have taken the child across states lines, heading for the South, possibly to one of the Carolinas, where he was originally from.

This particular source was a close friend and co-worker of Renee's.

There were a lot of newsworthy stories where these folks resided, very sad ones, also lots of violence, including armed robberies and carjackings. Laylah had made several acquaintances in the area. Many of them had become her personal contacts. No one was paid for any kind of information, but most of the folks believed they were helping out.

She took a minute to open the fat letter she'd received by special delivery first thing this morning, slitting one end of it with a razor-sharp letter opener. Although she had been highly curious about its contents earlier, since it was from a television station, she had tended to the most pressing issues first, which had also included her morning fix, a cup of delicious hot coffee.

Eyebrows shot up as Laylah perused the letter. Her surprise grew more and more after each line she read. It fascinated her that a television station wanted to hire her as a special correspondent, handling newsworthy stories and events. Her communications license was always kept current so she was okay there. She had often thought about doing television news. Brandon had even encouraged her countless times, offering to put in a good word for her with one of the producers at his network.

Taking the job would certainly help her get rid of the annoying March Riverton.

As Laylah continued to read, the letter stated she had come to their attention on high recommendations. *Brandon.* She smirked. She loved that lots of travel had been mentioned. She could live with that. While a dollar amount wasn't given, the promise of her salary being very worth her while caused her to smile. She could use a raise, but then everyone in the company could use one. Promising herself to give the letter serious thought, she folded the neatly typed pages and put them back in the envelope.

With so much stuff going on in her life, the exciting things along with the scary ones, Laylah decided to call Kelly right now instead of waiting until she flew in on Friday. Her best friend's number was loaded on her speed dial, so she clicked in the memory code, hoping Kelly was at her desk. Fat chance since the girl was always flitting about in and around the studio, which made it hard for Laylah to get her at work.

Surprisingly enough, Kelly answered on the second ring. "Hey, Lay," she sang into the receiver.

"Kell, how are you?"

"Couldn't be better. Something must be up, girlfriend. You hardly ever call me at work. Is everything okay with you?" Kelly sounded concerned.

"Actually, everything in my life is chaotic. You'll never guess in a million years what has happened to me." Praying for understanding, Laylah launched into her story.

Kelly released a deep sigh into the phone, sounding relieved. "Is that all? You had me scared there for a minute. I don't know why you're so surprised about being attracted to a homeless man. You've always picked up strays. That's your nature. This is how you've been all your life. Why are you freaking out over this one? Is he hot?"

"Sizzzzling," Laylah said in dramatic fashion. "I know I'm a compassionate woman and I'm always out for the underdog, but am I taking it too far with this one?"

"You have always listened to your heart, Lay. Just 'cause you're not normal doesn't mean anything…"

"What!" Laylah screeched. "Not normal! How's that?"

"Maybe I used the wrong choice of words. It's just that you

have this way of sensing things the normal person can't make any sense of. If this guy turns you on as much as you say he does, go with your gut instincts. They've served you well thus far. You've never been one to take stuff like this lightly. Trust yourself and your feelings."

"All I wanted was a little understanding, but you've given me so much more. I *do* feel good about this guy…and I guess it is okay to continue going with my instincts. There's just something about Chance that causes my pulse to soar. I also sense something really deep is going on with him." She went on and told Kelly about Chandler Kingston and how Chancellor was desperately trying to find his twin.

"This sounds like a great story for you to write. Are you entertaining the idea?"

"I've thought about it a time or two. It's a great human-interest story, but I'd need to know more about him before deciding to take the leap. I'd also need to know how he'd feel about me writing it."

"I'm not sure I'd tell him just yet, but keep thinking about it. We'll talk more over the weekend. Did you get the e-mail with my itinerary?"

"Got it. See you at one o'clock on Friday. I'm taking the afternoon off. Are you checking bags?"

"You've got to be kidding. Carry-on is the only way to go, sister. Baggage claim is always a huge nightmare. Oops, got to run. The intercom is buzzing. Later, Lay."

"Later." Laylah smiled as she cradled the phone. Thinking of how much she and Kelly loved each other gave her a warm rush. She felt both blessed and lucky to have such a good friend.

The only reason Laylah had even considered not telling Kelly about Chancellor was because of her own phobias over the situation. Kelly was truly a loyal friend and a great person. However, she had thought Kelly might've reacted a bit differently. That she hadn't reacted negatively made it so much sweeter. Laylah had purposely held back news about the job offer. It was something she wanted to discuss with Kelly in person, after she had let her read the letter of interest she'd received.

Out of pure curiosity, for no other reason than that, Laylah put the Kingston name into her Google search engine. In a matter of seconds hundreds of Kingston references popped up on her screen. Scrolling through the entries, she didn't know what she was looking for. Just as one particular document caught her attention, her intercom line sounded off. Upon hearing March's voice, she shook her head in dismay.

While Laylah waited for her brother, Brandon, to pick up the phone, she wondered for the umpteenth time why Chancellor hadn't shown up at the shelter to eat or to sign up for a bed. She had constantly looked out for him, all to no avail. Her disappointment had grown tenfold by the time she had realized he was simply a no-show. Still worried about Chancellor, she hoped he was okay and that nothing bad had happened.

Another bout of disappointment hit her when Brandon's message center picked up. She left a message for him to call her back, telling him it was really important. Besides wanting to talk to him about the offer she'd received from the television network, she also wanted to ask him if he had anything to do with it.

March had once again enraged Laylah when he'd summoned her into his office earlier in the morning. Apparently he'd been called on the carpet by the powers that be in administration. Needing someone to blame for the bad situation, he had accused her of filing complaints against him. She hadn't done so. She'd told him that, but he hadn't believed her. A heated argument would've ensued between employee and boss, but she had sensed he was trying to get her to overstep the boundaries so he could fire her.

Although there were many times Laylah had thought of filing grievances against March, she had held back, thinking it was just a matter of time before he cooked his own goose. He was the best candidate for getting himself fired. He couldn't continue covering up his lack of knowledge about his job and his nonexistent skills in employee relations. His inability to relate to the people he supervised was quite apparent to everyone who worked under him. March simply didn't measure up as a leader, on any level.

Looking upset and confused, Chancellor stood outside Laylah's front door, having used the security code Laylah had given him to the gate so he could tend the lawn when she wasn't at home.

The day had been an unpleasant one for him. Tired, physically and mentally, was an understatement for how he felt. He had searched high and low for his brother, hitting shelter after shelter, showing Chandler's picture, asking if anyone had seen him. To try to stay away from Laylah had been his intent, before he'd admitted to himself that it would be impossible to toss her out of his life. His deep feelings for her wouldn't allow it.

Whether or not to ring the bell hadn't been decided yet. Chancellor wanted to see her, needed to spend time in her company, but he was fearful that his feelings for her were starting to get out of control.

If what he felt for Laylah was love, Chancellor hadn't felt anything like this ever before. She was constantly in his thoughts and in his prayers. Thinking he should have called before coming there, he chided himself for his rash behavior. After pulling out from his wallet the card she'd given him, he turned it over and looked at her phone number. Another act of insanity; he didn't have a phone.

As Chancellor turned to walk away, the garage door started

upward, startling him something awful. A tad calmer now, he took the few steps leading him over to the driveway. That's when he saw Laylah standing inside the garage with her back to him.

Hearing something behind her, Laylah turned around, screaming at the top of her lungs before she saw it was Chancellor. Upon recognizing him, her hand instantly went up to her mouth, hoping no one had heard her yelling her head off. This was a pretty tight town-house community, one where the owners looked out for each other. The last thing she and Chancellor needed was for one of her good neighbors to call the police.

Having seen the terror-stricken look on Laylah's face, he rushed over to her and gathered her into his arms. "It's just me," Chancellor soothed, hugging her. "It's okay. Sorry I scared the daylights out of you. I should've called first. Are you all right?"

Loving the feel of Chancellor's arms wrapped so tightly around her, Laylah clung to him, basking in the warmth of his security. "I'm fine. Sorry for my reaction. I thought an intruder had gotten into the complex. I didn't know you were coming."

Chancellor laughed nervously. "I didn't know either, not until after I found myself standing here at the front door. I've been doing a lot of crazy things since I met you." He pressed his lips into her right temple. "Think someone might've heard you screaming?"

"I hope not. I had wondered the same thing. I was about to put the trash out on the curb for pickup tomorrow morning. Let's get inside in case a neighbor calls to see if I'm okay instead of phoning the police department. If my next-door neighbor thought I was in trouble, he would've been out here by now, .357 Magnum in hand. If the police do come, we'll just calmly tell them what happened. No big deal."

"Good idea. You go ahead inside. I'll follow once I put the trash out for you."

Grateful for Chancellor's suggestion, Laylah looked all

around the area. "Maybe I should wait out here until you're finished just in case the police *do* show up."

"Okay. Is everything already in the trash barrel I see over there in the corner?"

"That's only one of them. I have three." She pointed out the other two on the far side of the garage. "They all need to go out. Thanks."

"Not a problem." Chancellor left Laylah standing outside as he went into the garage and grabbed a hold of two of the larger trash cans. All three were on wheels, which made it easier for him to get them down the driveway and out to the curb.

Once Chancellor had taken care of putting out the trash, Laylah again invited him inside. His presence was something she'd been hoping for. He gladly accepted her offer, glad the evening would begin with them on the same page.

Having just prepared herself a steak dinner, Laylah went into the kitchen, where she'd left her food in the oven to keep warm. Her intention had been to sit down and enjoy her meal once the trash had been tended to. After removing the pan from the lower oven, she cut in halves both the baked potato and the steak. Each half of the meal was set on the lovely but casual square plates she always kept on the table. With that simple task accomplished, she yelled out for him to join her in the kitchen.

Once Chancellor appeared in the room, Laylah threw caution to the wind by lighting the candles nestled inside a wooden centerpiece, accented with a bunch of polished stones. "I love to eat in an intimately lit atmosphere. What about you?"

Chancellor grinned, shrugging. "I'm for whatever makes you happy. I also enjoy dining by candlelight." He laughed when he saw the halved portions on each plate. "You *do* believe in sharing, don't you? This is nice." Without uttering another word, he walked over to the sink and washed his hands, drying them on a paper towel.

Upon Chancellor rejoining Laylah, he took her hand and then offered up a humble prayer of thanks. After pulling her chair out for her to be seated, he also sat down.

The minute Laylah picked up her fork she realized she'd forgotten the green beans, steaming in butter and herbs in a pot on the stove. She rapidly excused herself and headed straight for the built-in, gas-range top. Back at the table, Laylah practically skipped back across the room and took her seat. With fork in hand, she looked over at Chancellor and smiled beautifully. "How was your day, dear?" she asked on a giggle, enacting one of the scenes from the film *Pretty Woman.*

Chancellor loved the sultry voice she used in delivering her question. She never failed to make him laugh, which made him feel good all over. "My day could've been better, but it also could've been much worse. I'm blessed. However, I had the experience of all experiences today. I got more than I bargained for at the doctor's office." He moaned. "My behind still doesn't feel so good."

Laylah looked confused. "What does that mean?"

"You know, the things they do to men during a physical."

"Oh, that," she said, chuckling. "It can't be any worse than what happens to women. You guys should try having your feet uncomfortably propped up in stirrups for an eternity, with your intimate treasures exposed to all the elements."

"Compared to that, I guess the exam wasn't that bad. I survived."

"Wonderful! Let's eat." Laylah clapped her hands before digging in, glad Chancellor hadn't asked about her tough day.

Chapter 6

Drawing her closer to him, tilting up Laylah's chin with a closed fist, Chancellor's lips, starving to taste hers, engaged her mouth in a deliciously staggering kiss. The fire shooting straight up his spine made his whole body feel hot. Her fingers, tangled in his hair, tugging gently, had already fully aroused the lower half of his body. His manhood throbbed so hard he felt as if it might explode at any moment.

Wanting her in the worst way, he squirmed around on the sofa until he was in a horizontal position. As he brought her down on top of him, their desire for each other had already begun to heat up. As his lips gently seduced the side of her neck, his hands drifted toward her breasts, cupping them tenderly.

Laylah was still in control, but she was ready to free herself from all restraints. It'd be so easy for her to lose it completely with him. She was already so close to it. His wet kisses had her body on fire, making her want more and more of the white-hot treats he had to offer. When his fingers began to undo the buttons on her cotton shirt, she tenderly stroked the back of his hand. The sizzling sensations coursing through her body had her moaning and purring softly.

Encouraged by her unmistakable body language, as well as her whispered desires, Chancellor continued his tender exploration of her beautiful body. As he helped her out of her blouse, her hands itched badly to assist him in stripping off his restricting attire. Then he relieved her of her bra, making a seductive showing of it.

Laylah watched him disrobe, enjoying every delicious moment, though she wished he'd move a bit faster. Her breathing was already labored. As the bottom half of his attire was finally removed, she stifled the nervous giggle tickling her throat. He *is* strapped, she thought, though not surprised by the caliber of what his plain white briefs were packing. For sure, his body packed tons of heat.

Chancellor's lips pressing into the side of Laylah's neck made her want to tear off his briefs in one rapid motion. He lay back on the sofa, drawing her on top of him. As she squirmed around beneath his delicious hard body, she felt the bulge of his manhood growing more and more rigid against her thigh. The hardened flesh caused her spine to tingle with flashes of heat, as well as heating up other delicate parts of her anatomy.

Looking up into Chancellor's eyes, Laylah hoped he had read in hers what she needed from him. He'd have to be blind not to see how much she wanted him inside of her. But in case he didn't recognize the fire in her eyes, scorching red-hot for him, she decided to tell him exactly what she had on her mind. "Make love to me, Chance. I want you more than you can possibly imagine. I can feel how much you want me, too."

That was all he needed to hear. After carefully lifting her off him, he got to his feet. Hoisting her up into his arms, he carried her down the hall, relying on her to direct him to the master bedroom. Passionately kissing her all the while, he didn't seem in too big of a hurry to get her into bed.

The erotic union wasn't going to be a rush job, not if Chancellor had his way. His slow, thorough seduction of Laylah hopefully would make her desire him even more. He could hardly wait for their ultimate connection. He had every intention of burning his way into Laylah's heart and to unite their spirits forever.

The foreplay was nothing short of arresting. Chancellor's luscious mouth and dexterous fingers knew the exact spots on her body to touch, tease and taste. By the time he was ready to take things to a deeper level, she was ready to be taken.

He gently slipped inside her intimate treasures and her muscles flexed tightly around his manhood, causing him to shudder wildly. "Laylah," he cried out, "I need you so much." She felt so good to him, making him feel wonderful.

The onset of the journey into ecstasy had begun as easy and as lazy as a summer afternoon. No rush, just the way Chancellor liked it. He continued to kiss and caress her, stroking her up and down—and she couldn't seem to get enough of his gentle touch.

Then he suddenly turned up the heat, as his hips gyrated wildly. His strokes grew more intense. The power behind his deep thrusts caused her to tightly grip his buttocks as she hung on for the amazing finale. As he whispered her name over and over, the climax simultaneously rocked their world off its axis.

After slowly rolling off Laylah, he pulled her on top of him, burying his lips in the soft folds of her neck. To calm her breathing, he tenderly stroked her back, wondering if his own speeding heart rate would ever slow down. Chancellor had made love to many women in the past, but nothing compared to what he'd just shared with Laylah. It was the most beautiful and the only soulful experience he'd ever had.

He knew tears were falling from her eyes because he felt moisture on his chest. Hoping she was crying because she felt really good, and not out of any regret, he looked up into her eyes. "That good, huh?" He had wanted to make things light rather than make her think he was fearful of her reaction.

Laylah laughed softly. "Way better than just good. You are amazing!"

Chancellor sighed with relief. "Baby, so are you. You are truly awesome."

His lips connected with hers again. As the kiss deepened, his manhood throbbed to attention. Not wanting to wear out his welcome, or make himself seem greedy, he didn't act upon his renewed desire. As hard as it was to resist making love to her again, he thought it was best. Just lying there next to her was a wonderful feeling.

With their bodies comfortably entwined, they soon fell off to sleep.

Laylah awakened in the early hours of the morning. Chancellor was gone. She didn't know what to make of it, but she made the decision not to dwell on it. She would only end up second-guessing his disappearance anyway. She didn't know why he'd left her side after such an awesome sexual encounter; speculating on it might bring about negative thoughts. She didn't want to do that. Only he had the answers.

She didn't know where she and Chancellor would go from here, but she hoped they'd have lots of repeat performances. She *was* in love with him. She wouldn't have made love to him if she hadn't already fallen in love with him. There was not one ounce of regret over what had occurred between them.

She had earlier planned to ask Chancellor where they'd go from here, but she'd somehow felt it would take away from the beautiful, breathtaking moments they'd shared. It might also sound as if she was pressuring him about entering into a relationship with her. If she never saw him again, she'd always have the memories of their wonderful experiences, something she could definitely look back on and smile.

She was happy, thoroughly so. In fact, she'd never been happier and more content.

The bedroom door suddenly opened and in walked Chancellor. As naked as the day he was born, except for the towel around his neck, he pointed upward. "Just took a shower in the upstairs hall bathroom. Didn't want to wake you. Hope you don't mind."

Laylah's heart was too full to speak. That he hadn't actually walked out on her after such a beautiful experience had her floating. All she wanted to do was jump up and down in the center of the bed. Of course, she refrained from acting so darn crazy.

Misinterpreting her silence, Chancellor wasn't sure what to do next. His clothes were still out in the living room, so he couldn't begin dressing. He pointed toward the bedroom door. "I guess I'd better go up front and get my hand-me-down clothes."

Laylah smiled lazily, sorry he was so nervous. "What's your hurry?"

Chancellor's heart skipped several beats as it rejoiced over her question. She hadn't verbally invited him back to her bed, but he'd interpreted her body language as an invitation. As he rapidly closed the distance between them, he couldn't wait to hold her in his arms, couldn't wait to feel what he'd felt last night. It didn't matter if they made love again or not, he just wanted her next to him so he could caress her softness.

Laylah went straight into his arms after he'd settled down in bed. She thought her head fit perfectly into the well of his arm. He smelled so good. She laughed inwardly as she recognized the scent. He had used the lavender shower gel she kept in all the guest bathrooms.

Chancellor stroked her hair as they lay there in total silence. Being next to him was a total joy for her. They both felt content. Regardless of the lack of conversation, a lot of wonderful things were definitely being communicated between the two.

In two hours or so Laylah knew she'd have to get up and get ready for work. She wasn't sure of his schedule, but he'd probably leave when she left. Even if she told him he could stay as long as he'd like, she knew he wouldn't take her up on the offer.

Chancellor was a very proud man.

Pleased that he was helping her fix breakfast, Laylah couldn't stop looking at him as he stood over the stovetop grill preparing silver-dollar pancakes. He had already cooked the sausage links and had put them in the oven to keep warm. She was genuinely surprised to find that he knew his way around the kitchen as she scrambled the eggs and brewed coffee. In the mood for tea, she also had water boiling.

This was anything but a typical morning for Laylah, yet everything felt normal to her. No man had ever slept in her brand-new bed or spent the night there. Since her town house was fairly new, ten months old, no men other than those in her family, and a couple of male friends and co-workers, had sat down to eat in her kitchen. Chancellor being there with her was very real and sometimes surreal—and she liked having him around.

They were both fully dressed. They had showered together before slipping into their attire. She had a power suit on and he wore the jeans and shirt he'd had on from the previous night. She still didn't know if Benjamin had handed out clothing to him, and she didn't feel right about asking him. It really didn't matter to her where the used clothes came from. They were clean and he looked good in them.

After pouring steaming coffee into a mug, Laylah carefully carried it over to the table. Before she could go back to fix her tea, Chancellor was already pouring hot water over the peach-mint tea bag she'd placed in the mug earlier. She kept her eyes on him as he brought the cup over to her and set it down. He then sat across from her at the table.

This time Laylah passed the blessing over the meal.

After taking her first bite of the fluffy pancake, she closed her eyes expressively. "So good," she said to him. "They are so light and airy. I could eat a couple dozen."

Chancellor grinned. "Wouldn't recommend that, not if you care about your waistline. These babies are fattening, especially with all the syrup you put on them."

"Won't you still love me if I fatten up these hips and thighs?"

Stroking his chin, Chancellor narrowed his eyes at her.

Laylah wished she could take that question back. She'd been teasing, yet she didn't think he had taken her remark as a joke. "I'm sorry. I shouldn't have said that."

He stared hard at her. "Said what?"

"You didn't hear me?"

"I heard you. Just want to know if you're bold enough to repeat it."

Laylah didn't know what to say to that. Her breakfast was starting to be ruined by her nerves running amok in her stomach. "Whatever."

"Will that be the answer to everything you don't want to deal with?"

Laylah looked nonplussed. "I don't know what you're getting at."

"Yes, you do. You asked me if I'd still love you if you got fat. Why are you trying to pretend it didn't happen, when it did?"

"I know it happened. It's how you may've taken the question that worries me."

"How'd you intend for me to take it?"

Exasperation was quickly taking over Laylah. "I made a stupid blunder, okay?"

"Is that what you call it, a blunder? Why is it stupid?"

Close to tears, Laylah jumped up from her seat. Breakfast was now a fiasco; it was all her fault. Why had she gone and said the L word. He was upset with her about it, but not as much as she was disappointed in herself. Oh well, this little affair was certainly short-lived. She probably would have to kiss him off after he left her house.

Before Laylah could leave the room, Chancellor came up behind her and grabbed her around the waist. "Hey, hey, what's the matter, babe? Sorry I upset you. I was only kidding. I thought you'd fire right back at me, like you always do. I didn't know you were so sensitive." He rested his chin on her shoulder, begging her for forgiveness.

Tilting her head back, Laylah looked up at him. "I guess I overreacted, huh? I thought you were mad at me for saying the L word. You looked upset."

He pressed his lips onto the top of her head. "But we've discussed the L word before. Don't you recall us talking about love?" He turned her around to face him. "Don't you remember me telling you I want to love you?"

Her heart nearly burst open from the excitement his comment

generated. Of course she remembered. How could she ever forget? "So you're not mad at me?"

He grazed her lips with his fingertips. "I'm mad, okay, but not about that. Mad about having to leave you. That's what I am. Can I come back this evening?"

She put her finger up to her right temple. "Hmm, I'll have to think about that one." She then leaped right into his arms. "I get home around seven-thirty."

Chancellor cracked up. "That's some rapid-fire thinking you got there, girl. We might want to can that quickness and sell it on the black market."

"I doubt anyone would pay one red cent for it." She got a glimpse at the clock, yelping in response to the time. "I've got to get out of here." She looked over at her barely eaten breakfast. "I don't even have time to finish my pancakes, unless I want to be late, and I don't. You worked so hard to make them for me."

"Not to worry. We'll just put everything away and eat it for dinner. Then I won't have to get in line down at the shelter. Sound like a plan?"

"A brilliant one," she responded, smiling.

Laylah and Chancellor began cleaning up behind themselves. She stacked the dishwasher while he put the food in plastic containers. He liked how well they worked as a team. His late grandmother and grandfather couldn't be in the kitchen together for more than ten minutes before she started yelling for him to get out. Yet they had loved each other without end. Being in the kitchen with his family was only one of millions of fond memories he carried around inside his head, ones that he wished he could relive.

Never going to happen again, he thought sadly. The wonderful memories only fueled his desire to find Chandler. Locating his brother was a must. He couldn't allow himself to think he'd never see him again. He would see him. He had to.

* * *

Laylah hung up the phone and reared back in her leather chair. As she looked around her office, she thought about how she'd feel if she gave it all up. There were a lot of sentimental memories within the walls of *L.A. Press*, yet the unpleasantness was really getting to her. She was tired of allowing March to make her miserable.

Although she would feel as if she was deserting her co-workers, she had to be happy wherever she worked. She was no longer happy at *L.A. Press* and not at all happy with the current boss. The television job was becoming more and more appealing to her. Now that she knew Brandon wasn't behind the offer, and that the network wanted her because of her excellence in journalism, it made it so much easier for her to start seriously considering a move. The interview had been set up for a week from now.

Wanting to take a look to see if her aunts had written back to her, Laylah logged on to the Internet under the same screen name she'd used to send the letter. With the numerous screen names she'd created, she had hard times remembering them all. Her eyes lit up as she saw the e-mail from her aunts.

Dear Young Lady:

Please excuse the greeting above. You failed to sign your letter, so we can't address you in a more personal manner. Thank you for writing to us. You help keep us in business by using our services. We appreciate you supporting our newspaper column.

As for your dilemma, we've never had anyone write to us about something like this. The subject of your letter is very interesting. You gave us a lot to think about, and think about it we did. All we could do was mull it over during the past couple of days.

You are obviously a very compassionate person. There

aren't too many people who would even consider getting involved with a homeless man, let alone actually going for it. However, we can think of one other person who would champion your young man, a beautiful someone very near and dear to us.

You are definitely to be commended on having such a pure heart. Let your heart of gold continue to lead you. If you honestly have romantic feelings for this man, we believe you should explore them. If you don't go with your instincts, you'll never know.

We wish you the best of luck. Please keep us posted on future developments..

God bless you,

Cora and Gertrude

Laylah fingered the computer screen, outlining the broad strokes of her aunt Gertrude's signature and her aunt Cora's thinner one. Cora's handwriting was smaller, often hard to read. Thank God she typed her letters on the computer, but she could remember a time when her father's adorable but tough sisters had handwritten all their correspondence.

Laylah had to wonder if her aunts, the Versailles sisters, would have answered the letter the way they'd done if they had known it was from their very own niece.

The big staff meeting was scheduled for less than an hour from now. She cringed at the thought. She used to love staff meetings. They used to be so much fun, until March had come aboard. Now they were boring as could be, because all he talked about was himself and his outstanding accomplishments.

None of the staff ever received any accolades from March on a job well done. He didn't know how to give out deserving compliments. He barked out orders and yelled when they weren't carried out to his satisfaction. Leaving notes about his complaints on the desks of his employees was his personal way of addressing issues that displeased him. Lately, laughter was rarely heard around the *Press* offices—and he seemed to love bringing the female employees to tears whenever he needed a lift in his day.

Folks could hardly wait until the staff meetings were adjourned and Laylah was sure that today would be no exception, especially for her.

Chancellor sat behind a beautiful mahogany desk, imperiously stationed inside a beautifully decorated office with all sorts of state-of-the-art equipment. Innumerable leather-bound books were housed in heavy wooden bookshelves with smoked-glass doors. On the other side of the room was dark red leather furniture: a nail-studded sofa, love seat and two wingback chairs. The wood-and-glass coffee and end tables were carved into the shape of a dollar sign, an unusual design that definitely made a bold statement.

As Chancellor read through a stack of mail, he hoped to find a letter from Chandler. Wishful thinking. It was as though his brother had vanished off the face of the earth. Other than what Laylah had shown him, not another clue had been found. Chandler's letter to her had been written a good while back. He couldn't help worrying that his brother might be sick or in big trouble. His stomach let him know when something was wrong and it had really started giving him more of a fit a few days ago. Sucking up the pain was something he was a pro at, but this was a different set of circumstances.

After picking up the long typed list of shelters, Chancellor began checking off the ones he'd already visited. There were several dozen more to go in a city the size of Los Angeles. He even planned to extend his search up north if warranted.

Chandler also loved to hang out nearby in Las Vegas and also at the resorts of Sedona, Arizona.

Chancellor knew he had to pick up a scent, one that might put him on the right track and keep him there until he found Chandler. Although his brother, who wasn't opposed to hitch-hiking, could be in another country by now, he had to continue to let hope abide. He lowered his head for a moment of silent prayer.

Before leaving for work, Laylah had taken out a nice cut of beef from the freezer to roast for dinner. On the way home, after a tiring full day, she stopped off at the grocer's to pick out a few tiny red potatoes to bake. She didn't know Chancellor's choice in vegetables, but a lot of folks liked corn on the cob in the sum-mertime. Thinking that it might be too many starches, she switched from corn to fresh broccoli. Salad greens and tomatoes were always on her menu. The roast was slowly cooking while she tended to her duties at the shelter. She had stopped off at home after leaving the store.

She had to laugh at herself as she stepped behind the serving counter. She was suddenly acting like the little loving housewife, the kind who had her man's meal on the table when he walked through the door after finishing up a hard workday. Laying a soothing, relaxing massage on her significant other might earn her a dozen red roses, or maybe even two. She had even caught herself singing a couple of times today.

If this was what love felt like, Laylah wanted to feel this way forever. She might not have been in love before, but she would surely welcome it with open arms. She'd heard that love made people do all sorts of stupid things—and she believed it to be true. She'd lost count of all the weird, brainless things she'd done since meeting Chancellor.

Upon feeling her cell phone vibrating in her pocket, Laylah sighed as she turned away from the counter to answer it. It was March, which she wasn't too happy about, yet she hung on to every word he was saying in an excited manner.

A breaking story needed to be covered and March needed Laylah to handle it, stat. Hearing him telling her he wanted her to get right on the story because she was the best and that the very best was needed for this one surprised her. These remarks weren't offhand ones, either. He truly sounded sincere in praising her great work.

"Think you can handle it, Versailles?"

"I know I can."

"That's what I want to hear! Ready to copy the address?"

"Ready." She had removed the pen and small pad from her pocket the moment he'd mentioned the words breaking story. She rapidly penned the address and then told March she was leaving the shelter as soon as she could gather up her personal stuff.

The moment Laylah disconnected the line she went in search of Benjamin. After locating him in the kitchen, she let him know she had to leave and wouldn't be able to work the serving line. Regret was awash in her eyes.

Benjamin's forehead was crunched with worry. "Is everything all right?"

"Just been assigned a breaking story. I doubt that I'll be back, so you'll have to get someone else to assign beds. Have a good evening. I'll see you tomorrow."

"Go, Laylah. I know how important your job is to you. I've got this covered."

Laylah smiled. "Thanks." She turned and walked away.

She then stopped, but only for a brief second. She had thought of telling Benjamin to tell Chancellor that she had to leave, but then she'd recalled what he'd said after she'd told him it was okay to come back to her place that evening.

"Then I won't have to get in line down at the shelter," he'd said to her.

While Benjamin didn't know the exact nature of Laylah's relationship with Chancellor, she was almost sure he suspected them of having a personal interest in each other. However, he wasn't the type of man to pry into the private affairs of others.

It was still hard for Laylah to believe what she had been witnessing for the past hour. If she hadn't seen this tragedy with her own eyes, she would not have believed it. Inside a small house, with the filthiest conditions she had ever seen, there were sixty or so frightened illegal immigrants packed into three tiny rooms.

As if that wasn't amazing enough, Laylah learned that these poor people had been held against their will. They had paid a certain amount of money to be smuggled into the country, but after they'd arrived, they were brought to this little house of horrors and put into bondage, where they were forced to stay until they paid their oppressors even more money to buy the rest of their way to freedom. The women, young girls and boys were told they would be prostituted to pay off the debt thought to have already been paid in full. Some of the male victims were even bound and gagged.

INS had also been called to the scene of this horrendous crime against humanity.

This was definitely front-page news in Laylah's estimation. Rarely did anything that happened in Los Angeles shock her, but this one had taken the cake. Seeing these poor folks terrorized like this had her sick to the stomach. She was already geared up for the interviews, glad she knew a couple of foreign languages, Spanish included.

Laylah was sure she'd gotten all she'd needed from the six detainee interviews she had conducted. Lucky for her, there had been one woman in the group who spoke impeccable English. When she didn't quite comprehend something being said, the young lady had helped her out tremendously. This woman had been a great asset to Laylah.

It was really late when Laylah finally entered her home from the garage. Pretty sure she had missed Chancellor, she felt really bad about it. Praying he was down at the shelter, hoping he'd eaten, since he'd planned to have breakfast leftovers with her.

As Laylah made a mental note to give Chancellor her cell and work numbers, she went back into the bedroom and unloaded her gear. Then she turned on the computer. After turning on the tape recorder, she inserted the mini tape into the transcribing machine and placed the earphones into her ears. Once she'd taken a few deep breaths to calm down, she began to type her feature story, a heartrending one.

Laylah's anger pounded inside her head as her fingers flew across the keyboard. Some of the insufferable injustices people had to endure were shocking. That slavery and human smuggling still existed in this day and age was a worldwide tragedy. Innocent people had been rounded up and smuggled into the country like cattle. She had heard many stories like the one she was writing, but she hadn't seen it this up close and personal.

Money should've been made red instead of green, she thought, as it was surely a sign of the devil, representing the worst of evil.

Hot tears rained down Laylah's face as she continued to transcribe her story.

* * *

The phone was ringing when Laylah stepped out of the shower, which had done very little to ease her bone weariness. So much stuff had happened between writing her story and getting into the shower. Brandon had called to say he was down from San Francisco and wanted to drop by the next day, leaving the phone and room numbers of the hotel he was in. Her brother normally stayed with her, so she didn't understand the hotel stay.

She laughed, thinking Brandon probably had one of his bozo girlfriends with him. He sure knew how to pick them. The girls he dated were definitely not the marrying kind, by design. The designer playboy was scared to death of commitment. He had come close to getting hooks into him about two years ago. After he'd escaped a trap that had been well laid for him by a known gold digger, boyfriend did his best to steer clear of the so-called marrying-kind perpetrators. At any rate, Brandon was a riot, kept her laughing. Even with all his character flaws she loved her big brother like crazy.

"Hey, where are you?" Her eyes lit up like diamonds. Hearing Chancellor's voice had her insides melting like candle wax.

"Not too far from your place. Is it too late to come by? And what happened to you earlier? Don't answer that. You can tell me all about it when I get there."

Laylah laughed heartily. "Your last remark sounds like you're assuming I'm going to say you can come on over. Am I right?"

"It's called the power of positive speaking and thinking."

"Okay, whatever. It must work 'cause I can't wait to see you."

Chancellor chuckled. "Let me put my superhero cape on so I can fly right over."

Laylah could hear him still laughing as he disconnected the line. Two minutes later the doorbell rang. Wearing nothing but the towel she'd wrapped around her after her shower, Laylah ran for the door. Chancellor had already come through the gate when talking to her, she figured, laughing at how he'd duped her.

Seeing tall, gorgeous Brandon, impeccably suited down, standing there with a woman on his arm, had Laylah fleeing the scene like she had just committed a serious crime. "I'll be right back," she yelled. "I thought you were someone else."

"Obviously," Brandon shouted back to her, laughing. He came on inside and guided his new girlfriend, Sierra, into Laylah's immaculately kept living room.

Chapter 7

Laylah was too embarrassed, so much so, that she hated to go back out there and face her brother and his companion. Answering the door with nothing on but a towel had been downright insane, no matter who she may have thought it was. After slipping into blue jeans, she took a neatly folded T-shirt from her drawer and pulled it down over her head. What was she going to say to Brandon to explain her actions? He was definitely going to rib her about it. Teasing his little sister was one of his favorite pastimes.

Then Laylah realized her problem was much bigger than just her embarrassment. Chancellor was on his way over there and she hadn't talked to Brandon about him yet. Fearful of the questions that her brother might ask Chancellor, she prayed for immediate deliverance from the situation.

As if some sort of bad spirit was acting in defiance of Laylah's request, the doorbell rang again, sending her flying out of the room and tearing up the hallway. "Ugh," she moaned, realizing she still had on her shower cap. *Could things get any worse?* She surely hoped not.

She ripped the butterfly-patterned shower cap from her head, and quickly tossed it into the hall closet. Knowing she could do nothing about the state of her mussed hair, she still thought it would be nice if a comb or brush suddenly appeared. Laylah pasted a passable smile on her face, and opened the front door. When Chancellor reached for her, she backed up a step or two, but all she really wanted to do was fall into his arms.

Chancellor looked puzzled. "Something wrong?"

She pointed toward the living room. "I have company," she whispered. "My brother and a girlfriend of his, one I haven't met before, just dropped in."

"I see how it is." He backed out the door, wishing she wasn't ashamed of him. Maybe she wasn't as real and compassionate as she'd made him believe. Normally he couldn't be fooled that easily. "Maybe I'll see you at the shelter tomorrow." The deep disappointment in his voice couldn't have been any clearer.

Laylah reached for his hand and tried to pull Chancellor back inside. "Where are you going? Don't you want to meet my brother?"

Chancellor looked surprised, yet he didn't believe he'd entirely misread her initially. She had just made a quick recovery. "That might be a bad idea."

She stretched her eyes. "Why? Why's it a bad idea?"

"Are you sure you want me to meet your family? Because I'm sure I'm not what they have in mind for you as a love interest."

Wishing this wasn't happening, Laylah looked exasperated. "I make my own choices and decisions." She sighed hard. "This is so silly. Are you coming in or not?"

"Not." With that said, Chancellor turned and walked away.

Unable to believe he had taken the easy way out, Laylah

stared after Chancellor, trying to decide if she should go outside to try to get him to change his mind. Instead, with her heart breaking, she closed the door and headed toward the living room.

The only thing a woman could ever change on a male was his diapers.

Before Laylah reached the living room, the doorbell rang again. Hoping the man she loved had had a change of heart, she ran back to the door and threw it open.

Chancellor apologized with his eyes. "I'd love to meet your brother."

Without saying a word, she looped her arm through his. When they walked into the living room, she didn't hesitate in introducing him as her boyfriend. Brandon shook Chancellor's hand and then introduced his lady friend.

Brandon wrapped up his sister tightly in his arms, his skin glowing like he'd just received a facial. His smile was wide and bright white. "I didn't know you could run the fifty-yard dash so fast. It was like somebody had lit a fire under your crazy butt. What's up with greeting guests in only a towel?" His eyes went straight to Chancellor.

Laylah's cheeks turned fire-engine red. "Can we talk about something else? Why don't we discuss the reason you're here in L.A., Brandon."

Chancellor had raised both eyebrows at Brandon's question about how Laylah had come to the door. As he laughed inwardly, he could only imagine the look on Brandon's face when he saw how his sister was dressed. Laylah must have thought it was him ringing the bell, Chancellor surmised. The thought made him feel pretty good. He already vividly recalled what she looked like in only a towel: adorable and sexy.

"Business, baby sister," Brandon boomed in a baritone voice. "I couldn't come to the big city and not drop in on you. I also wanted you to meet Sierra. We've been seeing each for a couple of weeks now."

I know how that goes, Laylah thought quietly. She hoped this one lasted longer than all the others…and would like nothing more than to see her brother find the right one. He deserved the best woman, but first he had to learn how to be the best man.

Conversation flowed at a relaxed pace for the next thirty or so minutes. Then, when Laylah remembered to mind her manners, she offered her guests something to eat and drink. She was willing to bet that Chancellor was starving, at the same time hoping he had gotten something to eat after he'd come by the first time.

Brandon declined Laylah's offer of refreshments, saying it was time for him to leave. He got to his feet and then helped Sierra to hers. Brandon hugged his sister again and also shook Chancellor's hand. The ladies chatted on the way to the door, the first time Sierra had said anything, other than the polite remarks right after being introduced.

At the door Brandon took Laylah into his arms yet again. "I plan to be in the city until Sunday. I'll call in the morning. I want to know all about him," he whispered softly.

Laylah cringed inwardly, wishing he'd forget to call, yet knowing better than that. If nothing else, Brandon was a man of his word. When he did call, she would tell him the truth about her relationship. Hiding it from everyone wasn't her style.

Chancellor deserved to be treated with dignity regardless of his standing in life. Her family could accept him or not accept him. It was all up to them, but she was keeping him in her life regardless. They had raised her to love everyone. She wasn't taught to love based on what a person had or didn't have. She wouldn't have a problem letting her parents know what they'd taught her if they dared to object to her being with Chancellor.

Once the farewells were said and the door was closed behind Brandon and Sierra, Laylah stood on tiptoe and gave Chancellor a wet, spicy-hot kiss. "I missed you."

Lacing his hands though her hair, he brought her back to him for another passionate kiss, firmly holding her head. "Same here, babe." He looked down at his watch. "It's late. I'd better let you get to bed. Work tomorrow for both of us."

"You can't go. You haven't been here that long. Did you eat?"

"Had a bite to eat at Josh's place. I stopped by there after you weren't here when I came by. But that was a long time ago. Still have those leftover pancakes I made?"

"They're waiting just for you. Come on in the kitchen while I warm them up."

After taking her into his arms for one more kiss, he followed along behind her.

Chancellor had eaten way more than he had intended. His stomach felt bloated and he hated the uncomfortable feeling. "We've talked about my brother, but we haven't talked about yours. He said he had to get back to the hotel. Where does he live?"

"San Francisco. My parents, Jack and Selma, and Dad's sisters, Gertrude and Cora, live there also, as does my best friend, Kelly. I grew up in Frisco and went to college there."

"How is it that you ended up in L.A. with everyone else in San Fran?"

"This is where I landed a job. Plus, I wanted to be out on my own. I couldn't do that at home. My parents and aunts would've popped in on me day and night, dropping by unannounced. Living somewhere other than in the family home would've been miserable for me. I don't mind admitting I'm spoiled. I really don't like it, though. I'm the only girl in the family. My mother has three sisters and they all have boys. Mom's sisters and their families live up in Tacoma, Washington, but they see each other often."

"A close-knit family must be awesome. My grandparents raised Chandler and me. We had a great upbringing, but with them gone on to the afterlife, I constantly wish things were the way they used to be. I miss my grandparents. Chandler is the only family member I have left, as far as I'm concerned."

"What about your mother? I haven't ever heard you mention her."

"Purposely," he strongly stated. "The topic of Lavonne Kingston is taboo. The less I talk or think about her, the better off I am."

Laylah was stunned by the things he'd said angrily in reference to his mother. What had happened between mother and son? she had to wonder. In concurrence with his wishes, she didn't ask the dozen or so questions she had ready to fire at him.

Chancellor observed Laylah, eyeing her intently. This woman was something else, someone to reckon with, and he wasn't sure he was the right man to do the reckoning. She needed so much more and deserved the moon and the brightest stars. Comparing her to the lyrics in "Lady," written by Lionel Ritchie, was fitting.

He certainly wanted to be Laylah's knight in shining armor. If she felt as strongly about championing the underdog as he did, then nothing would turn her away. However, if she could easily be swayed by others to disregard the less fortunate, she simply wasn't the woman for him. How he hoped otherwise. He definitely wasn't looking for a wishy-washy woman. The only lady for him was one of substance, one that knew how to plant her feet firmly and then dare anyone to try and move her.

His expression turned thoughtful. As much as Laylah was strong, he sensed that she still needed to be needed. Was volunteering down at the shelter fulfilling a particular need in her? Did she also champion the underdog out of that same need? Perhaps he should ask her.

He propped his elbows upon the table and rested his face between his hands. "Hey, do you think you're hanging out with me because you feel I'm needy? If I wasn't down on my luck, do you think you'd be as attracted to me? What if I was a corporate type, with lots of money? How would you feel about me then? I'm still having a hard time accepting the fact you're hanging out with a homeless person without an ulterior motive. I personally think you need to feel needed to feel whole. Am I even close to being right?"

What a mouthful! Laylah certainly thought that Chancellor's questions and observations were bizarre, yet she considered them, anyway. As she slowly mulled over things in her mind, his comments began to seem less strange. "Do you see yourself as needy?" His reaction of surprise let her know he hadn't anticipated a turnabout.

"I have a few unusual needs, so I guess that makes me somewhat needy. But we were supposed to be talking about you." He swallowed softly, realizing not one of his questions were the ones he'd intended to ask. He'd gone in a completely different direction, making it more about him than anything, more personal.

"I *am* also needy, Chance, but not to any dangerous degree. I am with you because I was attracted to you, not because of anything you might lack. I'd have to see you in a corporate setting to decide if I'd still be as interested. I'm normally not into the power-suited types, but I can't say for sure since I've not been involved with one. The artsy-creative guy has always suited me better."

He sharply angled an eyebrow, though he wasn't surprised. "Really?"

Roderick Blackmon suddenly came to Laylah's mind. Despite

being a professional architect, all he'd ever worn were jeans and casual clothing. What an interesting blast from aeons ago. Well, maybe a year or so ago wasn't all that long, yet she rarely ever thought of the charming devil.

She and Roderick had been compatible in so many ways, but none of the ways important to the survival of a romantic relationship. He turned out to be a cheater. He'd claimed it had only happened that one time, and in a moment of utter weakness, no doubt. That it shouldn't have happened, period, was all that had mattered to her when she'd removed herself out of his life faster than the speed of light.

"Really. No power suits in my past or present." She shrugged.

"Care to expound?"

"It'd serve no purpose. I can't speak on something I haven't tried."

"Let me get this right. You've never dated a man who wore a suit?"

Laughing softly, she rolled her eyes dramatically. "I didn't say that. Just haven't dated one who lives and breathes that particular dress code." She threw up her hands. "Where is this going, anyway?"

Chancellor had to laugh. "I don't know. I have gone astray, haven't I?"

"I'd say so."

He then decided to go ahead and ask the questions he'd initially thought of. "Are you volunteering down at the shelter to fulfill a particular need in yourself? Do you give of your time out of a desperate need? Do you also champion the underdog out of the same kind of need?" There, he thought, that's better; more to the point, less personal.

"A resounding yes to all three of the questions you put to me." She momentarily hooded her eyes. "The shelter definitely fulfills my need to help others who are in need. As for the desperate part, I'm desperate to try to help make a difference in what goes on in this country as well as all over the world. It's now over two years since Katrina and the needs of the citizens of the disaster areas have yet to be met. Championing the underdog is what I do best. A part of me is also fulfilled by it because I'm one of them."

"You see yourself as an underdog?" Chancellor would be surprised if she did.

"It's what I am," she stated as a matter of fact. "Like it or not, most men think women will always be second best to them. While I don't see myself in that light, I'm an underdog simply because I'll always have to work twice as hard in this testoster-one-run society to prove myself. Don't think it's a bad thing, either. Keeps me on my toes, keeps me striving toward excellence. If you can't beat 'em, you can sure as hell join 'em."

"Hmm. Nicely stated." Chancellor pointed a finger at his temple. "Do I recall you mentioning a homemade apple pie recently? Or was my imagination at work?"

"I thought you were too full to have another taste of anything."

His eyes locked with hers, smoldering darkly. There was something sweet on her that he'd very much like to taste. As his eyes appeared to emit plumes of smoke, he kept them fastened on her. In one swift motion he made it over to Laylah, scooping her up into his arms, making sure he held her secure.

While he carried Laylah back to the bedroom, he bumped into the wall and into this or that inanimate object until he reached his destination. After laying her upon the mattress, he settled himself down alongside her. Once he'd removed her casual shoes, he rapidly got rid of his own, locking their toes together in a playful way.

Keeping up the intense eye contact, he lazily traced her lower lip with the pad of his thumb, loving how pliable her mouth was. His hungry mouth then replaced his thumb, but only for a minute or two. He just wanted to touch her, nibble on her sweetness, and hopefully raise her body temperature way past normal. His desire would then be to turn her hot body into liquid putty, molding her femininity against his throbbing sex. "Been thinking about what happened between us a couple of days ago?"

Can't think of anything else, barely able to wait for an encore. Laylah did her best to try to remain collected. That was so hard to do when her body was an absolute inferno of lust and sexual desire. The smoke curling in every direction between her legs and under her top would be visible any minute now. Being on fire like this for a man was downright sinful. *Where was one of those church fans when she needed one?*

"What do you mean by that, Chance? What happened between us?" she asked, shrugging with indifference to show she didn't know what he was talking about.

Highly suspicious of her response, his eyes narrowed to tiny slits. Refusing to get caught into the pitfalls of her devious little game, he shrugged with the same sort of nonchalance. "I thought shopping for chandeliers would've been just as memorable for you as it was for me. Too bad it wasn't. I had a blast. Can't stop thinking about it."

"Chandeliers…" Realizing she had been about to lose her cool, she quickly recomposed herself, wishing she hadn't begun this stupid little game.

If he could just go back to looking at her in the same desirous way he had stared at her only moments ago, up until she'd decided to play cutesy with him, they'd probably be rumpling her sateen sheets by now. The raging fire he'd had in his eyes then was the only reason her body was still smoking hot beneath her attire. Had she allowed him to get on with seducing her, which had obviously been his plan, he just might be all dressed up in his birthday suit right now. Slipping into her own birthday gear was something she was more than ready for.

As though Chancellor had read Laylah's mind, he slowly came down on top of her, gently pinning her arms over her head. His lips wasted no time in a search-and-seize mission. As his mouth, tongue and hands fervently explored her alluring anatomy, he seized every possible opportunity to taste and touch each of her engaging body parts.

Better than sweet, sweeter than honey, Laylah tasted utterly divine.

Closing her eyes in order to enhance the enjoyment she felt over his exploration of her body, she just lay there, still as could be, allowing him to have his every way with her. Oh, what a way it was… He had already made an art form of passionately manipulating her belly button and her supersensitive nipples.

Was it even possible to have an orgasm from the navel?

"Yes," she screamed out, her mind spinning from the heat of lust, every single nerve in her body tingling. Yes, she silently cried, succumbing to the unrelenting expert hands of one Chancellor Kingston. The boy sure knew his way around a woman's body. With all the enlightening discovery matters he had thus far introduced to her, she thought he would've made an excellent legal eagle.

As Chancellor's tongue tenderly laved Laylah's left ripened breast, with his hand gently kneading the opposite nipple, her insides quivered, making her fight hard to keep from screaming out his name. "Please take me" was already sitting right there on the tip of her tongue. Tremendously enjoying the highly addictive foreplay was the only reason she didn't request his speeding things up. This was way too pleasurable for her to want it to end. Keeping her eyes closed kept her relaxed and savoring every moment.

Laylah's heart rate nearly went through the roof as Chancellor's lips suddenly wrapped around a couple of her toes, sucking gently and then harder. Trying to control the waves of ecstasy steamrolling all through her, she inhaled and exhaled slowly. These pulse-pounding, mouthwatering sensations were alien to her. As if her toes had the same sort of orgasm as the one with her navel, they pulsated and twitched uncontrollably.

Who the heck knew toes were such an amazing erogenous zone?

Hungry for the taste of Chancellor's mouth on hers, Laylah reached down and gripped the back of his head, pulling it toward her face, her eyes all but pleading for him to passionately kiss her until she stopped breathing. As his lips slightly parted, her mouth was quick as lightning, wildly roping his tongue with her own.

Kissing Laylah always brought Chancellor great pleasure. Her tongue wrestling with his own had him on fire. It was almost as if her mouth had been deprived of any personal attention, since it seemed she was starving for the union of his mouth with hers. Their hot and moist kisses were deliciously tormenting. She had his manhood harder than tempered steel. He couldn't imagine ever getting enough of her. Being around her was gratifying in every way. What Laylah had brought to Chancellor's life was already incomparable to any other situation he had experienced in his personal life. No other woman had ever had Chancellor confused about which end was up.

Mentally wishing she still had on nothing but the towel she'd earlier answered the door in, beneath him Laylah matched stroke for stroke his wildly grinding hips. As his belt buckle cut into her bare flesh, she thought it was time for him to part ways with it. In one rapid, jerking motion, she stripped the worn brown leather from the large loops on his jeans. While she was at it she thought it was okay to go ahead and help him out of his shirt, too. Having him before her totally naked was on top of her agenda.

Closing her eyes, she instantly conjured up a beautiful scene of them making heart-stopping love outdoors in a field of flowers, atop a bed of purple and red tulips. She wanted to just lie there and let him take her places she had never visited before. Touching him and having him touch her like this felt so splendid. The way he looked at her made her feel as if she was his very own fairy-tale princess.

Chancellor gently rolled Laylah over onto her stomach. Lying atop her back, his lips teased the nape of her neck and the outer edges of her ears. His tongue played hide-and-seek with her inner ear, desperately making her want him nestled deep inside her. His manhood was harder than she'd ever felt it. He wanted her, too, urgently. They wanted and needed each other.

What they felt when together was nothing short of beautiful. Her heart sang sweetly to the steady beat his major organ of life tenderly strummed so harmoniously. Smiling softly, Laylah thought of the poem she had recently recited at Bella's. This was her tonight, their tonight, a night to never forget, one she hoped they'd always remember.

After Chancellor rolled away from her, he lay flat on his back and then he slowly brought her atop him. Their eyes, glazed with lust, locked in an intense stare. Covering her with his overheated body, he unhurriedly entered her with infinite tenderness. As his mouth came crashing downward to meet up with her eagerly awaiting lips, she thought she heard him whisper her name. Moments later he breathlessly breathed it again.

While Chancellor gently thrust himself inside Laylah, pulling slowly out of her sweetness time and time again, it was all he could do to keep from climaxing. This woman had his world all atilt, but that didn't matter in the least. He didn't care if his life was ever again righted as long as she stayed by his side. She would always keep him terribly off-kilter. That's what made her so darn special. It was also her who caused his heart and spirit to act so crazy and unpredictable. He could do crazy, he could do unpredictable; he just couldn't do any of it without her.

Kissing Laylah over and over again had Chancellor feeling as though he were floating on top of the world. As their breath and tongues continued to mingle, he kept her wrapped up tightly in his arms. Her softly whispered moans had him nearly out of his mind with desire. To hear her purring with contentment because of the way he tended to her physical needs made him feel as if he was indeed very special to her.

The diamond-shattering explosion came for them simultaneously, causing their bodies to shake uncontrollably. Another passionate kiss left them both utterly breathless.

Falling asleep on Chancellor hadn't been done purposely on Laylah's part. She had been totally weakened from her spent desires…and it hadn't taken her long to fall into a restful state. Looking over at Chancellor, she saw that he was out like a light.

Still naked as the day he had been born, he wore only a contented expression upon his handsome face. His hair was in disarray and she itched to run her fingers all through it. The urge to reach out and touch every part of his anatomy was so strong. Feeling his nude flesh beneath her hands would only make her want him again. She was too weak to love him anew, yet she was still fulfilled beyond explanation.

Would her full strength ever return to her? Laylah couldn't imagine being this physically ineffectual on a regular basis, yet she desired to make love to him as often as possible. As tired as she was, she still felt empowered by the intimacy they'd shared. After kissing the tips of each of her fingers, she blew them toward him. "I love you."

Chancellor had clearly heard her whispered, heartfelt confession, but he didn't dare open his eyes for fear of embarrassing her. "I love you, too," he whispered lowly to himself. He loved every diminutive inch of her.

Falling in love with a woman was an altogether new experience for Chancellor. Laylah had caught him totally unaware, had taken his heart unexpectedly. She was his unpolished diamond, but he'd soon have her shining brilliantly and sparkling like a perfect day in heaven. Their very first meeting had been destiny at its finest hour. Destiny was incapable of letting them down, which meant they would be together forever. If he had his way, forever would start for them today, at this very moment.

He reached for her hand, taking it, squeezing it reassuringly. "We belong together, Laylah, just you and me. There are a lot of things we need to work out, but I'm willing to give it all I have. Are you willing to give us the same?"

Laylah was absolutely speechless, but that didn't stop her from nodding her head in agreement. It'd be so easy to give all she had to him and to the survival of their relationship. They had a lot going for them. Well, at least she thought so.

It probably mattered to most that she and Chancellor had somewhat different lifestyles, not to mention their barely knowing each other, but they wouldn't let it make a difference to what was important. That they were extremely eager to get to know everything there was to know about each other was a check mark in their plus column. Giving their relationship all the energy they had should take them far into the future.

Suddenly, Laylah felt like crying. There were so many people who wouldn't understand their romance. A lot of folks would only look at the surface, failing to recognize what the couple experienced deep down inside. This was an interesting and unusual journey they were about to embark upon.

Although they would probably be constantly reminded by others that he was homeless, with a mediocre job and no permanent residence, she felt certain they could overcome such startling facts. He wasn't the first person to face life with an uncertain future, nor would he be the last. Overcoming any and all obstacles was paramount to the success of any intimate relationship.

Sensing her sudden melancholy mood, Chancellor quickly scooted as close to Laylah as he could possibly get, before taking her into his strong arms, holding her tight. "We'll be just fine, lovely lady. Our strength will carry us through the good, the bad and everything else tossed our way. Are you up to the challenge? I know I am."

Laylah gave him the thumbs-up sign. "I'm in."

"That's nice to know." He planted a kiss on her earlobe. "I'm hungry. Are you?"

Laylah nodded. "Just for snack food." She started to get up. "You want a sandwich and chips?"

As he grabbed on to her hand, she gave him a puzzled glance. "Lie back down. I got this one. Okay?"

She grinned from ear to ear, loving any form of pampering. "You bet." She was still weak as a newborn, anyway. Chancellor had put something hot and heavy on her, leaving her with one of the sweetest memories she'd have of them together.

Seeing how languid Laylah was, Chancellor rushed into the bathroom and began preparing a hot bath for her. He made sure the water temperature was just right first. He couldn't have her cute little tail burning or freezing off.

After Chancellor checked a couple of obvious storage places inside her private bathroom, he reached down and stuck his hand in the cabinet under one of the sinks and removed a large plastic bottle of lavender-scented bubble bath. Once he located a bottle of baby oil, he dripped a few drops under the spigot. Since her tub had whirlpool jets, he already knew to only use a very small amount of bubbles and oil. Removing a large fluffy towel from the linen closet, he placed it on the dressing-table chair, next to where her bathrobe had been haphazardly thrown.

Now that Laylah's hot bath was ready, Chancellor thought it was time to carry her into the bathroom so she could enjoy her special surprise. While he went off to prepare the snacks, he wanted her to just lay her head back on the bath pillow and totally relax. Before leaving the bathroom, he closed all the shutters and lit a variety of scented votives and tea-light candles. Taking a minute to check things out, he stood back and looked at his handiwork. The romantic ambience made him want to join her.

Chancellor walked back into the bedroom and strolled over to the bed. He bent over and kissed Laylah's forehead ever so gently before picking her up and carrying her into the bathroom. Her eyes lit up as she surveyed the room, surprised at how much of a romantic he was. The huge smile on her face let him know she was pleased.

As Chancellor lowered Laylah into the bathtub, he kissed her softly on the mouth, extremely happy to see her thrilled and so comfortable with him. "Relax, sweetheart. I'll have the snacks all ready for you when you come out." He stood up and blew her a kiss.

Laylah's lower lip trembled slightly. "I can't believe you're not joining me. I want you in here with me. Please stay. The snacks can wait."

Chancellor didn't need Laylah to ask him twice.

Chapter 8

The green Granny Smith apple slices were cool and crisp, just the way Laylah liked them. Chancellor had made a beautiful fruit plate consisting of juicy watermelon chunks, ripened blackberries, banana slices and plump strawberries. A small dish held flavored yogurt for dipping. He had also made a refreshing pitcher of peach iced tea.

As the couple sat at the table in the bedroom, Laylah could hardly keep her eyes open. Her eyelids fluttered every time she took a bite of fruit. The steamy bath had her feeling very much relaxed, making her body feel like jelly. The Jacuzzi jets had also given her muscles a darn good workout. Once Chancellor had carried her back into the bedroom, he had dried her off completely. Massaging her entire body with hot oil and lotion had come next, relaxing her even more.

Laylah stared over at the phone, trying to decide whether to answer it or not. She chose to ignore it and listen to the message after she finished eating. Chancellor seemed pleased with her decision. He liked having her undivided attention. She made him feel important and he did everything possible to show her how invaluable she was to him.

Climbing into bed had been a real chore for Laylah since her muscles were so relaxed. As she waited for Chancellor to come out of the bathroom, she picked up the phone and dialed into the message center. Even with all her numbers registered on the no-call list, she still received annoying telemarketing calls, but rarely did they leave messages. The first call was from a popular department store announcing their upcoming weekend sale. She erased it when prompted to do so.

Her mother's voice always made Laylah smile. When she heard her reason for phoning, her smile quickly turned into a frown. The family was all coming down from San Francisco this weekend. Since Brandon would still be in town, her parents and both aunts thought it would be nice to have a small family reunion dinner at her place.

Laylah thought it would have been nice to have been consulted before her family had finalized their plans, but she wasn't surprised it hadn't occurred. When they got into their heads what they thought was a brilliant idea, they just began the execution.

Kelly would also be in town, so Laylah thought it might be a bit overcrowded if everyone decided to stay with her, which was more than likely the plan. She'd give up her bedroom to her parents, and her aunts could stay in the guest rooms. That meant she and Kelly would sleep together on the queen sofa bed in her office.

As much as Laylah was annoyed by this little surprise family visit, she knew they'd have a great time. Upon hearing the toilet flush, she wondered if Chancellor was up to meeting so many members of her clan all at one time, as well as her best friend. This visit could get real interesting, she thought, hoping everything would go smoothly. Her family wasn't one to hold its tongue, the same as she was. She'd learned from them to speak her mind or plan on spending her entire life taking crap from others.

When Chancellor came out of the bathroom, she was surprised to see him fully dressed in the same clothes he'd been wearing the last couple of days. It bothered her to know he was leaving. "Going somewhere?" It was too late for him to get a room at any shelter, she knew, praying that he wouldn't go out there and walk the streets. Perhaps Joshua's home was an option. She sure hoped so.

"Don't worry. I'll be fine." He came over and sat down on the side of the bed, brushing her hair back from her face with his fingers. "Would it be okay if I called you at work tomorrow? It's hard on me when I don't get to talk to you through the day."

Laylah sat up in bed. "Of course it's okay, but why are you leaving now? We've had such a sensational evening. I want you to stay here with me."

He shook his head. "Not tonight, babe. I don't want to wear out my welcome."

She cocked her head to one side. "Who says that's going to happen?"

Gripping the back of her head, he pulled it forward until her lips lined up with his, kissing her thoroughly. "No one said it…and I want to make sure it's never said. Come lock the door behind me. We'll talk tomorrow. I promise."

Too weak to put up a fight she didn't stand a chance of winning, Laylah slipped out of bed and quickly slid her hand into his. She hated to see him go—and she would worry, no matter what he said. He dropped his arm around her shoulder as they made it up to the front of the house. At the door they kissed good-night. As he slipped out into the darkness, she was already missing him—and he had barely cleared the doorway.

After making sure the locks were all in place, Laylah set the alarm and trudged her way back to the bedroom. With tears in her eyes, she slid into bed and buried her face in the pillow. Loneliness was not a nice feeling. She'd been lonely before Chancellor had come into her life; she was lonely now. *Why was that?* Why wasn't the void ever filled? Why was the hole so deep? She lay back to reason out things.

Maybe it was because she'd never really been in a committed relationship. She then had to clarify that for herself. She wanted to entrust her heart to someone, had wanted an exclusive relationship badly; no male she'd ever dated had seemed to want the same. She'd heard more excuses than she could remember why men felt they couldn't be in a monogamous affair. A couple of men had even pretended to want to date just her, only for her to find out later that more than two people were involved in the relationship.

This was the first time she'd found someone who seemed to want to give back all that she gave out, someone who was as passionate as she was. Chancellor didn't mind sharing his time with her. In fact, it seemed he'd rather be with her than anywhere else. Then why did it hurt so much that he didn't spend the entire night with her? Why did she feel so rejected because he'd left? She prayed to God that she wasn't coming off as needy, but she had to wonder if she was just that. She didn't need Chancellor; she wanted him. She didn't need to be with him, she wanted to be with him.

There was a definite difference between need and want, a big one.

This homeless thing was a big problem for her, too, she had to admit. Why was he homeless? He had never said, though he'd promised to tell her everything one day. That day hadn't come and she was getting antsy.

Chancellor was obviously upset and preoccupied over the

disappearance of his twin brother, but he hadn't explained to Laylah any of the circumstances of that situation either. She really had nothing to go on. All she knew was his name, Chancellor Kingston. And that didn't necessarily have to be his real name.

Was she naive enough to be duped into believing his story without an ounce of proof? Was he with her because he had nowhere else to go or had no one to go to? There had always been something about him that didn't quite fit the homeless story.

Here Laylah was ready to present Chancellor to her family, yet she couldn't tell them a thing about him. They would ask her questions regarding him, many of them, dizzying ones. There was nothing she could tell them about him or his background because she didn't know anything. Yet she'd already slept with him, had already fallen madly in love with the man she knew absolutely nothing about.

Chancellor sat at the table inside the extravagant kitchen of his friend Joshua's opulent mansion. His brow was creased with worry as he tried to explain to Joshua how he felt about Laylah. "I think I'm already in way too deep."

Joshua looked perplexed. "Explain."

"I've fallen in love with her. If she loves me back, she's in love with a stranger. I know so much about her life, but she doesn't know a thing about me. I've never seen a person so accepting of others, one who takes people at face value, someone so nonjudgmental. I didn't set out to deceive her, but I have. How do I undo all of it?"

Joshua shook his head. "You can't, but you can go to her and explain what you've been doing. For whatever reason, you've felt that you *had* to do things this way. You feel you need to protect yourself and Chandler, especially if your brother is in some sort of serious trouble. I can understand you not wanting people to know who you are. Someone could try to take you for a serious ride if your true identity is revealed."

"She has my true identity, but my name doesn't seem to mean anything special to her. That's interesting in itself, especially with her being a well-established reporter. I didn't lie about my name to her because I couldn't. She's so pure at heart. When she asked me not to leave her tonight, the sadness in her beautiful eyes just about did me in."

"Perhaps she knows exactly who you are and is working you from that angle. This city is chock-full of gold diggers and man-eaters. Maybe she's hiding something, too."

"Not this girl. I know I've made some poor choices in women in the past, but not this time. Laylah is everything I've ever dreamed of, all that I've ever wanted. Her compassion and love for others is real. There's nothing fake about Laylah Versailles."

"You said she's met Chandler. Did you ever follow up on it?"

"It *was* his handwriting on the card he'd left her. Chandler even mentioned how kind she was to him, leaving behind a note and a gift to show his appreciation. We both know he's not the sentimental type so Laylah must've had a profound effect on him."

"For your sake, I hope she's as real as you say. But that doesn't solve any of your problems. You need to get back to work before the corporation begins to suffer because of your absence. I know you have loyal employees, but you've been gone awhile now. You're the man, Chance. And you have no good leads on Chandler's possible whereabouts."

"He's out there, Josh. I know it. I can feel it. If I don't get to him soon, he could get himself killed." A blank stare appeared in Chancellor's eyes. Moisture and deep emotion replaced the blankness. "I haven't said this to anyone because I'm having a hard time accepting it." He swallowed hard, wishing he didn't have the need to share his deepest fears. "I believe Chandler has mental-health issues, serious ones. No one walks away from a great way of life to take on one of uncertainty. No one opts to live on the streets when they have innumerable liquid assets. Signs of his mental health deteriorating were all there, but I ignored them. I just couldn't deal with the possibility."

"You've walked away from your great way of life, so how do you explain that?"

"I'm doing what I'm doing for my brother. I have to see and feel why he was so suddenly attracted to living on the streets and roaming from pillar to post. If I don't live his new way of life, I won't be able to get a handle on it. I won't understand him or it."

"I disagree. You can do exactly what you're doing to find your brother and still lay your body in your own bed. You don't have to live on the streets to prove anything to anyone. You're the one who's acting like you have mental-health issues. Your behavior is bizarre. Your way won't help you find Chandler. And it won't help you win the heart of this so-called compassionate woman you've just gotten yourself involved with."

Hating the way in which Joshua had referred to Laylah, Chancellor bristled, jumping up from the table. "Don't ever speak of her in that way or in that tone. There's nothing *so-called* about her. She is just who I said she is. And she's far more real than any of the chicks with the fake anatomies I've seen you hanging out with."

Joshua had a look of regret in his eyes. "I'm sorry, man. I shouldn't have gone there. I'm really worried about you. Nothing you're doing is making any sense to me."

"It doesn't have to make sense to you. I'm out. Talk to you later." Without even glancing at Joshua, Chancellor walked out, steam still rising from under his collar.

Outside in the cool night air, Chancellor let go of his emotions. He walked and walked and cried and cried. His anguish was deep. His heart was weighted down with his deep feelings for Laylah. Fear of losing her over this situation had him shackled. Even though she was the most compassionate and fair-minded woman he'd ever met, he felt she'd be angry with him, rightfully so, for not telling her the truth from the beginning.

In his mind, over and over again, Chancellor kept telling himself to go to Laylah and be honest with her, to not let another day pass without her knowing everything there was to know about him. She deserved to know who he was and how he had lived his life before Chandler's disappearance. Once he'd made up his mind to come totally clean with her, he felt a tremendous weight lifted from his heart. All he had to do now was to find the perfect way to reveal the entire truth to her, without pulling any punches. Laylah was a very special person—and he wanted to treat her just the way she deserved.

After finding the nearest pay phone, Chancellor dropped in the proper amount of coins to connect him with Laylah. The phone rang and rang, causing him to worry. He knew she was at home when he'd left, had been ready for bed. Then again, she was a reporter. There could've been a breaking story. He thought of hanging up before the message center came on, but he waited and waited for it to kick in. Nothing occurred.

Worried about where she was at this hour of the night, he hung up the phone and waited for his money to return, which he redeposited, and dialed her line again. While holding the phone on his shoulder, he pulled out his wallet to find the card with her cell number. The moment he came up with it, he hung up and dialed. No answer came from those digits either, but he was able to leave a message. "I need you, Laylah. I love you. We have to talk. I'll try back in the morning. Hope you're safe."

* * *

Laughing excitedly, Kelly slid into the passenger seat of Laylah's car, having already stored her bags in the trunk. She was a pretty, caramel-complexioned woman, around five foot six. Her lovely brown hair had well-defined streaks of golden highlights running throughout the shoulder-length style. Although many people thought her plump lips were cosmetically enhanced, they were as natural as sunlight. Men loved her juicy, pouting lips. Most women would kill to have a full, shapely mouth just like Kelly's.

Before pulling the car away from the curb, outside of the arrival area, Laylah leaned over and kissed both of Kelly's cheeks. "You look great! I can see that you're taking your work-out program seriously. Girlfriend got muscles."

Flexing the well-toned muscles in her upper arms, Kelly laughed heartily. "Girl, if you'd get a glimpse of Antoine Ledger, you'd work your buns off for him, too. The man is fine, with a capital F. Sexier than that hot behind Shemar Moore. In fact, you'll get more than a glimpse of him. He's coming to L.A, too. I can't wait for you to meet him."

Laylah was having a hard time finding her voice. She cleared her throat to try to do so. "You're involved with your personal trainer? Where the holy heaven is Max?"

Maxwell Hunter, the hunky, starving musician, was Kelly's long-term boyfriend.

"Max is in the wind. I've been dating him for four years and it's gone nowhere. He's not interested in marriage. I am. I want children before I'm sixty, you know."

Though she was sort of in a state of shock over Kelly dumping the gorgeous Max, Laylah chuckled lightly. "Does your fitness trainer have personal feelings for you?"

"I assume so."

"You dumped Max on an *assumption?* Why am I just now hearing about all this?"

"Wanted to wait and tell you in person. Besides, I've only recently admitted to myself I have a real jones for Antoine. The boy is hotter than an Indian summer in Hades. I hope I get the chance to douse his burning flames. Can't tell you how many times I've already envisioned it."

Laylah was still a bit stunned, but she absolutely loved how excited and happy Kelly sounded. She'd always had a great sense of humor, but it had dulled a bit lately. The zesty fire in her dialogue had finally returned. Her friend had given her all to Max, but he'd never seemed to appreciate some of the sacrifices she'd made on his behalf. Kelly followed that man all over San Francisco just because he wanted her at every one of his gigs. Then all he'd do was flirt with his groupie chicks right in front of her.

"How is it that Antoine's also coming to L.A.?" She hoped Kelly didn't plan on him staying at her house, since her rooms were already fully booked. However, if that was the plan, Laylah wouldn't disappoint her friend by turning her down. She had a couple of air mattresses they could blow up with the vacuum cleaner.

"I casually mentioned I was coming down to L.A. to see you this weekend. He's heard me talk about you a lot. Out of the blue he said it'd be nice to come down, too, just to hang out. He also has a college friend who lives in L.A., Malachi Jennings. He'll be staying with him. I hope you don't mind all of us hanging out together a time or two."

"Of course not." Inwardly, Laylah gave a sigh of relief over the accommodations. "I get to meet Antoine and you get to meet Chance. Should be fun. By the way, do you remember me saying I'm doing open mic tonight down at Two Brothers'?"

"Can't wait! You know I love poetry bars, Lay."

Laylah frowned slightly. "There's more. Like I told you, Brandon is in town. And I just learned that my parents and my aunts are coming to L.A., too. So you see, it seems there'll be a passel of us hanging out together. Lovely, huh?"

"Absolutely! Hanging out with your family is always a riot of fun. I'll need the address to Two Brothers' so I can call and give it to Antoine. His friend might already know where the bar is since it's so popular with the locals, but I want to make sure."

Once Laylah helped Kelly get settled in, she put a call in to Brandon's cell phone. He should have picked up their parents and aunts from the airport by now, and she wanted to know how long it would be before they got to her place. Before his cell had a chance to ring, the doorbell pealed. Sure that it was her family, Laylah ended the call and ran for the front door. Excitement flared inside her as she opened the door, beaming from head to toe.

Falling into her father's strong, protective arms came first. Jack held on to his daughter like it might be the last time he'd ever do so. He was always so worried about Laylah living in L.A., especially when all her family resided up north. A day didn't go by that he didn't pray for his baby girl to return home to San Francisco.

Laylah enthusiastically hugged and kissed her mother, Selma, who was a classic beauty, her clothing stylish and sophisticated. She worried about her daughter, too, but she also trusted and believed that she'd truly gotten all the things they'd taught her about life. In Selma's opinion, Laylah was a smart girl and had made wise choices so far. She couldn't wait for her daughter to one day marry and make them grandparents. When that did occur, Selma wanted it to be a forever kind of holy union, just like her own.

The two stunning, elderly aunts, also stylishly dressed, their faces made up beautifully, patiently waited their turn to fill their arms with the niece they both adored. Laylah always reminded the spinsters of themselves during the different stages of their lives. No one could be any prouder of the loving, compassionate woman their beautiful niece had become. Gertrude and Cora were also just as crazy about their handsome nephew, Brandon.

Laylah felt the tender warmth and unconditional love from her aunts permeate her entire being. They were two wonderful souls, spicy and full of life and always quick to speak their minds. There wasn't anything they shied away from and each one could hold her own in confrontations. Not many women their ages were on top of every aspect of their lives. These sisters traveled all over the globe, via plane, ship and train, to exotic places, those off the beaten tourist paths. Visiting the oldest of European cities was their favorite thing to do. Both sisters spoke several languages.

Gertrude lifted Laylah's hand and placed an airy kiss into her palm. "I hear we're going out partying tonight. What's the hot spot for this evening?"

"Two Brothers'. I'm on the poetry program. You all get to hear me do my thing."

Gertrude clapped her hands. "What a treat. You are a wonderful poet. Well, I haven't stayed this beautiful and healthy by not getting my proper rest. Please lead me to where I can lay my head for a short spell. I want to be able to hang tonight."

Though used to Gertrude's sense of humor, no one could keep from laughing.

Once Laylah got her family assigned to the rooms where they'd spend the weekend, she went into the room that she'd share with Kelly. Finding her friend asleep didn't come as a big surprise. Kelly often burned candles at both ends, wearing out her pretty little self in the process. When attending college, they both had burned the midnight oil more often than not.

After Laylah had tiptoed around the room to get a few things she needed, she went in search of a quiet place to work on her poetry presentation.

Because Laylah had decided to dedicate a poem to her parents, after finding out they'd be coming down, she decided to write a new one in their honor rather than use one of the ones she'd given them before. She was always writing a special poem for her parents, whom she credited with the majority of her personal success.

It was Laylah's assertion that she had learned just as much from her father as she had from her mother. Because Jack treated Selma so well and with the utmost respect, she had learned and seen firsthand what special ingredients it took to have a successful romantic relationship. Their marriage was amazing to observe and study. After thirty-three years of matrimony, the Versailles union was still strong.

First and foremost, Laylah's father had taught her to show respect for herself at all times and to also demand deference from everyone she came into contact with, no matter how long they were present in her life. Rarely did folks respect those who didn't revere themselves, Jack instilled into his daughter. One of the very reasons why Laylah believed she wasn't married was that she'd set such high standards.

As Laylah thought of her sweet Chancellor, her heart fluttered wildly. Whatever he was or wasn't he was kind and respectful to her. The more she was around him, the more she was able to closely observe the type of man he was. He may have secrets, but he held her in high esteem—and vice versa. Laylah couldn't be with anyone she didn't respect. She'd rather just walk away from someone she couldn't feel good about.

March was one of those people Laylah had very little respect for, yet she wasn't disrespectful toward him. She had her feisty moments with her boss, but for the most part she didn't cross the boundaries that should exist between supervisor and employee.

In just a couple of hours she would be in Chancellor's company. He planned to meet her at the poetry bar. He had thought it was best for her to introduce him to her family there rather than at the house. The informal setting would allow them a chance to relax and not scrutinize each other too closely. The last thing he'd said to her was how much he looked forward to meeting her family and her sister-friend, Kelly.

Laylah smiled out at everyone in the audience as she stood in front of the microphone, having already been introduced to the patrons by one of the poetry bar owners.

"What's up, people?" she asked with enthusiasm, verbally acknowledging each of her co-workers seated up toward the front. "Thank you so much for coming out tonight. This is a special evening for me. My family from San Francisco is in the audience.

"In fact, the poem I plan to read is dedicated to my mom and dad, Selma and Jack Versailles. A special shout-out goes to my brother, Brandon, my aunts, Cora and Gertrude, and my best friend, Kelly, all of whom are here to support me." She blew a kiss right at Chancellor. "I also have the support of my man, Chancellor. Thanks, Chance, for being here to cheer me all the way to the end. You are always such an inspiration to me.

"Let's also give a warm L.A. welcome to Antoine," she enthused.

Chancellor grinned, loving the way Laylah had acknowledged him. Her man, indeed. She looked hot in the sexy black, low-cut, figure-clinging dress she wore like a second skin. While she wasn't showing too much cleavage, he wouldn't want the top of her dress cut any lower. The rounded twin mounds were well defined. He liked how the hemline rested high above her knees, showing off well-toned thighs and legs.

The large, gold diamond-cut hoops she wore in her ears were nice accents. With one side of her long hair pushed back behind her ear, the visible earring swayed every time she moved. Taking his eyes off her wasn't even an option for him. His hazel eyes were stuck to her like glue. Everything about Laylah was beautiful, picture-perfect.

Laylah raised her hand to have the music start up. She closed her eyes to get in the groove. "'I Love You' is dedicated to my parents." She opened her eyes and allowed herself to get swept up in the performance.

After she delivered the emotionally charged poem, she blew kisses to her parents and the audience, and then Laylah bowed gracefully, turning to leave the stage. Tears welled in her eyes, but when she saw Chancellor walk up and hold out his hand for her to take, just as he'd done before, the moisture spilled over.

He wasted no time in folding the emotional Laylah into his arms.

Because Laylah hadn't yet introduced Chancellor to the family, she took him right over to where everyone was seated. Kelly had made sure she had saved two chairs for them at their reserved table. As Laylah quickly made the introductions, Kelly discreetly took hold of her friend's hand and squeezed her fingers gently. Laylah was sure her best bud had no idea what that little gesture had done to shore her up. Only moments ago she had spoken of courage, endurance, withstanding everything that came her way, but she felt none of that at the moment. The introduction of Chancellor was the test of all tests.

Interestingly enough, Chancellor didn't seem the least bit

worried about meeting Laylah's family and all the others. Since the program was in between poets, he took the opportunity to extend his hand to each person, emitting rays of warm sunshine with his bright smile. He kept a steady arm around Laylah's waist as he made everyone's acquaintance. Once all the formalities were out of the way, he and the woman he adored claimed the two empty seats.

Chancellor would normally order drinks all around, but until he got a chance to tell Laylah his entire story, he couldn't do that. He didn't want to do anything to ruin her night. This was her time to shine—and what a brilliant start she had already had. He had been moved by the touching poem, wishing his parents had loved him like hers did.

The twins didn't even know their father. From what little they'd heard about him, he was just someone their mother had specifically picked up at a bar for a one-night stand, a meaningless roll in the hay that had turned into the birth of two unwanted children.

While Laylah observed Kelly and Antoine interact, she was impressed by how well they seemed to get along. He seemed to really be into her, paying close attention to everything she said. It was hard to hear with all the background noise, but he'd just move his mouth intimately close to her ear when he spoke. Her eyes flashed and sparkled at whatever he was saying. Kelly was like a beam of moonlight, straight-up brilliant.

Chancellor nudged Laylah to get her attention. "What're you thinking, babe?"

"How glad I am you're here. Are you okay?"

"Couldn't be better. Where's everyone staying tonight?"

"With me. Where else?" She saw a flicker of what looked like disappointment in his eyes. "Is something wrong?"

He shook his head. "Not really. Just wishing we were spending the night together. I guess that can't happen until after Sunday," he whispered in her ear.

"You could've stayed last night, but you didn't. Regrets?"

"Deep ones. Did you miss my sexy, hard body in your bed?"

"Every hardened inch of you," she growled lowly. "I made hot, passionate love to you in my head. Boy, you were good, even in my thoughts. You were working my body like you owned it. What a night to remember!"

Chancellor laughed hard. "I'll never forget one single moment of any of our nights together. You're a little spicy freak in the bed, you know."

"And a lady in the streets," she said, thinking about one of the popular songs.

A slow song came on, and Antoine and Kelly instantly got up and headed for the dance floor. Brandon and Sierra were the next to leave the table.

Chancellor extended his hand. "We can't let them outdo us. Besides, I'm itching to hold your body close to mine. Think I can hide the rising evidence of my desire?"

Laylah grinned. "Not with the size of what you're packing. Don't worry. I'll make sure I stay in front of you to cover you up." Laughing, she blew on her fingertips. "Boy, it's getting so hot up in here. You feel the heat?"

"Gobi Desert–like." Laughing also, Chancellor brought her into his arms. "We'd better stop talking all this trash since we can't do anything about it tonight."

"We can pull over and park before we get to my house. I'd love for us to test out my backseat for comfort. I even have a pillow and blanket in the trunk," she joked.

Chancellor shook his head. "You're losing it, girl. Lay your head on my chest and shut your eyes so we can do some subtle bumping and grinding. I want you close to me."

Laylah kissed him softly on the mouth. "If I get any hotter, I'll burn this place down. There's already a brush fire going on down where you know I burn for you."

Chancellor had to laugh again. He loved how she kept him in stitches.

After introducing Chancellor to each of her co-workers, Laylah made sure she sat down and mingled with them for a spell. Their coming out to support her meant a lot. Not one of them had failed to encourage her. She'd heard their cheers when she'd performed.

Marina, Tom's girlfriend, told Laylah she loved the birthday poem he'd given her, complimenting her on its touching content. Cherise had purchased a few poems also and Erika was still encouraging her to write a poetry book. Kaye, March's assistant, gave praise to Laylah's work, too. Before she and Chancellor headed back to join her family, she thanked Manny for pulling the group of supporters together, giving him a big hug for making her evening a grand success. Laylah loved having her co-workers present.

Chapter 9

Laylah saw that her parents' heads were really close together as they chatted nonstop. The possible topic of conversation concerned her a bit. She couldn't help but wonder if they were talking about her and Chancellor. They had to be curious about him. That was only natural. She wasn't exactly looking forward to when they'd all sit down and talk, when everyone could actually hear each other. That was the only way her parents and Chancellor could get better acquainted.

Chancellor pointed across the dance floor. "Get a load of that."

Laylah laughed at the shocked expression on his face. "They dance together all the time. My aunts love to shake a tail feather. Those two women are so free-spirited. They know exactly how to live their lives to the fullest. People are always fascinated by their style and their ages."

"I'll definitely ask them to dance. I'd love to whirl those two lively girls around the dance floor a time or two. How old did you tell me they were? I forgot."

"Aunt Cora is sixty-seven and Aunt Gertrude is sixty-nine." She rested her mouth against his ear to whisper into it. "I have reason to think they're older than that. A long time ago I overheard Dad accusing them of lying about their ages. He said they were three and four years older than what they'd made everyone believe."

Laylah's father was the youngest child. She told Chancellor how Jack had been an unexpected pregnancy, yet a very much wanted addition to the Versailles clan.

Chancellor and Chandler had been unexpected pregnancies, too, unexpected and unwanted. It saddened him that he hadn't seen his mother in several years. If she passed them on the street, he wasn't positive she'd know who they were. She had lost complete contact with her two sons, right after their grandmother's funeral, who had been the last one of the two grandparents to pass away.

Lavonne was none too happy to learn how much money her two boys had been left, which had been many times over what she'd received. When she talked to an estate lawyer about contesting the will, she had been told the will was ironclad and there wasn't a single loophole available to her. In fact, he'd told her she'd needlessly burn up a lot of her own inheritance to try to challenge it. The information had changed her mind.

Mary Kingston had been of sound mind and body when she'd rewritten the will. She'd also secured a few witnesses, besides her lawyer and the mandatory notary. Chancellor and Chandler were the rightful heirs to the Kingston fortune. Although Lavonne had vehemently vowed to get what was rightfully hers, she hadn't attempted it thus far. Lavonne couldn't insult her sons any more than she already had.

Quickly snapping out of the funk Chancellor regrettably found himself slipping into, he turned all of his attention back to the happenings with the folks around him. The Versailles family seemed solidly united, he mentally noted. They had each others' backs. He loved the way Jack and Selma could still openly flirt with each other and indulge in romantic notions after all their years of marriage.

As Chancellor tried to assess Brandon, and what motivated him, he found that Laylah's brother was hardly an easy read. Although he acted as if her was into Sierra, the woman who seemed to adore him, he got the feeling he'd shower the same kind of nonchalant attention on whomever he was with. Sierra was only a queen for the day.

Chancellor thought it was rather sad, especially when he compared it to the kind of everlasting relationship Brandon's parents had going for them. Laylah's brother was still rather young, but Chancellor didn't think youth should be used as an excuse to treat anyone as disingenuously as Brandon treated Sierra.

The two sisters whisked Chancellor out onto the dance floor, dispelling all his thoughts for the moment. The song was fast paced and he hoped he could keep up with the ladies. He'd already seen some of their moves. He'd be willing to bet the farm they were frequent viewers of *Soul Train* and BET. As he was the meat for the sandwich they'd made, he thought he should do his best to provide a bit of flavor.

Laylah was amused by her aunts. She was used to their antics, but they were doing a serious number on Chancellor. He looked as if he didn't know what to expect next.

Kelly nudged her. "Looks like you need to rescue your man. By the way, I really like him, Lay. He seems like a genuine guy. He's also gorgeous. The boy is fine."

"Thanks." Laylah smiled. "I like Antoine, too. He's so attentive with you. I like that he hangs on to your every word. Maybe we've both found the kind of men we've been looking for. God only knows it's about time. Chance is the ideal man for me. If I don't want to lose him to those two live wires I love, I'd better get out there and cut in."

The two women laughed at that, looking over at the energetic Cora and Gertrude.

Chancellor was both happy and relieved to have Laylah rescue him. His feet were tired and his soles burning. It was his guess that the two sisters could last through another complete set. He'd already danced three songs, welcoming the slow number now playing. Laylah wrapped her arms around him tightly as he guided her head onto his chest.

There was no conversation between the happy couple as they swayed to the slow, romantic music. With foreheads touching, both had their eyes closed. Neither of them could have felt more content. Laylah thought the night was going much better than she'd initially expected, though she hadn't thought it would turn out badly. She had just been worried about things getting complicated for Chancellor. No such thing had occurred. He looked happy enough to her, seeming to fit in very well with everyone.

Back at Laylah's place, Kelly helped her friend serve coffee, tea and slices of the golden pound cake baked by Cora. Cora had brought along the moist delight as a present to her precious niece, whom she knew loved it.

Everyone was closely seated at the table or the breakfast bar inside Laylah's kitchen. The room wasn't so big that it made it difficult for all the guests to converse with each other. It had been designed for comfort and everyone looked at home.

Upon seeing Jack and Chancellor now involved in what

appeared to be a deep conversation, Laylah got more than a little nervous. *What questions was her father asking him?* Hopefully nothing offensive, because she didn't want Chancellor insulted.

"What line of work are you in, Chance?" Cora suddenly asked out of the blue.

Sucking in a deep breath, Laylah looked back and forth between Chancellor and her aunt, awaiting his response. Her heart fluttered nervously as it went out to him.

Chancellor looked a bit uncomfortable. "I'm kind of between lucrative jobs right now. Odd jobs here and there keep me afloat. However, I recently started working at Home Depot. I hope to get full-time hours there very soon."

Those unsettling remarks caused everyone's concerned gazes to land right on Laylah. It appeared that her family was having a hard time believing she was dating a man employed by Home Depot. Had he not gone into any detail, for all they knew, he could've been a top banana in the corporation. Working there wasn't anything to cause an employee embarrassment. In these hard times having a job, period, was a blessing.

"Home Depot," Gertrude reiterated, as though she was positive she hadn't gotten it right the first time around. She also acted as if what he'd said was downright unsavory.

"Home Depot," he reiterated with a smile, making sure he kept direct eye contact with the inquisitive Gertrude. He could tell that her mind was spinning like a windmill.

Laylah was aware that Chancellor had left himself wide open for speculation, but she couldn't help wondering if he'd done it purposely. *Was he testing them in the same way they were obviously examining him?* She steeled herself for the next question to come his way, pretty sure she could easily guess what it might be.

"Where do you live?" Cora inquired, one eyebrow angled sharply.

"He's also between homes," Laylah responded just above a whisper, right on target about the next question she'd thought they might've asked Chancellor.

"Actually, living homeless is more like it," he told Cora, with everyone else listening intently. "My situation is very difficult to explain at best, but I plan to tell Laylah everything very soon. I have so many serious issues to discuss with her. In the meantime, please pray for me, for us."

Laylah had been observing everyone very closely. Aunt Cora wasn't having a coronary, but she sure looked as if she was. Gertrude's expression revealed nothing, while Brandon looked as if he was in total shock. Jack and Selma had kept their eyes fast on Laylah from the moment Gertrude had asked Chancellor the first bombshell question.

All Kelly could do was to be there to support her best friend when this inquisition was all over. Laylah was who she was and she was a darn good person. It didn't matter whether she was in love with a homeless person or a rich man. Laylah was the very best person she could be. There was no one more caring and compassionate than the woman who'd give someone in need her last dime, even the shirt off her back.

"I can't imagine Home Depot pays too much," Cora said nonchalantly. "Is that the only source of income you have, dear boy?"

Color flooded Laylah's cheeks. "That is the most insulting question you could ever ask anyone. I'm ashamed that you resorted to something so awful." Laylah clenched and unclenched her fists. Of course she wasn't going to whack her aunt, but just thinking about it provided her some relief from the steadily mounting tension.

All of a sudden Laylah ran from the room and rushed down the hall to her bedroom, from where she retrieved the response letter her aunts had sent her. As she made her way back up front, she prayed fervently, hoping she'd say the right things. She didn't want to offend anyone, but she wasn't going to allow anyone to insult Chancellor, especially in her own home. Family or not, they needed to show some respect, too.

Once Laylah returned, she stood in the middle of the room, sighing hard. "I need everyone's attention." She looked over at Kelly. "Please turn off the stereo for me so I can be heard clearly." Kelly nodded. "Thanks." Laylah winked at her dear friend.

Taking in a deep breath, Laylah read the letter she'd written to Cora and Gertrude. She then held up another letter and read it. "This is the note you sent to me when I wrote in to your column a short time ago. How you're acting toward Chance since learning where he works and lives does not correlate with the advice I just read from you."

Chancellor was stunned by her candor—and he was not the only one.

Moving over next to him, Laylah took Chancellor's hand. "He is homeless, very much down on his luck right now. His living and job situations don't make him any less of a man. For your information, I love him. He's treated me like a princess from day one. I've dated a lot of professional, well-to-do, financially independent men, but not one of them makes me feel special like Chance does. Because I love you all, I care about what you think and how you feel. I also care deeply about Chance's feelings. No one, and I mean no one, gets to hurt his feelings or insult him because of his economic and social standing, especially not here in my home. If there is anyone who can't accept that I'm having a love affair with a homeless, orange-vest-wearing, Home Depot working brother, a man who also takes on other odd jobs to try to make ends meet, all of you know where the front door is."

Smiling gently, Laylah squeezed the stunned Chancellor's

fingers. His own flesh-and-blood mother had never stood up for him like this. "I love him. No ifs, ands or buts. If you love me, and if how you've raised me isn't just a load of meaningless crap—and insincere teachings about how to love others uncon-ditionally—then you'll stay and wish us well. You'll also pray for the best to come our way. In my life, Chance stays put."

Without a moment of hesitation, Jack raised his glass in a toast. "Here's to Laylah and Chance. Your mother and I wish you the very best of everything. May God richly bless your relation-ship. We'll always be here for you. Never doubt that for a second."

"Hear! Hear!" rang out from her aunts and Kelly. Brandon said and did nothing.

Laylah fought the good fight to keep from crying. Realizing that her parents were exactly who they'd always shown them-selves to be, she lost the battle to her burning tears. At the same time she lodged herself snugly into Jack's arms, she reached out for her mother's soft, warm hand. These people had raised her the exact way they'd lived their lives. No one in need went without when Jack and Selma were aware of their plight. Giving their last dime to those in need was commonplace to them. Selma and Jack had taught Laylah to practice what she had constantly seen them preach.

While Laylah guided Chancellor out into the hallway, her face ached from grinning so broadly, her heart bursting from grati-tude. Leaning into Chancellor, she landed a passionate kiss on his mouth. "I'm so happy you're here." The back of her hand reached up and tenderly smoothed its way across his cheek.

He looked deeply into her eyes. "You amaze me. That was quite some speech you just made. The funny thing is I believe every single word of it. My grandparents are the only people I know who would've given up everything for me. You went to the mat for me, kid. I thank God you won't have to give up a thing because of it. Your family supports you. That must be one hell of a feeling."

"It is, Chance, it really is. I was pretty sure about how they'd react, yet I always knew it could go the other way. I had prepared myself for both outcomes, thrilled that the way I'd been taught showed up." Brandon's silence had been painfully noticed by her.

"They raised you, Laylah. They instilled in you the best of each of them, the best of what they know is good and right. Your parents couldn't have let you down."

Chancellor went on to tell Laylah he could see how her family would be worried about her getting involved with a man whose future looked bleak and uncertain. "My life is not as forlorn as I've portrayed. There's a lot for me to explain. I hope you'll give me that chance. The day your family leaves, not one day past it you'll know it all. Okay?"

Extremely curious about his comments, Laylah only nodded. "Sure."

"Thank you." He kissed her forehead. "Let's rejoin the others All the bad stuff has been addressed, though I still have lots of stuff to prove to you and your family."

"Only to me and only because I want to know what's going on with you. I've always known there was more to you than what met the eye. If I'd turned out to be wrong, my heart is already okay with that. I promise to listen to all you have to say. Although I'm worried and a little bit scared, I trust you. I believe in you."

Terribly sorry that he had caused her concern and fear, Chancellor brought Laylah to him for a warm, reassuring hug, hoping he wouldn't ever disappoint her. He desperately wanted her to understand the method to his madness. "I'll do my best not to lose your trust. Knowing you believe in me is an awesome feeling. I've never had anyone give their trust to me as easily as you. Let's finish up on a positive note."

Sunday morning came in amidst a heavy rain shower. The Versailles family had planned to go out to breakfast and leave for the airport from the restaurant, where they'd have plenty of time to continue visiting since the flight wasn't until noon. Because of the heavy downpour, the women had decided to stay inside and prepare the meal at home.

They had spent most of Saturday shopping at various malls and taking in a window-shopping stroll down Rodeo Drive. Jack and Brandon had gone off somewhere nearby Laylah's place to play golf. The entire group had met up later and had ended up hanging out on the Santa Monica Pier, where they'd had an early-evening dinner.

Chancellor was not present for any of the family festivities. Until he had told Laylah everything she should know, he had decided not to intrude upon her time with her family. He didn't like the tension she'd already had to endure because of him. If he was going to make it work with her, all his cards had to be laid on the table. Laylah was the only woman for him. He now had to show her that he was the right man for her.

Now that Laylah's company had gone home, though Brandon was still in town for a few more days, she lay in bed thinking about the interruption she'd had when she'd done a Google search on the Kingston name. She thought it was time for her to try it again since there'd be no interruptions this time. Although she felt a little guilty about snooping around to find information about the Kingstons, she pushed it out of her mind.

With that settled, Laylah jumped up and ran across the room. She retrieved her laptop then slipped back into bed. Within a couple of minutes she was on the Internet. After getting onto Google's Web site, she put in Chancellor's first and last name. She would also check on the name Chandler Kingston.

The number of entries that came up with Chancellor's name was astounding. It would take her a month or two to search all the information. But she didn't need to search it all, she told herself. Just going through a few of the entries might be able to tell her something. Perhaps there was even a picture of him on one of the sites, if in fact this was the same man who'd swept her up into his comforting arms, the man she loved like crazy.

Laylah's body was tired and her eyes bleary from sitting up in bed and reading entries on the computer all night long. The things she'd learned about Chancellor still had her in a state of shock. The man she loved had been wearing a mask from day one, but that was all about to change. As sure as she was breathing, she intended to unmask him. She sighed hard as she took a glance at the mountain of papers she'd printed out from the Internet; all of them had to do with the intriguing Kingston twins.

Laylah's tear-swollen eyes had begun burning like fire a couple of hours into the research, but she had kept on reading. The Kingstons' story was as interesting as any fiction or nonfiction novel she had ever read…and she read plenty. Since Chancellor hadn't told her much of anything, she couldn't decide what was fiction or fact.

All through the night Laylah had wrestled with what this information might mean. The Kingston family was rich beyond her wildest imagination. The twin brothers owned a very popular line of state-of-the-art fitness salons called Fitness First. Interestingly enough, Laylah was a member of the one closest to her home, which was also in proximity to her office. She'd often run over there for a good workout during lunch or after work.

Was it possible that Chancellor and Chandler had lost their lucrative business holdings and were homeless because of it? If so, not a single word had been written about it. It was highly unlikely that a story of this magnitude on such high-profile people would go unreported. The media would have been all over a juicy story like this one. She also knew business buyouts didn't always make it to the media, so that could have happened. Silence was often a part of those kinds of deals.

The truth was, Laylah didn't know what to think. But if she stopped seeing Chancellor she might never know the true story. He just didn't seem like an outright liar, but she had to admit he'd lied to her. Not really, she thought, since he hadn't told her anything she could label blatant. He had never said if he was rich or poor. Thinking back on their conversations, she had assumed a lot about him, she realized.

But he'd taken money from her for the motel and for the lawn work. Why would he do that if he was rich? He certainly wouldn't have needed her few measly dollars. She also thought about his insistence on paying for the meals they'd eaten out. That counted for something. *Didn't it?* She cringed inside when she thought Chancellor could've moved into her place with her had he been trying to scam her. If he had asked to move in with her, she would have agreed to it. She knew it would have been dumb of her, but love often made people act stupid; she loved Chancellor.

There were people who moved in together after only knowing each other one night. There was a time when she thought that wouldn't have been a good idea, but she understood it a lot better than she had before. Some emotions just couldn't be controlled. She once thought that people really needed to get to know each other and be in a relationship for a long time before they even considered cohabiting. She had also thought she was a definite holdout for marriage. Surprisingly enough, Chancellor had walked into her life and swept her off the planet with just a beautiful smile.

As silly as it might seem, Laylah now actually believed in love at first sight. Chancellor had compromised her heart the moment she'd laid eyes on him. She could see his smile as clear as day, not to mention his other wonderful attributes, those of the physical kind. Although she thought she should be stark raving mad at him for keeping secrets, she wasn't. There were two sides to every story— and she wanted to hear Chancellor's version of things before she decided to condemn or exonerate him.

Laylah thought she owed him at least that much.

Chancellor couldn't wait for daylight to appear so he could put his plan to see Laylah into action. This had to be a special evening. He couldn't decide whether to make it public by going out to a restaurant or keep it very private by having dinner prepared for her in his home, of all places—a palatial home he hadn't been inside of for months. No one knew how much he missed his residence and the over-the-top luxury it had afforded him and his brother.

Sleeping in motels and shelters had been difficult for Chancellor, but not nearly as hard as it was for those who didn't have anywhere else to go. He could've called this off at any time. But he'd been so sure he could locate his brother by living the style of life he'd been living for the past few months. Going undercover had seemed like such a good idea at the time. While he still had high hopes of finding Chandler, he was starting to accept the fact it wouldn't be as easy as he'd once thought.

The floor-length gown was stunning, sexy and valentine red. Laylah tenderly fingered the exquisite material as she tried to imagine herself wearing it. It was almost an exact copy of the dress Julia Roberts had worn in *Pretty Woman*. Had Chancellor taken a clue from the scene she'd enacted for him from the movie? She was still amazed by the way he intently listened to her and paid such close attention to everything she said and did.

The gold-embossed invitation to have dinner with Chancellor was rather ritzy. She was quite impressed with the handwritten note that told her a limousine was to pick her up at her home at six-thirty, though it didn't say where she'd be taken. He had also pleaded with her not to turn down his invitation. He wanted to tell her everything she wanted to know about him—and he couldn't do that if she didn't give him a chance to be heard. "I love you" written on the note in his own hand brought tears to her eyes. She had listened to his message from last night, right before she'd researched him. He had said he loved her then, too. That meant they loved each other, because she sure loved him.

Then Laylah thought of all the obstacles they faced. While she had no intention of turning down Chancellor's invitation to dinner, she wasn't feeling very optimistic about the outcome. Why she felt that way, she didn't know. Hearing what he had to say might clarify everything for her. Then again, she might not learn anything more than what she'd read online. Until she heard him out, she promised herself to stop second-guessing issues related to their relationship. Everything would soon be revealed, but she wouldn't tell him what she knew until after he'd laid out his subject matter on the line.

As the limousine whisked through the streets of Los Angeles, Laylah watched the sights pass by through the tinted windows of the longest car she'd ever ridden in. Just to calm her nerves, she had accepted the glass of white wine the driver had offered her.

Everything seemed so surreal to Laylah, but it wasn't. She wore the most beautiful red dress in the world and she was in a white stretch limousine on her way to a destination she wasn't sure about. The one thing she was sure about was that Chancellor would be there to meet her. There was not an ounce of doubt in her mind about that. If for no other reason, though many existed, curiosity had her seated in the back of this limo.

Laylah's eyes darted everywhere, shining like precious jewels. She'd never been inside a house like this one, not even on the mansion-home tours she and Kelly used to take in San Francisco during their college tenure. They had seen some magnificent places, but nothing compared to this. She had never seen so much marble, granite, beveled mirrors, sparkling chandeliers and elegant European-style furnishings.

Chancellor knew he had picked the perfect dress for Laylah. It was made just for her. She looked positively regal in it. The small diamond bezel-style earrings dripping from her ears and the matching pendant caught his eye, making him wish he had thought to also present her with a set of jewelry, though what she wore was perfect for her.

Deciding to show Laylah the entire place before they dined, Chancellor thought she should know how he really lived. He had already admitted to her that this home was co-owned by him and his brother. He'd had a hard time of it when he'd shown her Chandler's living quarters. Memories of his twin came at him from every part of the grand suite, making him miss Chandler's presence even more.

Watching her ever-changing expressions, Chancellor finally guided Laylah out to the sweeping terrace, where she stared at the beautiful settings. Exquisite dinnerware graced the table, along with magnificent lace table linen and a golden candelabrum centerpiece. A red, long-stem rose was placed on both china plates.

A variety of other candles burned brightly all over the remarkable terrace, sheltered in holders that kept the wind from snuffing them out. Colorful flowers were everywhere, even looped through the railings of the white balusters of the balcony. Though she probably shouldn't have been, she was surprised by the decent-size marble and flagstone dance floor off to one side of the balcony. Chancellor's home had it all and the panoramic view from the top was nothing short of glorious.

Chancellor pulled out Laylah's chair, concerned that she hadn't said a word. However, he had heard several astonished gasps pass her lips. The dazed look in her eyes was easy to read. She was captivated by his home, mesmerized by its grandiose style.

Before seating himself, Chancellor pulled out a cell phone and punched in some numbers. No sooner than he had taken his seat, opting to sit right next to her, than a group of formally dressed waiters came out of all four exits leading to the terrace. Sparkling wine and cheese was the first course served, along with stuffed mushrooms and other dainty hors d'oeuvres. The delicious scents were heavenly.

Chancellor reached over and covered Laylah's hand with his. "You haven't said a word since you greeted me when you first arrived. I hope you're not at all displeased. Hopefully, after I explain everything to you, you will be able to understand my actions."

Wishing her stomach would calm down, Laylah smiled weakly. God only knew how much she wanted to understand everything about him. Just seeing him again had her insides trembling. He had no idea the intense effect he had on all her senses. The love she felt for him was fathomless. "I'm speechless. Anyone would be mum after touring this mansion. I haven't even seen the grounds yet, so I'm sure I'm in for more of a shock. Your home is beautiful, absolutely magnificent."

Sounding as if a live orchestra performed for their entertainment, romantic stereo music played softly in the background. The ambience couldn't have been more perfect.

Once the couple finished the showily displayed garden salads, a rack of lamb, its presentation exquisite, was served next, along with accompanying mint jelly. Steamed baby carrots and butter-whipped sweet potatoes looked divine. Celery sticks and a variety of olives had been carefully placed in a crystal relish dish. Knowing how much she loved macaroni and cheese, he'd had a small, personal-size casserole baked just for her.

Savoring every tasty bite of the exquisitely prepared meal, Laylah ate slowly. As hard as she tried not to look at Chancellor, she couldn't help it. Seeing him in a traditional tuxedo was quite a contrast to the casual attire he normally wore. From head to toe, he looked marvelous, every bit the debonair, wealthy entrepreneur.

Unfortunately, Chancellor's mask was still partially in place, even though he had confirmed for her that he was a filthy-rich man, one who obviously had inexhaustible means. Outside of that, she didn't know a whole lot more. He may have lost his business, though she doubted it, but he still owned this unbelievable piece of priceless real estate.

The home alone had to be worth its weight in gold. Prices of real estate in California had flown off the charts.

Chancellor laid down his fork. "Please continue to eat while I tell you the history of my family and the reasons why I was masquerading as a homeless person."

Masquerading. Good word choice. Laylah was eager to hear all that he had to say. She simply nodded at his remarks, too emotional to speak.

Chancellor started out by saying that the Kingston brothers had taken the world by storm. Owners of a chain of fitness and spa centers, the two men had invested vast amounts of the money they'd inherited from their grandparents. The business had later become a successful conglomerate, allowing the brothers to heavily invest in stocks and bonds.

Then Chandler had one day stormed out into the world without Chancellor. Over two months had passed since the last time he had laid eyes on his twin. Fearful that his brother might be hurt or even dead, he had decided to try to solve the mysterious disappearance of his beloved sibling.

Life just wasn't the same for him without Chandler.

Oddly enough, Chandler had taken a strange shine to living as a homeless man on the tough streets of Los Angeles. At first he had just drifted from place to place, calling nowhere in particular home. He'd return home for a week or two, only to leave again, without any warning. He would call from time to time during his absences, but he wouldn't always say where he was. He'd never returned home after his last departure.

After giving it much thought, Chancellor had decided to join the ranks of the homeless to try to figure out the mysterious disappearance of his brother, since the police hadn't seemed interested in pursuing the case.

Chapter 10

The history of the twins had been filled with pain, anguish, love and joy.

Raised by their maternal grandparents, Mary and David Kingston, Chancellor and Chandler had been an unwanted pregnancy by twenty-year-old Lavonne Kingston, a wild, uncontrollable young woman. Because of all the money at her disposal, she wasn't the least bit interested in raising her kids as a single parent, though that wouldn't have been a struggle for her. Soon after the birth of her twins all she had wanted was to continue in the jet-set lifestyle her parents' wealth had always afforded her.

Because Mary and David had never denied Lavonne a single one of her desires, they sought legal custody of Chancellor and Chandler not long after their birth so Lavonne could go on with her life. Although the parents had hoped their daughter would come to her senses, they hadn't held out much optimism, so they'd adopted the twins.

With tears rolling down his face, Chancellor closed the photo album he had pulled out to share with Laylah. Finding his twin was imperative, he'd told her. He couldn't go on with his life in a normal manner until he had some answers. Although he had been heavily involved in the day-to-day operation of their conglomerate, they had a very capable staff. A leave of absence for him had been warranted, but only for a short period of time. Time had run out on him. He needed to get back to business as usual.

The majority of the employees had been with his company, Fitness First, from day one and had earned their employers' complete trust. Now that neither he nor Chandler was around to oversee the business, Chancellor had been relying heavily on their staff.

As Chancellor had thought about how to go about putting his plan of living on the streets into action, he had figured he should allow a week's worth of growth to amass on his face so he'd look kind of scruffy. Forgoing his weekly hair salon appointment would more than likely produce a mop of unruly, wavy hair in just a couple of weeks. Those plans had eventually pretty much fallen by the wayside. Old habits were very hard to break. He was who he was, though he had thought he needed to learn how to be someone else for the sake of understanding Chandler while trying to find him.

Every article of clothing Chancellor owned was a designer label, so he had figured he should get some less flattering items from the Salvation Army. He had also thought he might need to wear the same clothes a week straight, without washing them, so they'd become somewhat soiled and smelly. That idea hadn't played out either, he had informed Laylah.

Chancellor had known that pulling off this homeless feat wasn't going to be easy because he was so clean-cut, but he had thought it was necessary. He loved and missed his brother something fierce. He hadn't gone back to the police because Chandler had left and returned so many times already that the authorities had started to show doubt. He had also figured that his brother might be out there on the streets simply because he wanted to be. Chancellor still didn't know what to think and still had no reasonable answers.

Getting the police involved again wasn't something he was sure he should do since he also feared Chandler may have unwittingly or wittingly gotten himself involved in something illegal. It was also possible he was staying away just to protect the home front, fearing that he could bring trouble back to his brother.

His worst fears had begun to come home to roost after he'd started to closely observe his twin's odd behavior. That Chandler might suffer from a mental illness became his biggest concern. There wasn't any other logical reason for his twin's strange, unexplainable actions. Chandler was like a stranger at times.

Although he could afford to hire a team of private detectives, he had decided not to go that route just yet. He'd feel foolish if his brother was fine and just didn't want to come home. Chandler had always been a free spirit. Even in showing up for work he'd set his own hours, which wasn't the same schedule every day.

Chancellor's gut seemed to tell him differently, but he couldn't be sure that Chandler wasn't in some sort of serious predicament. Time was of the essence and he now had to speed things up if he was to find out what had happened to his twin. He hoped Laylah would decide to stick by his side, but her silence definitely had him worried. Especially getting dead silence from a woman who loved to talk nonstop, one who always had a lot of interesting stuff to say, a reporter by profession, no less.

Chancellor eyed her curiously, wondering what she had been

thinking during his emotional presentation. He wished he had been able to hold his emotions in check, but he hadn't been able to contain his feelings. Her expression hadn't changed a bit since he'd first begun his story. "I want to hear your thoughts on this situation, but it's only fair I give you time to take everything in. A lot has been said by me, all of it true. Hope you can forgive my deception, but I can also understand why that might be hard for you."

Before Chancellor forgot to give Laylah what he had earlier put away for her, he reached into his inside jacket pocket and removed an envelope, which he handed to her. "It's the money you've given me since we first met. It's all there, every single dime."

Feeling horribly sick inside, Laylah got up from the table and strolled across the terrace. After placing both her hands on the balcony railing, she leaned forward and rested her abdomen against it. The life story of the Kingston twins had been touching, gut-wrenching, truly believable, but she was still scared beyond understanding. He had put some of the puzzle together for her, but she felt there were many more missing pieces.

Laylah thought it was strange that Chancellor still hadn't once mentioned any kind of true feelings for his mother; that continued to bother her something awful. He had shown very little emotion when he had talked of Lavonne Kingston, showing far more deep-seated sentiment over his feelings for his beloved brother and loving grandparents.

Walking up behind Laylah, Chancellor rested his chin on her shoulder, circling her waist tenderly. "I love you. Please don't desert me. I need you in my life. We can work this out. I believe that with all my heart and soul. Ours was not a chance meeting."

Reaching back, Laylah gently took a fistful of his hair in her hand. She then put her head back, resting her cheek against his. She didn't believe their meeting was by chance either. As much as she wanted to turn to him and tell him she'd be there for him every step of the way, she couldn't commit to that, not with so many blank spaces left.

Besides the commitment issues, Chancellor lived like a king. Laylah thought he needed a sophisticated queen to share in his life, not a newspaper reporter. She wouldn't know how to act around the kind of people she imagined he hung out with. She was all that and so much more, but she hadn't been groomed to be the wife of an extremely wealthy man, who probably attended a lot of important engagements, business and social.

Laylah loved wearing jeans and T-shirts and loved wearing nothing best of all. Did the fabulous, grossly expensive gown he'd purchased for her represent the way he'd want her to dress? Dressing formally was okay now and then. In fact, she loved to dress up occasionally, but she didn't see it happening as a regular part of her lifestyle.

As Laylah thought about how she used informal dishes and glasses, she wondered if he ate on china and drank from crystal stemware all the time—and in a formal setting like the one they'd just dined in. Everything in his home was perfectly placed. All the furnishings were dust free and each piece glowed from regular dusting and waxing.

Though Laylah was neat and clean, she had the tendency to let things at her place get a bit untidy from time to time. She also ate all over the house, but she didn't think it would be acceptable in his mansion. There were times when she didn't wash clothes for two weeks, which meant the dirty laundry often got piled up. Besides all that, her place was her castle, the one place where she could find peace in the valley at the end of the day.

Chancellor turned Laylah around to face him. "Please say something. The silence is killing me."

"I know what you're feeling. It's awkward for me, too. You

said you'd give me time…and I'd like to take you up on it. My head's spinning from all you've shared with me, throbbing from all I still don't know. Time, Chance, a little time is needed here."

Chancellor kissed her softly on the mouth. "Laylah, take all the time you need. Just know that I love you and I believe we belong together. Do we have to stop seeing each other completely while you think things through?"

Laylah had to laugh inwardly at the adorable expression on his face. "We can't see as much of each other as before. Being close to you keeps me from thinking clearly." *Especially when all I want to do is strip you naked and take you to bed.*

"That's fair enough." He kissed the tip of her nose, smoothing back her hair.

"I'm glad you met my family." She eyed him intently. "My parents and I have talked about this situation, but no one else has even tried to discuss it with me. Kelly won't allow me to remain silent much longer. You were very courageous with everyone and I respect how dignified and courageously you handled yourself. It could've turned out to be a disaster. By the way, Kelly thinks you're great. She feels good about us."

Laylah was happy she'd tested her family's reaction to his misfortunes. She had really wanted to see how he and her family interacted. If he wasn't the real deal, she'd known he wouldn't have been able to dupe them for long.

"I'm glad I got to meet your family, too. I tried hard not to disappoint you." His eyes suddenly locked passionately with hers. "May I have this dance?"

Whitney Houston's "I'll Always Love You" playing in the background made Laylah fearful of going into his comforting arms. Being that close to his body just might cause her to lose total control. It was already hard enough being as near to him as she was right now. With her willpower failing her completely, she went right into his arms, resting her weary head against his broad chest. The scent of his cologne was sexy and manly and she inhaled deeply of it, hoping to never forget how he smelled.

As Chancellor slowly guided her over the dance floor, holding her tenderly, the gentle winds played in her hair. The romantic atmosphere had her intoxicated and she just couldn't fight the delicious feelings. When his mouth met up with hers in a passionate union, she offered no resistance whatsoever. Kissing him back felt so natural to her. She had many feelings to sort out, but she was sure of one thing: her unyielding love for him.

Loving him so deeply and so unconditionally made her feel whole.

A few minutes later, Chancellor guided Laylah into the grand master suite, causing her to once again gasp in disbelief at such luxurious splendor. She didn't know why she hadn't refused to go into the room when she'd realized where he was taking her, but she had proved herself to be extremely weak against his romantic arsenal.

As Chancellor pulled back the comforter, Laylah watched with bated breath, wishing she had the guts to run away. But she didn't want to flee. She wanted to be right there where she was, lying with him in his own bed. He tensed a little as she waited for him to begin disrobing her, fearful of how she might react. Instead of undressing her, he picked her up and lay her in the bed fully dressed, climbing in beside her.

Chancellor turned on his side and brought Laylah's body fully back against his, circling her waist, resting his chin in her hair. "It's okay, sweetheart. I just want and need to hold you near me. Close your eyes and dream. No harm will come to you."

Laylah couldn't recall the last time she'd called off work sick. Lovesick was more like it, but she simply hadn't wanted to go into the office today. As she lay in Chancellor's bed, still fully dressed, she wondered where he was. He couldn't have been gone long because he'd been there a half hour ago, when she'd first awakened, only to drift back off to sleep minutes later.

Chancellor and Laylah had slept in each other's arms all through the night—and neither of them had taken off their clothing. She was sure the beautiful dress was probably wrinkled, but dry cleaning should restore it to its natural state.

Laylah had never slept on a more comfortable, deluxe pillow-top mattress. It had been like slumbering in the lap of luxury. She was surprised at how easily she had fallen off to sleep, especially when her mind her been so turmoil filled. Knowing she should go home, yet wanting to stay with him, had been a tough decision for her to deal with. The last thing she wanted was for Chancellor to think he could make a fool of her. He couldn't. She for sure knew that much about herself.

Laylah would walk away from the man she loved before she'd be made a fool of.

Dressed in a burgundy and gray silk robe, carrying in his hand one of his perfectly pressed shirts, Chancellor came into the bedroom. Leaning over the bed, he kissed her gently on the mouth. "Why don't you slip into this shirt while we have breakfast. I'm sure the formal gown has you feeling really uncomfortable."

Laylah nodded. "Can't believe I slept in this magnificent dress." Her eyes blinked uncontrollably. "Maybe I should just skip breakfast. I really should be getting on home."

Taking her hand in his, Chancellor sat down on the side of the bed. "I'll take you home after you eat. I promise. Go ahead and slip into the shirt. I'll be right back."

It was important to him to protect her dignity. Having her undress in front of him would have been unfair to her, which was why he'd put her into bed fully clothed. He wasn't going to try to make love to her or do anything else to spook her, not when she was so confused about everything.

He knew he had to do all within his power to bring her back to him, back to the way they were, madly in love with each other. Winning Laylah's heart anew and finding Chandler were his top priorities. Chancellor simply didn't want to live without the two people he loved most in the world.

As Chancellor passed through the foyer on his way to the kitchen, Effie, his middle-aged personal assistant, friend and confidante, handed him a special-delivery letter. "This just came for you, Chance." She handed him the letter. "Are you and your young lady ready to have breakfast served? Harold has everything prepared for you."

Harold, Effie's husband, was the main chef and nutritionist. There were also three housekeepers and several groundskeepers employed at the Kingston home.

Chancellor looked at the envelope and read the name up in the left-hand corner. His gasp was audible. His expression suddenly turned to one of total confusion. He then looked up at Effie. "We're ready to eat. Please have Harold serve breakfast in the dining alcove off the master bedroom, unless, of course, Miss Versailles prefers to eat on the terrace."

Chancellor dropped down in one of the dozens of chairs strategically placed throughout his palatial home. As he perused the letter from his mother, he gritted his teeth, unable to believe her nerve. She must need something, he thought, wondering if she was now stone broke. He couldn't believe how recklessly she'd handled her entire life.

Lavonne was requesting to pay a visit to her sons. She didn't know Chandler was missing. Of course she didn't know; she didn't know anything about her two sons. For the most part, she had never been around for them to consult with about anything. Knowing he'd have to give her request more thought, Chancellor folded the letter, put it back in the envelope and stuck it in the pocket of his robe.

Pleased that Laylah had opted to have breakfast on the terrace, outdoors where the weather couldn't have been more pleasant this lovely morning, he took a seat across from her. The food was already laid out on the simple but colorfully set table. The scrambled eggs, sausage and homemade biscuits smelled delicious. Harold had also put out a couple of miniature boxes of cereal, ripened bananas, flavored yogurts and glass pitchers of ice-cold milk, orange and cranberry juices. A carafe of hot coffee was also available.

Chancellor frowned. "Sorry I didn't order hot tea for you. I can still get it done."

Laylah held up her hand. "Not necessary. There's enough here to drink already. I met your chef. Seems like a really nice guy."

He nodded. "Great man, with a wonderful wife. Ms. Effie's my personal assistant. Actually, she's more than that to me. Both are loyal employees, but I think of them as family. My grandmother hired them a couple of years before her death. She loved the couple like they were her own children. Chandler is extremely fond of them, too."

Not looking too pleased, Laylah stared openly at Chancellor. She licked her lower lip. "Your job at Home Depot, do you really work there? Or is that a fabrication?" She didn't want to refer to him as a liar.

"Sure do. Hardest physical work I've done in a long time. Not used to lifting heavy products." He lowered his head for a moment. "I'm giving notice, though. My employees need me back to operate the company. Everything's not running smoothly."

"Sorry to hear that. I belong to one of your fitness centers, the one nearest my house at Oak Forest Boulevard. In fact, I believe it's one of your newer ones."

"You're correct. Oak Forest is actually the last one built, the finest one yet. We keep trying to improve on the design and the offered amenities. Consider yourself a life member. I'll personally take care of changing your membership at no cost to you."

She narrowed her eyes. "And if it doesn't work out between us?"

"It will." His eyes showed love. "I need you to believe that as much as I do."

Laylah no longer knew what to believe, yet he definitely seemed to care an awful lot about her. The fact still remained that their lifestyles were totally different—and she wasn't sure that wouldn't eventually get in the way of their happiness. The only thing she could really commit to was helping him find his brother, no matter how much she loved him. The deep compassion inside her heart wouldn't let her ignore his need for her help.

"Thanks, but no thanks. This girl is used to paying her own way. I can afford my current membership at Fitness First or I wouldn't have joined in the first place."

He had offended her, he realized—his last intent. "As you wish." He shifted his weight until he retrieved the envelope from his pocket. "Today I received a special-delivery letter from my mother. She wants to see her sons after all these years."

Laylah recognized the deep, agonizing pain in his eyes. "You don't seem so keen on it. You won't ever get closure over her bailing out on you guys if you don't see her. Don't you want some sort of closure with her?"

"I don't see what good it'd do after all these years. My mother didn't want us, would've given us up for adoption had my grandparents not taken us. She's either stone broke or her conscience is starting to kick her butt. She is getting older now. Her desire to see us only complicates our lives even more. I have no desire to know her."

"Don't you think she should know Chandler is missing?"

He hunched his shoulders. "As if she ever cared. We both could be dead, for all she knows. Not even so much as one measly birthday card from her in thirty years. Does that sound like a woman who gives a hoot about the children she birthed?"

Laylah's heart went out to him. The pain in his voice was as raw as the hurt in his eyes. If only she could shelter him from it all, she would. The only thing she could do was make sure she didn't cause him any undue pain. She really didn't want to hurt Chancellor, still didn't know if they could remain a couple, but she was willing to explore all their possibilities. It was scary to get in any deeper with him than she already was, but her heart was telling her he was her destiny. The thought of being wrong was frightening.

"If it'll make you feel better, I'd be willing to be with you when you see your mother. Will that help any?" She ran her hand down his arm.

He stared at her in disbelief, knowing he was right about her being an angel of mercy. Her halo had never shone brighter. "It'll help tremendously. I haven't decided whether to see her or not. If I do, I want you there with me."

"You got it. Just let me know your final decision." She looked at her watch. "I'd better get going. The day is getting away from us."

"You've called off work already, so please spend the day here with me. We can go by your place to get you some suitable clothes. Just like you didn't want me to leave you a few nights ago, I don't want you to leave me now. I understood it then, just as I do now, but I'd thought it was better to go. Please stay with me. There's so much more I want to share with you. It just can't be done all at once."

His last statement reeled her in. As much as he seemed to want to share more with her, she was so eager to hear all of what he had to say. He was right about it taking time. She laughed. "I feel stupid dressing in a formal gown just to go home, no matter how stunning it is. But I do need something casual to put on. Can we go now?"

"Sure. Have you had enough breakfast?"

"More than enough, Chance. Thanks."

"I'll wait for you out here. Go ahead into the bedroom and get dressed."

Because she needed it as much as she thought he did, she leaned over and gave him a lingering kiss. His totally surprised reaction wasn't lost on her. "Be right back."

All changed into jeans and a plain white T-shirt, Laylah was busy returning phone calls from her home office while Chancellor watched television in the family room. There had been an unusual break in the story about little Ashley. There had been so many negative things said about her father, but it was now looking as if her mother might be more than culpable. Apparently, young Ashley was last seen with her mother's new boyfriend, not with her biological father. It had been reported that the boyfriend had served time for child molestation and was a recently registered sex offender.

This story was ever changing. Laylah didn't know what or who to believe. However, a friend of Laylah's, an active-duty police officer, had confirmed for her that the new boyfriend, Roger Hogan, was indeed a pedophile. He had done hard time in state prison over a young handicapped girl he had been found guilty of molesting. The child was the daughter of a past girlfriend. It amazed Laylah how some women let boyfriends get too close to their precious young daughters.

After writing the latest version of her story about Ashley, Laylah saved it on her hard drive and also on a CD. She then returned Brandon's phone call, but to her dismay he wasn't in his hotel room. She left a message for him to get back to her whenever his schedule permitted, though she really wanted to talk to him.

Once she turned off her computer, she went into the family room where she found Chancellor totally engrossed in what appeared to be a movie thriller. Seconds into viewing the television screen, she realized he was watching Denzel Washington's movie, *Déjà Vu*. She plopped down on the sofa next to him and his arm immediately went around her shoulders. Keeping his eyes plastered to the television, he kissed her temple.

Laylah kept quiet while he finished viewing the movie. She was thinking she should be red-hot mad at him about a number of things, but if anger wasn't in her nature she probably shouldn't force herself to act it out. The wrong he'd done wasn't so egregious to warrant her being unforgiving. People made mistakes. Human beings were fallible. She couldn't count all the mistakes she'd made, nor could she recall all the people she'd hurt unwittingly. Only on Judgment Day would she learn all of her misdeeds. Even then, God was forgiving.

Seated in a lounger outside on the flagstone and marble terrace, it was still hard for Laylah to believe Chancellor owned such a magnificent home. Her instincts about him were right. From the very beginning she'd thought he was a special person who'd somehow gotten down on his luck. Sophistication was hard to cover up, but he'd done a pretty good job of pulling it off. Believing he had fallen on hard times was easy for her because it happened a lot. Losing fortunes wasn't an unusual occurrence.

As her cell phone rang, she quickly reached into her bag and pulled it out. Brandon's name popped up on the screen. "Hey, what're you up to?"

"Just got out of a meeting. What's up with you? You sounded stressed-out on the message. Are you okay?"

"Actually, if I were any worse, you'd probably need to admit me to a sanitarium. I'm having an incredibly hard time of it. I need to talk. Do you have any free time?"

"I'm always available to you. Want me to come by your place?"

"No, no," she said, her voice quaking. "I'll drop by the hotel." She looked at her watch. "Is about an hour from now good for you?"

"That's fine. You know the room number. See you then."

Laylah put her cell phone back in her purse, glad that she'd insisted on driving her own car to Chancellor's. Knowing that Sierra had already returned to San Francisco also made her happy. She wouldn't think of talking to Brandon about Chancellor in front of a stranger. Although Sierra was her brother's girlfriend, Laylah knew very little about her despite the fact she'd been around her a lot during the weekend.

Just as Laylah stored her cell phone in her purse, Chancellor came back onto the terrace. He stretched his hand out to her. "Come with me, please. I want us to walk around the grounds together." Because it looked as if more rain was threatening, he wanted to show Laylah the large pool area on the back side of the home.

Right after she got to her feet, he took her into his arms. Looking into her eyes, he smiled. "Is it okay if I kiss you? My lips miss yours."

With a bit of reluctance, Laylah went into his arms, offering up her lips to him. Kissing him always brought her great pleasure. Her lips had missed his, too. The kiss deepened and she stood on tiptoe, molding herself closely against his hard body. The rigidness of his manhood had her libido going crazy. It had been a while since they'd made love and her body was definitely letting her know it.

Drawing her head back slightly, Laylah looked up at him. "Where do we go from here, Chance? Do we even have a shot at some kind of future? There's so much I don't know about you, but I want to know it all. Are you ready to bare your soul to me?"

"It's already in progress. Don't you feel that I'm trying to bare all? There's just so darn much muck to get through. I'd wished me loving you with all my heart and soul was enough for you, but I can't expect that. I'd want to have all the missing pieces, too."

She eyed him curiously. "Is there anything criminal in your past? Anything you are so ashamed of that it'll cause you to lie to me?"

"Not one thing. I've never been in trouble with the law. The only thing I'm ashamed of is that I didn't come to grips earlier with what was happening to Chandler. I really believe he has mental-health issues." He cleared his throat. "According to my grandparents, my grandfather's mother resided in a sanitarium from the age of thirty-two up until her death many, many years ago. I never gave it much thought until lately, never thought about mental illness being hereditary. Now that's all I can think about."

She felt so sorry for him. Fear of the unknown invaded his eyes right as she looked into them. His sadness was deep. She laid her head on his shoulder for a couple of seconds before making eye contact with him again. "Can you excuse me for a moment? I need to make a call to Brandon."

"Not a problem." Chancellor stepped over to the balcony railing and leaned on it.

Laylah punched in the code to Brandon's cell. As soon as his voice came on the line, she told him she'd have to postpone their meeting, promising to call him later.

"Is everything okay?"

"Yeah, I believe so. Chance needs me right now. If I don't get back to you today, I'll definitely call tomorrow. Can you hang in there with me?"

"Long as you need me to be there. Be careful, baby sister. I'm a little worried about this relationship you're in. I'm assuming that's what you want to talk about."

"It is. And I already knew how you felt. You've never been able to mask your feelings. My gut and my heart are telling me Chance is a very honorable man. I just need to give him the chance to prove me right or wrong. No pun intended."

"You're a smart cookie, Laylah. You'll figure it all out. Instead of completely leading with your heart, let your head in on the action."

"You know I will. Talk to you later."

Laylah walked across the terrace and circled Chancellor's waist from behind, laying her head against his back. His linen shirt felt soft to her skin as his manly cologne scent sailed on the air. One hand left his waist and found its way into his hair, lightly massaging his scalp with her fingernails. To kiss the back of his neck she had to stand on her tiptoes again. She wanted all of him and she was ready to have him pleasure her body in the way only he knew how.

Chancellor turned around to face her. Catching her lower lip between his teeth, he sucked on it gently. His desire for her was as deep as hers for him, yet he wouldn't think of making a move on her at a time like this. They were standing on too much unproven ground and he didn't want either of them to sink.

While he demonstrated to her how she could trust him completely, he also wanted to show her every day how much he deeply loved her. Because they'd gotten off to a rocky start didn't mean the playing field couldn't eventually be leveled. All in due time, he told himself. All she had asked for was time, which he was willing to grant.

He kissed her forehead. "Ready for that walk?"

She slid her hand inside his shirt. "What I'm ready for is your body to walk all over mine. Tenderly," she whispered, rubbing her hand over his chest. "I've never needed you more than I do right now. Please don't ask me if I'm sure. I am."

Hiding his surprise at her unashamed request was impossible, his eyebrow lifting considerably. Making love to her was the last thing he'd thought she'd request of him.

Chancellor didn't know what to do. If he turned her down, he could hurt her feelings. If he did as she requested, would she later have regrets? This was such a confusing time for her and for him, yet there was no way he could tell her she didn't know her own mind. *I'm sure,* echoed in his head. He was sure, too. He wanted her like crazy.

Instead of waiting for him to decide one way or the other, Laylah took his hand and guided him in the direction of where she thought his bedroom was. The layout of the enormous place was complicated, since there were so many rooms inside. Bent on seducing him, she really didn't want to mess this up. She covertly looked around her as she tried to recall which way they'd gone when they'd gone to his bedroom from the terrace last evening. The high-arched hallway made her think she was on the right track. Then she saw the massive double doors.

Bingo. You go, girl!

Chapter 11

Just to keep his burning hands busy, Chancellor turned on the stereo, pressing in the number for "Falling," the cut he liked a lot from Alicia Keys's first CD release. The love he felt for Laylah was the kind that didn't become burned-out. If he had his way, what was between them would only continue to grow deeper and deeper, for the rest of their natural lives.

Once in the bedroom, Laylah looked around to see what she could use as props to make things hotter for Chancellor. Spotting the silver ice bucket on the built-in bar, she strolled over to it and poured a half-glass of water. Smiling devilishly at him, she soaked her T-shirt with just enough water to make it wet and clingy. Feeling her erect nipples straining against the cotton material turned her on as much as him.

Making a seductive showing of stripping off her T-shirt, Laylah kept her eyes fastened on Chancellor, who looked as if he didn't know what to do. He'd been looking that way a lot lately. His woman had him mesmerized and confused, all at the same time.

She slowly lowered one strap of her bra and then inched the other off to bare her golden-tanned shoulder. As she circled the tip of her forefinger with her tongue, she summoned him to come hither with a slight wiggle of a digit on the opposite hand.

Trying not to disobey the wishes of a woman he wanted in the worst way, physically and soulfully, Chancellor darn near ran a marathon to close the short distance.

Curling her hand around the back of Chancellor's head, Laylah brought him to her, kissing him hard on the mouth, her coiling tongue providing and receiving the sweetest of pleasures. Taking a few steps back from him, she popped the top button on her jeans, rolling down the waistband just a tad. Posting one finger on her zipper, she gazed at him as if she was inviting him to do the honors.

When Chancellor looked fearful of moving a fraction of an inch, she laughed wickedly at his boyish reaction. Lowering the zipper just enough to reveal her navel, she circled her belly button with her fingernail. Provocatively, she wet her luscious mouth, allowing her flirtatious tongue to linger languidly on her bottom lip.

It felt to Chancellor as if every muscle in his body had solidified like petrified wood in response to her sexy exploitation of his flaming desire. He was ready to get it on, prepared to take things to the next level. But he wasn't ever in that much of a hurry with her. He loved it when they took slow, easy rides to ecstasy.

Seeing this side of her personality was intriguing beyond description to him. He desired her like crazy, yet he also wanted this beguiling show to go on and on and on, until he had no choice but to give in to the fiery temptation. Only then would they take the unhurried journey into paradise and beyond.

Laylah had other ideas. Unable to keep her distance from Chancellor another second, she slowly unzipped her jeans the rest of the way, sliding them down her thighs and over her feet. After twirling the denim in the air for a hot second, she tossed them aside. Each thumb went into a side of her white lacy bikinis. "I'd love for you to separate me from these babies." She looked down at her intimate apparel and then back at him.

While Chancellor tried to control his ragged breathing, he locked his lustful gaze onto Laylah's, hoping that what they were about to indulge in was the right thing. He wanted so desperately to revere her in every way possible. At the moment his manhood wasn't thinking about honor. The urge to be inside her was stronger than it had ever been.

Covering her thumbs with his own, he slowly stripped the bikinis from her trembling body. He would love to give her the same kind of sexy routine she'd seduced him with, but it was obvious that neither of them could wait another second. Quickly, he removed a packet of protection from the nightstand drawer to keep her safe.

As he practically tore off his clothes with one hand, the other one had her meshed tightly against him. Totally nude now—and protected—Chancellor brought Laylah fully against him. As he lifted her, she wrapped her legs up high around his waist. Their mouths came together in a riveting kiss, their tongues entangling in a burst of passion. He slowly walked over to the bed with her stuck to him like glue.

Glad that the comforter was still turned down from earlier, he sat on the edge of the bed and then worked his way near the center. Raising Laylah slightly, he brought her down onto his manhood slowly, gasping in delight. Her moisture-filled inner core covered him like a second skin, making him burn like fire for her. He lay back in the bed and she fully stretched out atop him, bent on taking control of the helm. As she moved over him fervently, deliciously torturing every inch of his bare flesh, she ravished his mouth with hot, wet kisses.

His hands tenderly caressed her creamy breasts, before he took one into his mouth, switching back and forth between the perky ripened peaks. His tongue laved and sucked on hardened nipples until they were bathed in moisture.

Wanting to take over before he completely lost control, in one quick motion Chancellor flipped Laylah over onto her back. His mouth feverishly went to work, teasing and nipping her heated flesh. Determined to cover every inch of her nudity, he kissed and delightfully tortured her sensitive erogenous zones, his fingers twisted up tightly in her hair. Her pleasurable gasps and wild shudders further excited him as he continued to fulfill her in ways she hadn't ever imagined.

Tender thrust after thrust sweetly pounded into her uncontrollably, causing her to dig her nails into his flesh to keep from screaming. So close to being swept over the edge, she did her best to hang on for a simultaneous, earth-moving climax. She didn't have long to wait. As his long, hard shudders suddenly shook him to the core, she eagerly gave herself up to the moment, her fulfilling release coming the same time as his.

Laylah's and Chancellor's soft moans and pleasurable panting rent the air as they held on to each other as though there was no tomorrow in sight. He lifted her head and kissed her passionately. Bringing her even closer to him, he guided her head onto his chest and soothingly massaged her back in circular motions. Within minutes, the physically worn-out yet completely fulfilled couple fell asleep in each other's arms.

Awakening before Chancellor, Laylah propped up her head on one hand to study his handsome features. She stilled the desire to feather her fingers across his pleasure-inducing mouth. Her body still tingled all over from their unbelievable rendez-vous. He had made her feel as if she were in heaven. There was no doubt she had returned the favor.

Canceling her meeting with Brandon had occurred because she'd felt that Chancellor had needed her to be there with him. She needed him, too, every bit as much, in more ways than one. He filled a huge space inside her heart and deep down in her soul. Massive, gaping holes never before occupied.

As her fingers crushed the silk sheets she lay upon, she basked in the boundless bliss she felt. She also understood the true meaning of happiness. The fireplace against the wall directly in front of the bed wasn't lit, but tiny white lights shone from some-where inside the framework. Though it was still early, the bedroom shutters had been completely closed, causing it to appear as if twilight was filtering into the room.

The decor of the room was masculine yet she saw soft feminine features that should delight any woman. Thinking of other ladies, she had to wonder how many females had slept in the place where she now lay nude and fully satisfied. *Does it matter?* His past history with women wasn't a big concern. That was then. This was now, she concluded. She truly believed Chancellor was hers exclu-sively. If he wasn't, he sure made her feel as if she was the only one.

There were many issues they had to get through, but him loving her and vice versa was not one of them. She saw love in his eyes for her every time he looked at her. She felt it in his touch and sensed it in his demeanor.

Chancellor awakened and looked up at her. His eyes softly scanned her face and body before coming back to meet her bewildered gaze. She was beautiful and he loved everything about her. Reaching out his hand, he drew her close to him. "Have I ever told you how beautiful you are, inside and out?"

Smiling gently, she nodded. "You have. Numerous times. You're beautiful, too. My life is so much better because you're in it. Thanks for revealing things never before revealed to me."

He looked puzzled. "Such as?"

She lowered her lashes briefly. When she raised her lids and stared into his curious, watchful gaze, her breath caught. "I never knew I was so darn emotional. Never knew I could be filled from head to toe with love for another human being. I love my family, of course, but this kind of love is different. I feel so alive and there are times when it feels like all this love is going to explode right out my chest. I've never seen such vulnerability in a man, have never known one so gentle and caring."

Chancellor could only stare at her, for he was speechless. She had a way of sayings things that made his insides quiver with excitement. He loved how alive she was, but he couldn't imagine her being any different before he'd met her. Her effervescence didn't just appear overnight. She was probably champagne-bubbly all along, but he didn't doubt her when she said he'd brought love into her life. It was the same way with him.

Laylah moved over an inch or so and curled up even closer to Chancellor, laying her head on his chest just so she could hear his heart beat. It sounded like a healthy rhythm, a steady one. When his hands came to rest in her hair, combing it gently with his fingers, she closed her eyes. The daylight hours were practically gone and dusk would sweep in and take over soon, but she didn't want to move a muscle. She had so many things to do at home, but none of them seemed important at the moment. Being with Chancellor was everything to her. They still needed each other. If they were to get through all that had thus far transpired for them, they had a lot to come to terms with.

His head leaned forward until his hungry mouth came down over hers in one sweeping gesture. As his tongue connected with hers, she rolled over on top of him and wedged her legs snugly between his. His bare flesh was every bit as heated as hers. Laylah knew making love wouldn't solve a single one of their problems, but it sure would put them in the right frame of mind to deal with whatever they had to.

Their very future was at stake. If Laylah ran from the things she feared, ran away from what she might learn about Chancellor, she'd never know what they could've accomplished together. Of course, she knew love wasn't always enough, but they also had so many other special things going for them.

She lifted her head slightly to make direct eye contact with him. "I want to work out everything with you, if that's at all possible. Are you willing to see how deep our feelings really are for each other? Do you want us to work out the tough issues we both know we face, the ones we keep putting off by making love at every turn?"

His mouth captured hers once again. "Yes to both questions. As for putting stuff off, I think we're doing that out of fear. Let's try to overcome our issues one at a time. Like we've already said, we can't solve it all overnight. I want you, all of you. I'm not talking about dating you or us trying to build a relationship. We're in love, so we're already past the initial stages. I'm talking about forever. I want to marry you, Laylah. Forever is all I'm interested in with you. Now that I've made my agenda crystal clear, I'm making love to you until we're both too weak to do anything but fall back to sleep."

As much as Chancellor wanted her to comment about his wanting to marry her, he knew she wasn't prepared to give him an answer. His love for her allowed him to be patient. She had a lot to mull over and to come to grips with. They both did. She looked like a doe caught in the headlights of a fast-approaching car.

Chancellor wants to marry me. She truly believed he loved

her, but she hadn't known he loved her enough to make her his wife. As much as it thrilled her, she was also terrified and very apprehensive. He was a rich man, one who ruled a successful conglomerate. They were far from equals in that regard. Although she made a darn good salary, she made nowhere near the revenue one of his spas brought in in a single day.

If they were to marry, she'd be married to a man whose very presence would be in demand at such events as board sessions, staff meetings, business seminars and lots of fitness conventions, which meant endless travel.

Unable to resist Chancellor's wonderful lovemaking proposal, Laylah simply smiled her approval. The answer to his marriage proposal, which hadn't been posed as a question, would have to wait until she was thinking a whole lot clearer. Chancellor had blown her mind with his voiced intent. A bit of recovery time was definitely needed.

Brandon stretched his eyes in disbelief. "Your homeless guy is rich?"

"Filthy rich. Chancellor may not have Oprah's and Bill Gates's money, but he has substantial wealth and he and his brother own the Fitness First health-spa chain. I still haven't gotten over the shock," Laylah said, shaking her head from side to side.

"So he's been straight-up lying to you all this time? I hope you've kicked his dishonest behind to the curb. He should be downright ashamed of himself."

She looked down at the floor in Brandon's hotel suite. Her brother probably thought she should be ashamed of Chancellor, too, but she wasn't. While she didn't like him not coming clean with her from the start, his reasons for such were sound. Besides, had she known he was a corporate tycoon, she probably wouldn't have given him the time of day. It had once again reinforced her belief to never judge a book by its cover.

Well, she thought, smiling inwardly, the instant attraction she'd had to Chancellor would've happened before she'd ever found out his profession. The man had turned her on long before she'd learned his name. Her curiosity about him had been high that day. Nothing would've deterred her from finding out exactly who Chancellor was. Corporate executive or not, she had fallen in love with him instantly.

"Does that guarded look on your face mean what I think it does? You're still involved with him, aren't you?" Brandon looked totally dismayed.

"Not only am I involved with him, I'm crazy in love with Chance. He's not the type of man you might think he is. Listen up for a minute." She went right on to tell Brandon the upside and downside of everything she'd learned about the Kingston twins.

As Laylah talked in depth about the brothers, she realized she knew a lot more about Chancellor now than she had just twenty-four hours ago. He had poured his heart and soul out to her in a very believable manner. The man she loved was hurting something awful and she didn't think he'd ever be whole again, not until he found his twin. Not even she could make him feel complete.

Although the truth of the matter saddened her, reality was reality—and that simply couldn't be changed. The brothers had been together all their lives, with the exception of the first couple of minutes when one had left the womb without the other. According to Chancellor, he and Chandler had been inseparable.

As brothers often did, they fought battles and fussed with each other, but the disagreements were always cleared up in a relatively short period of time. They hadn't been able to stay mad at each other for too long. In reality, after their grandparents had both died, they were all the family each one had left. That they didn't seem to consider Lavonne a part of their family was so unfortunate. Apparently, as the mother, she was the one who'd laid down the ground rules for the type of relationship they'd have.

"I see your point, but I'm still scared for you. You don't know this man."

"Yes, I do. I know his spirit. It's a good one and his soul is also a good and kind one. I love him and he loves me. Can you please just accept that? Can you just continue to love me as your sister and best friend and not judge me one way or the other? Just like we've always done with each other?"

Brandon couldn't stand to see any woman in his family cry, especially his mother and sister. Before the first tear cleared Laylah's chin, he was off the sofa in a flash, folding her tenderly into his arms. "Let's not do this, baby sister. You know I can't take the tears. Like I said earlier, I'm here for you. Always. I'll do my best to give Chance every benefit of every doubt. One thing I believe is that he loves you. I've seen the way he looks at you. It's hard to fake emotions welling up from deep within. I'm sold on the love part of this deal." Laylah's love for Chancellor was also apparent to Brandon. "But the jury is still out on this homeless, false-identity mess."

"I'll accept that." She looked at him with tears in her eyes. "He wants to marry me, Bran. Can you believe that?"

Brandon hid how shocked he was very well. "Of course I can. You're only the smartest, hottest chick around. The boy would have to be crazy not to want you as his wife. But if he's the corporate type, how'll that work for you?"

"Not interested in his credentials, only his heart." Fear suddenly settled in her eyes. "Yet I'm horribly afraid of his wealth and prestige. You know me. I can't stand uppity people, those who are too full of themselves to make room for others. I imagine he runs into a lot of counterfeit folks in his line of work. I have zero desire to sit around and sip tea with a bunch of stuffy, white-glove-and-stylish-hat-wearing corporate wives."

Brandon chuckled, loving the adorable expression of intolerance on his sister's pretty face. "I know at least that much about you. You're a blue-jeans-wearing kind of girl. I know you don't mind the occasional dress-up event, but with him as CEO of Fitness First, there'll be plenty of formal affairs you'll have to attend."

Laylah frowned, turning up her nose. "'Have to attend.' See, that's what I don't like. And I'd definitely be obligated to attend as his wife." She blew out a gust of shaky breath. "Love does not come without its share of demands and obligations. If I truly love him, I'll do whatever it takes to fit into his world. But *can* I fit into it? That's the issue."

Brandon stroked Laylah's hair. "If you and Chance are meant to be together, you will find your place in his world. On the business end of things, he may not expect as much of you as you might think. I sense that he's a fair man, one that wants to please the woman he loves. I think you'll be okay."

"Thanks, big brother. I needed a bit of reassurance." Laylah kissed Brandon's cheek. "Now I want to hear all about Sierra and you."

"There's nothing to tell. It's over already."

Laylah wasn't the least bit shocked, though this one was over much quicker than most of his noncommittal relationships. "What was the deciding factor?"

"You'll never guess the reason, so I won't ask you to. Sierra senses that I'm not the kind who can commit. Check this out. She ended our relationship. Not me."

Now Laylah was super-surprised. No woman had ever dumped Brandon, none that she was aware of. "How do you feel about that?"

He looked a tad perplexed. "Funny you should ask. I don't know yet. I don't think it's quite sunk in. I hate to admit it, but I'm surprised by it, also somewhat hurt."

Once again, Laylah was surprised. As she studied Brandon closer, she saw flickers of pain in his gaze. Perhaps he felt more for Sierra than he had believed possible. It looked as if her absence in his life had affected him. That Brandon might really care for Sierra began to suddenly cross Laylah's mind. Her brother was a player at heart, but an honest one. Before asking a female out on a date, he'd always laid down the ground rules.

"What hurts? Your ego or your heart?"

Uncomfortable with the question, Brandon swiped his tongue across his lower lip. "Maybe a little bit of both." He shrugged. "Emotions are new for me."

"Perhaps you should explore whatever you're feeling. Try to separate ego from heart. If you find that you miss her after you've accessed things, you should swallow your pride and try to get her back. The love bug could be at work here."

Brandon looked at Laylah like she was insane. "I admit to feeling something, but I'm not sure it's love."

"Since you've never fallen in love, how do you know it's not that?"

He hunched his shoulders. "I guess I don't know. You're in love so what *does* it feel like?"

Laylah's eyes lit up as they took on a dreamy appearance. "For starters, warm and wonderful, yet it can sometimes feel like you have a dagger permanently stuck in your heart. Love is multifaceted, as well as confusing. It's not just a feeling though. I wish I could explain it, but I can't. I just know what I feel for Chance is real. My love for him seeps out of my pores like sweat." She laughed. "I know that's not an attractive analogy, but it's all I could come up with."

Brandon laughed, too. "When stuff starts seeping out of my pores, I'm running into the shower to wash the funk off. Maybe you should try it, too."

"Laugh all you want, big brother. But if it's love you're feeling for Sierra, it will either wipe that huge grin off your face or fill your heart to the brim. It can also do both at the very same time." Laylah got to her feet. "I'd better go now."

"But you haven't told me what you're going to do about Chancellor."

"That's because I don't know yet. Right now I'm experiencing what I just said. My heart is filled to the brim, but I don't feel much like smiling, until I think of him."

Brandon got up and took Laylah by the hand. "Let me walk you down to your car. Maybe in time we'll both have our answers."

"Maybe so. And you stay put. I parked with valet service." She laughed at Brandon's stunned expression. "I'm not always cheap. I splurge every now and then."

"If you marry the man you obviously love, you won't ever have to second-guess a dime you spend. If marrying him will make you happy, I say go for it. You're deserving of everything he has to offer you, and then some."

After blowing Brandon a kiss, Laylah smiled softly. "Yeah, I am, huh?" She blew him a flurry of kisses. "Talk to you later. Love you, Bran."

"Love you, too."

Knowing that little Ashley had been found brought Laylah untold joy, yet knowing she had been placed in foster care disturbed her inner peace. Since she had resided with her mother whose boyfriend had been involved in serious crimes—kidnapping, etc.—the child was turned over to the Department of Socia

Services. Possible criminal charges were also staring the mother in the face. If sexual molestation had occurred, the police hadn't thus far revealed the story.

Laylah was happy that nothing as horrible as child molestation was reported in this case. Little Ashley had already gone through enough. The girl's picture had been plastered all over the world. If Roger Hodges had molested her, people would be able to identify her on sight. How terrible that would be for Ashley to have to live through.

When her thoughts switched to Chancellor, Laylah turned on her computer. If she wrote down all she knew about him and also how she felt about their troubling issues, it might help her sort things out much quicker.

As Laylah looked up at the office clock, she saw that she only had a couple of hours before her interview with the television station. She had decided to take the job. This would be a great breakthrough for her to join the ranks of televised media. If the money was right, and all cylinders were clicking, she would happily accept it.

Working in television wasn't something she'd given any thought to despite how successful Brandon was in the same field. The job sounded more and more appealing. Ridding herself of March was a must. Although he had been much nicer to her lately, she knew it wouldn't last for very long. His monthly cycle would return all too soon.

Laylah planned to type in her all her encounters with Chancellor from their first meeting up to the present. Writing it like a story made it easier for her to tell, though this was one tale she had no intention of printing in the newspaper.

While she had thought of writing Chancellor's story early on in their relationship, she now knew he'd never want that to happen. He was a very private person; she'd respect his privacy issues in the same manner as she'd protect her own. According to Chancellor, he had shared things with her he'd never told anyone. To breach that confidence was a criminal act, as far as she was concerned. As much as she had read about the twins over the Internet, no personal information had been reported, nor had there ever been any mention of their absentee mother.

Laylah listened intently to what the network's personnel interviewer had to say about the job they'd tapped her for. So far, so good, she thought. Mr. Glenn McGlone was very thorough. He had spelled it all for her. As if it had been handed to her in black-and-white print, she'd received everything with crystal clarity.

The salary and other benefits were so much more than what she had imagined. She had known that Brandon made a lot of money, but they'd never discussed the exact amount. As close as they were, each sibling kept some things private, respectfully so.

Glenn cleared his throat. "Miss Versailles, there has been one significant change to the job we've offered you." Nervous about what he had to say, he cleared his throat again. "It has just come to our attention that a news correspondent at our sister station in San Francisco has resigned without any notice. We'd like for you to take that position instead of this one. There is an immediate need there, whereas the position here doesn't have to be filled for another month. We'd be honored if you'd accept the other position."

Looking stunned, Laylah's mouth dropped open, her eyes bulging with disbelief. Disappointment filled her, since she had convinced herself to take the position. Never for a second had she thought the job would take her out of L.A.

She felt bewildered. "I don't know what to say. I never considered a long-distance move because I was told the job was in this city. My family lives up north, but I love where I've chosen to make my home. I just purchased my own place and I'd have to sell or lease it out. Not sure I want to do either. I need time to think about this."

"I'm afraid we don't have much time. However, I can give you twenty-four hours. We'll pay all moving expenses. I should also tell you I'm prepared to offer you an additional salary increase, a substantial one."

"How substantial?" Laylah raised an eyebrow in anticipation.

"I can add another fifteen thousand onto the yearly offer."

"Which means you could've offered that salary to me in the very beginning." She was dismayed by the game playing. "Sir, no disrespect intended, but this is my life we're talking about. Is the job here in L.A. still an option for me if I turn down the other one?"

He shrugged. "I'd have to consult with the head honchos to answer that one."

Laylah got to her feet. "Please do that. In the meantime, I'll think about the other offer, but I wouldn't hold out too much optimism. I have put down roots in this city. Leaving here might not be an option for me. It was nice meeting you, Mr. McGlone."

Without looking back, Laylah made a beeline for the door, leaving the interviewer in the same state of shock he'd put her in only minutes before. With Chancellor residing in Los Angeles, she didn't think there was a chance in Hades she'd leave the City of Angels. Even though their future wasn't settled, she couldn't imagine moving out of her town house. The fear of someone tearing it up wouldn't allow her to consider leasing.

Laying her head against the steering wheel, Laylah gave thought to everything that had just transpired between her and Mr. McGlone. She wished they'd told her about the change before the interview. That way, she would've had some time to think about it. However, he did say the resignation had just occurred.

Regretful about how she'd handled her disappointment in front of the interviewer, she wouldn't be surprised if they withdrew both offers. She knew she'd been somewhat unprofessional and a tad rude. She probably could've handled her disappointment better had she been forewarned. Anyone would've reacted badly to such a significant change.

Jack and Selma would be thrilled to have their daughter back in San Francisco, especially Jack. Brandon and Kelly would be excited, too. Her dad had been calling Laylah every day since he had returned home. She was sure the frequency had to do with what they'd learned about Chancellor.

Fear was constantly in her father's voice when they talked, but she was sensitive enough not to point it out. He was only thinking of her best interests. She hoped he'd one day come to understand that Chancellor also had her best interests at heart. He may not have gone about things in the right way, but she still didn't think he'd meant to hurt her.

During the drive home Laylah gave more thought to the job in San Francisco. That she had suddenly begun to consider it as a possibility came as a shock to her. If things didn't work out with Chancellor, perhaps it was best if she moved out of town. Then again, if she took this immediate position, she wouldn't be around to give their relationship every conceivable chance.

To talk the job over with Chancellor or not to say anything was then considered by Laylah. If she did go to him with the job offer, the fact that he'd asked to marry her might make him feel that his proposal wasn't being considered, that his love for her wasn't important to her. He had no idea how important everything about him was to her. She was so tired of thinking about all of this.

Instead of going home, she turned the car around to go back to the office, where she might be able to shut out her personal problems. Patricia Blakeley's retirement party was tomorrow night and Constance had asked Laylah for her assistance earlier in the morning. Maybe getting reinvolved in the celebration plans would cheer her up some. She had yet to ask Chancellor to accompany her to the dinner, but she now believed it might not be a good idea. Some time apart might do them a world of good.

Chapter 12

Reared back in her leather swivel chair, burned-out from the pressures of the day, Laylah stared at the paper mess piled high on top of her desk. She hadn't intended to print out any of what she'd written earlier. Yet she'd done so despite the fact that she'd have to shred it all before she left the office. Waiting on Constance to come in and go over the retirement-dinner itinerary for Patricia had her bored with herself and her disquieting situations.

Just as she was about to begin shredding the documents, Constance slipped into the office and took a seat at the small round table in the corner. Grabbing the handiest pen and pad, Laylah joined her co-worker. "So what you got going on?"

Constance read to Laylah the entire program for the dinner. The guest list had grown much larger than what was earlier anticipated. There were several bigwigs and their spouses who couldn't be left off the list. Whether they came or not, they had been sent invitations. The RSVP list included just about everyone who was sent an invite, which had been a surprise to March. Because he disliked Patricia so much, he thought everyone else did, too. There were a lot of people who hadn't cared for her, but after she started standing up to March, support for her came from employees company-wide.

The intercom buzzed and Laylah quickly answered the extension stationed right beside the table. "Who?"

The male receptionist, Leon Roberts, repeated himself.

"Give me a minute. Make her comfortable. I'll buzz you back when I'm ready." Laylah looked as if she'd been struck by lightning as she cradled the receiver. A second later she glanced over at Constance who was staring outright at her.

"What's wrong?" Concern was etched on Constance's face.

Laylah shook her head. "I don't know. There's a woman out there to see me and she says she's Chance's mother. Leon said she says it's imperative she speak to me." Fear began to march into Laylah's eyes, seemingly to the tune of her erratically beating heart. "Chance, oh, my God. I hope he's okay…."

Constance got to her feet. "I'll come back after you've handled your business, but please take a minute to wipe away the fear. It's glaring like a neon lamp."

Laylah frowned. "That bad, huh?"

"That bad! Buzz me when you're through. Looks like I'll be here half the night, anyway. A few people dropped the ball on their assignments and now it's all in my lap."

"Don't worry. I've got your back since I'm the original dumper," Laylah said.

Once Constance had cleared the room, Laylah pulled out her compact and hairbrush. After fixing her makeup and brushing her hair back into place, she pushed the intercom button to ask Leon to usher the surprise guest into her office. She had no idea why Chancellor's mother would be coming to see her, but there was no way she'd refuse to see her. Laylah continued to pray that nothing had happened to Chancellor, or Chandler for that matter.

Having nothing to go on as far as identifying Lavonne Kingston, Laylah couldn't help staring overtly at the extremely well-dressed, skinny woman with the ash-blond-streaked brunette hair. Although the lady had yet to identity herself to her, Laylah assumed she was who she said she was. However, the twins looked nothing like this person standing before her—no family resemblance whatsoever.

Lavonne looked much older than Laylah would've expected the Kingston twins' mother to appear, yet one could tell she came from money by her expensive clothing and footwear, all designer labels. The wide diamond bracelet and diamond studs, at least three carats each, were also a good indication of her financial status.

Remembering her manners, Laylah politely offered her guest a seat.

The lady sat down and crossed her legs at the ankles. "I know you're wondering why I came to see you, so I'll not waste any more of your time than I have to. I understand you are dating my son, Chance, whom I haven't seen in a long while."

Lavonne Kingston went on to formally introduce herself. She then told Laylah why she had come to see her and that she desperately needed her help.

"What makes you think I have that kind of influence over Chance?"

"Because it's my understanding my son is in love with you. Don't ask for my sources. I'll never divulge them. As a reporter, I'm sure you understand."

Oh, this is a clever one, Laylah thought, trying to use a reporter's code of ethics on her. *Where were her ethics when she gave up her boys?* Laylah wondered, quickly scolding herself for being judgmental. It wasn't fair nor was it her role.

"All I can do is ask Chance if he's willing to see you. Beyond that, I don't know how I can help. This really isn't something I want to involve myself in."

"That's understandable. How well do you know Chandler?"

"Your sources haven't informed you of that?" Laylah fired back.

Offended by the remark, Lavonne narrowed her eyes at Laylah.

That testy gesture briefly reminded Laylah of Chancellor. He had narrowed his eyes at her a few times already. It had been adorable coming from him. Lavonne looked like a cruel witch who'd love to cast a spell on anyone who dared to cross her.

"I won't press you about Chandler. If I get to see Chance, I'm sure Chandler will be there as well. Those two boys have always been inseparable." A look of deep regret flashed in her eyes, but it was fleeting.

Laylah couldn't help having a touch of sympathy for Lavonne, who must have no idea what she had missed out on by not loving her children and having a grand time with them. Her parents had delighted in their two kids.

Laylah couldn't help wondering what Lavonne had to keep herself alive. What hope did she have? What hope had she ever given out? Was she now one of the lonely hearts?

Lavonne stood. "Thank you for your time, Miss Versailles. You are a very beautiful woman. My son has chosen well for himself." She dropped a card on the table. "Please call me after you've talked to Chance." She then laid down another card. "Please give one to him. Perhaps you can convince him to call me personally." With her business stated, Lavonne was gone, closing the door gently behind her.

Laylah stared after the woman who had left her more shaken than she'd been when she'd actually found out who Chancellor really was and also the kind of power he wielded. She didn't know which of the Kingstons frightened her more. To keep from dwelling on this drama for another second, she picked up the intercom to let Constance know she was on her way to her office to finish up what they'd started.

Chancellor wanted to spend as much time with Laylah as possible. He didn't want to give her the opportunity to forget him. If absence made the heart grow fonder, he believed being in her presence every waking moment could make the heart burst with love.

As Chancellor looked over at the sleek, black satin-and-lace dress she'd hung on the door of her bedroom closet, he wondered where she planned to wear it. She hadn't mentioned any special event to him, but the sexy sheath indeed looked like special-occasion attire. "The dress, are you wearing it somewhere special?"

The impertinent way in which Chancellor had posed his question caused Laylah to rethink her decision about not asking him to accompany her to the retirement dinner. She shot him a curious glance, trying to see if he appeared upset. "Why do you ask?"

"You hadn't mentioned attending a special-occasion event to me. That's a pretty fancy dress. Seeing it hanging there aroused my curiosity."

"I'm attending a retirement dinner for one of my co-workers. I didn't ask you to go because I wasn't sure you'd be interested in attending that kind of function." Lying somehow seemed easier than to get into a lot of rigmarole on the subject.

"Would you change your mind if I said I'd love to go with you?"

"Consider it changed. Please accompany me to the dinner?"

"You already have my answer. When is it?"

"Tomorrow evening at seven."

"That means you're going to miss open mic. Are you cool with that?"

"No choice. I want to honor my co-worker. We've worked

together for several years. I'd never slight her by not showing up, though I'd rather go to open mic."

"I bet you would." He glanced at the dress again. "Does a dark suit, say, navy or black, work for you? What color are your accessories?"

"All silver. A dark suit is fine for you. I do need to be there early to help my colleague Connie make sure everything is set up properly. Should we meet there?"

"Is there any reason I can't get there a little early with you?"

"None at all." She sighed with relief, glad to have that over with, yet hating to admit she was thrilled about having him as her escort for an entire evening.

Knowing she had to get into a heavy conversation with Chancellor didn't make Laylah feel cheerful. Telling him his mother came down to the office to see her was darn hard. She'd rather talk to him about anything other than that.

He could tell she was having a hard time with something. The worried look on her face was one determining factor. The wringing together of her hands was another. "What is it, Laylah? What's happening inside your head?"

She took a deep breath. "I had a visitor show up at my office today—"

He jumped up from the chair. "Chandler? Did my brother come see you?"

Oh, how she wished he hadn't misconstrued her body language. "No, no, it wasn't Chandler. But it was a family member of yours—"

"Lavonne," he said, cutting Laylah off a second time. There was no one else it could've been. "Please don't tell me she had the nerve to come see you about me."

"She *had* the nerve." She moved over to the chair he was seated in and sat down at his feet. "She just wants to see you. It was obvious to me that she's sincere about a visit with you. She also gave me a card to give you. It has her phone number and address on it. The lady lives in Beverly Hills."

"Are you still advocating for a woman who has had absolutely nothing to do with her own kids for thirty years?"

"I'm *your* advocate. I think a visit with her will do you some good. As I said before, you need closure. Talk to her. Try to get some kind of understanding about why she did what she did. You owe that much to yourself. Don't do it for her. Do it for you. She also wants to see Chandler." She saw the question mark in his eyes. "No, I didn't tell her Chandler was missing. That's not my place."

"Thank you for that. What else did she say to you?"

"Nothing more than her saying she wants to see her sons. I didn't even have to ask her how she knew about me. She just said she had her sources, which she wouldn't divulge. She tried using the ethics code on me." Laylah blushed. "By the way, she said I was beautiful and that her son had chosen well for himself. Agree or disagree?"

"Agree, wholeheartedly."

He desired to tell her he still wanted to marry her, but then he thought better of it. She still wasn't ready to hear it again, at least not this soon. Not enough proving grounds had been laid yet. There were so many lovely gifts he'd thought of sending her, so much he wanted to do to show her how much he loved her, but he was scared she might think he was trying to buy her affection. There was nothing further from the truth.

Chancellor knew he could give her all or nothing when it came to lavish gifts, travel and romantic nights out on the town, however, whenever she wanted it. When it came to giving of himself, she had all of him. His heart belonged to her only.

As Laylah thought about some of the things she'd written down earlier, she decided to try to get answers to a few of her questions. She wrung her hands together, still feeling slightly anguished. "Do you mind if I ask you a couple of things?"

"I'll answer each one as honestly as I can. Let me hear them."

"I know you gave me back all the money I gave you, but where did the money come from when you bought drinks at Bella's and lunch at Friday's?"

"From money I earned." He tapped his foot up and down on the carpet. "Before I went out to try this homeless living I made a pact with myself not to touch any of the money I had at my disposal. Any cash I used would have to come from doing odd jobs. I really was trying to live this experience to see why Chandler was so attracted to it."

"What about the clothes you wore after our initial meeting? Some were designer labels, like the blue Izod polo shirt and the Dockers. Were they yours or did you get them from the shelter?"

He pressed his lips together, stifling a chuckle over what must've been obvious to her. "I donated them anonymously, never expecting to get back any of what I'd had delivered to the shelter. That's why they fit so well. I didn't want to take without giving something back. I am already supporting the Second Chances shelter."

Laylah was impressed with his spirit of giving. "The lighting-fixture place? Did you use Light Up Your World to furnish the magnificent lighting in your home?"

"Please don't make this about money and goods and services. It's not about any of that. I was trying my best, still trying every single day to find Chandler. Going undercover wasn't the best way to go about this, but I've admitted that. I never dreamed I'd meet someone like you when I started this venture. What is done is done."

She felt guilty for the pressure she'd just put on Chancellor, but at least she'd gotten answers. She believed him, still believed his sins were forgivable ones, definitely by God. She didn't know why she kept beating this dead horse. It wasn't about the things she'd been drilling him over, none of it. It was all about her loving him enough to marry him and live the style of life a rich entrepreneur lived. Either she could or couldn't.

It was really that simple.

Laylah turned sideways and laid her head on Chancellor's knee. "Have you ever been so tired your eyeballs hurt?"

Chancellor gently stroked Laylah's hair. "I know the feeling. I'm no stranger to burning the midnight oil. Why don't you take a hot shower and lie down. I'll call and order up takeout."

"Sounds nice." She moaned softly. "Will you lie down with me?"

Chancellor's heart skipped a beat. "If I lie down with you, we both know you won't get any rest. We'll be all over each other. What do you have a taste for?"

"Besides you, Chinese is good or even pizza, whichever you prefer."

If only she knew how ravenous his appetite was for her sweet body, she'd tempt his resolve every chance she got. He just wasn't strong enough to resist her wily charms. "I'll order a bit of both items. Orange chicken, steamed rice, no noodles. Mushrooms and black olives on a personal-pan pizza."

"Yep. I'm so impressed with how well you take notes on me. I'd also like to have hot-and-sour soup. Get the big one so it'll last me a day or two. I love that stuff."

He stood up and then helped her to her feet, nudging her toward the bathroom. "Off to the shower you go. I'll order the food in the meantime."

The steaming water pelting gently against Laylah's body had her feeling pretty relaxed, but it was time for her to get out and dry off. She still had to lotion down and she didn't want the food to arrive before she was all settled in bed. Chancellor had apparently turned on the stereo since she could hear soft music playing. If he wanted her to rest, he'd better not bring alive a romantic setting in her bedroom. It was hard being near him without wanting to make love to him. She had asked herself if what she felt for him was just about sex, but her feelings ran much deeper than the physical.

Before leaving the bathroom, Laylah massaged lotion all over her body and feet and then slipped into a pair of pearl-white silk pajamas. She loved the feel of soft things against her skin. Her lingerie drawer was filled with ultrafeminine sleep- and lounge-wear. Silk, satin and lace were her favorite fabrics.

As Laylah stepped back into the bedroom, hot blood surged through her body upon seeing Chancellor stretched out on her bed in nothing but black silk boxers. The boy had a body on him that seemed to scream for her attention. His physique was gorgeous and it had brought her unadulterated pleasure on more than one occasion. She hoped tonight wouldn't be an exception. Just as she crossed the room to lie down next to him, the scent of the food caught her attention. He lifted his head the same moment she made a U-turn in the direction of the table. "Come on and get into bed. I'll serve you, babe."

While Laylah fulfilled Chancellor's request, she couldn't stifle pleasurable giggles. When she neared the bed, he pulled the comforter back farther. Once she was settled down, he placed over her lap the breakfast tray she kept stored in the walk-in closet. As he stepped away from the bed, she reached out for his hand and pulled him back, offering him a taste of her lips. It was an offer he couldn't refuse.

Once Chancellor made sure Laylah was all taken care of, he got into bed with her and they began eating the still-warm food. He had also poured glasses of peach iced tea.

"Is your brother gone home yet?"

"Brandon's leaving tomorrow." She laughed. "Looks like the boy has gotten himself into some difficulty with Sierra. She dumped him."

Although Chancellor had figured out Brandon wasn't serious about Sierra, he was surprised to know she'd done the dumping. "Why'd she do that?"

"Bran says she felt he wasn't committed. Even though he'd told her how it was with him from the beginning, I guess she's like a lot of women who think they can change a man. Once she saw she couldn't do it, she moved on. I admire her for that. Some women stay too long, hoping for changes that never come."

Chancellor stroked his chin. "I clearly see what you mean." He didn't think it necessary to tell her what he'd thought about their relationship after only one encounter with Brandon and Sierra. "What's going on with Kelly and Antoine?"

Laylah threw her head back and laughed. "They've made a love connection. I never dreamed Kelly would commit to anyone, never this quickly. But she says she's agreed to an exclusive relationship with him. I'm happy for them."

"Me, too, especially if Kelly is happy. I like her. She's very genuine. Your parents and the aunts, what's up with them?"

"They're preparing for a seniors Caribbean cruise. They tell me lots of men will be aboard. My aunts Cora and Gertrude are happy about it. Those two are Spice Girls in disguise."

Laylah took a minute to think about her parents, trying to decide if she should be painfully honest with him. Jack and Selma would support her no matter which way the wind blew for her, but they had their concerns about a man who professed to be homeless when he was anything but. They didn't understand why he'd do that; Laylah did.

After polishing off the last slice of pizza, he studied Laylah's dubious expression. "Your silence has me concerned. Are your parents that disenchanted with me?"

"It's not about them. They know that. This is about you, about me, about what we feel for each other. I'm so over what others might believe were deceptive practices on your part. I know you didn't set out to deceive me." She bit down on her lower lip, unsure as to whether it was time to lay out her cards on the table.

It *was* time, Laylah quickly decided.

Removing the tray from her lap, she leaned over and set it on the floor. The empty pizza boxes were laid on top of the tray, as was the empty soup container. Chancellor had already closed the boxes containing the uneaten portions of Chinese food. Following her lead, he set the containers on the nightstand.

Laylah turned to face Chancellor, taking his hand nearest her. She told him she'd gone over everything he'd ever said to her and every move he'd ever made since their first meeting. She had analyzed and reanalyzed their relationship to the point of tedium, reliving every moment they had thus far spent together.

"The conclusion is always the same. None of what you did regarding the homeless issues matters to me. I love you, Chance. I love you for who you are. I love how you treat me with respect and kindness. I love how I feel when I'm with you, secure and beyond happy." She brushed her knuckles down the side of his face. "There is only one area of our relationship that brings me grave concern…"

"What is it? What have I done that concerns you so deeply?"

She smiled softly. "It's nothing you've done, unless making money and becoming wealthy is a crime. Yet it is the money. It's how you live and how I might be expected to live and how I might be asked to carry myself. I'm a simple girl with uncomplicated needs. In other words, your position in life scares the blue jeans off me. Living in your world is the only issue facing my decision to marry you or not to."

Laylah went on to explain how she wouldn't want to attend a lot of corporate functions and get involved with a bunch of stuffy corporate wives. She emotionally laid out to him all the things that disturbed her as it pertained to what he might expect of her. She blew out a gust of breath, glad that the confounded explanation was over.

The tears Chancellor felt in his eyes were in no way an embarrassment to him. He was busy remembering how he'd shied away from getting involved with Laylah, recalling his deep concerns about it, believing the timing for them to be a couple was all wrong. He had wanted to run away from his feelings for her in the beginning—and now she desired to flee from his lifestyle, not her feelings. *Was this poetic justice or what?*

He outlined her full lips with his forefinger. He then smoothed one of her eyebrows and the other one with butterfly gentleness. "There's nothing to fear, my lady. I could become the richest man in the world, but you'll always be wealthier than me. I'll never have your kind of riches, never." She looked puzzled. "Growing up, you had the love of your parents. You have their love now. I'd give up everything I possess for what you've had and still have. There is nothing in this world to compare to a parent's love."

Laylah's heart was so full of sorrow for him. His pain was so raw, still so fresh. How could anyone turn their backs on two darling babies, their very own sweet babies?

He told her that his grandparents loved their grandchildren dearly, but they hadn't conceived them or given birth to baby twin boys. He and Chandler knew who their mother was, yet they didn't know her. They had no idea who their father was because their mother didn't know who he was. He spoke of the teasing they'd taken from cruel kids who'd said they had no mom and dad and laughed at them because their grandparents were much older than the other parents. Riches didn't matter to the cruelest of kids then, just as Chancellor didn't want it to matter to his sweet Laylah now.

Leaning closer to her, he kissed the tears from her eyes. "Don't believe for one second that I want you to be anyone but you. I didn't fall in love with a fancy-faced girl, one dripping with diamonds and driving flashy cars and carrying around a purseful of plastic. Yes, you can have all that with me if you want it. But I know that's not who you are, nor is that what you want. All you'll ever be required to do as my wife is love me."

Laylah believed him yet again. "Yes, Chance, I'll marry you." Tears continued to fall from her eyes, intermingling with his. "All we have to do is set a date."

"Please, babe, as soon as possible. Whenever you can pull together the kind of wedding you want. I want you by my side for the rest of our lives. I love you, Laylah."

"And I love you, Chance!"

A passionate kiss sealed the happy couple's commitment to forever.

Loads of attention had been drawn to Laylah when she'd first entered the hotel ballroom holding on to the strikingly handsome Chancellor's arm. Her sexy black dress received a lot of male attention while his dark navy suit, pink silk shirt and white, navy and pink silk tie had many women overtly and covertly checking him out.

Wearing glowing smiles upon their faces, with eyes for only each other, the newly engaged couple looked absolutely stunning. The deep love between them was quite apparent. Although they hadn't picked out her engagement ring, something they wanted to do together, they planned to announce their upcoming nuptials to everyone close to them.

Laylah sat down at the table with the small group of co-workers she socialized with, the same ones who always supported her poetry performances and who had also saved two seats especially for her. Tom, Manny, Erika, Cherise and Kaye had a genuine affection for Laylah. Whether it was their spouse, lover or just close friend, everyone was paired off with someone from the opposite sex.

A co-worker slid out of his chair and made a beeline for Laylah. Once he reached her table, he leaned over and whispered softly into her ear.

Surprised by the news he had just shared with her, her eyes went straight to March. Amelia Markham was indeed seated right next to him, her hand hanging limply over his shoulder. *So, he'd finally read her easy-to-discern body language.* Amelia was smiling, looking as content as Laylah had ever seen her.

March and Amelia as a couple. Wow! It could've been a match made in heaven if March wasn't so evil and Amelia so jealous and possessive. Still, Laylah wished the new couple all the best, hoping his love affair with Amelia would keep him completely out of her hair.

As Laylah's cell phone went off, she frowned, believing she had set it on vibrate. She quickly and politely excused herself to the others and rushed out into the hallway, glad someone hadn't been presenting a speech when the phone rang. She planned to make darn sure it wouldn't ring again by turning it off after this call. The first hour of the event had been slated for mixing and mingling, a cocktail hour so to speak, so she had escaped total embarrassment.

Laylah couldn't believe her ears as she listened to what Detective Byron Gates imparted to her. After he told her he had a definite lead on Chandler, her heart rate started going bananas. Then she let out a loud moan. "In jail? For what?"

"Really can't get into this with you over the phone. Can we meet somewhere?"

Laylah knew there was no way she could walk out on the retirement celebration at this early stage, nor would she dare tell Chancellor what was happening until she had all the facts about Chandler's arrest. "How long will you be on duty?"

"Graveyard shift, all night long."

"Okay." She told him what she was engaged in at the moment. "As soon as I leave here, I'm on my way to the station. Should I call first?"

"Just make sure I'm here. If a service call comes in, I may have to leave."

"Thank you. I'll be in touch, Byron."

"Hope to see you later, Laylah. By the way, if something happens and you can't get back with me, I'll call your cell as soon as I get off tomorrow morning around seven. I never go right to bed after a graveyard shift, so I can meet with you then."

"Good deal. Later."

Byron was one of Laylah's best sources within the police department. He knew she was a responsible journalist, which made him confident he could trust her to do the right thing. She was the type of reporter who'd go to jail before giving up her sources. He had helped her out a lot with her stories by giving out details few were privileged to, including the Ashley Roberson story.

Slipping quietly back into her seat, Laylah reached for Chancellor's hand, giving him one of her brightest smiles. "Sorry about that."

"Is everything okay?"

She nodded. "This is the kind of unpredictable life a journalist lives."

He flashed a big grin. "And you're worried about my lifestyle.

Maybe I should worry about yours, especially if it's going to frequently take you away from me."

"Let's not worry about either tonight. We're here together, happy and in love."

"I couldn't have said it better."

The couple's attention was drawn to the podium when March's bass voice came over the wall-mounted speakers. He first thanked everyone for coming out to join in the retirement celebration for Patricia.

Hypocrite. Knowing how insincere March's remarks were, she rolled her eyes back. He couldn't stand Patricia and everyone knew it, including Patricia. Still he had to do what he had to do, even if he was a phony at it.

For the next thirty minutes the program ran smoothly. Everyone who spoke had nothing but kind and admirable things to say about Patricia and her dedicated service to the newspaper she loved. Laylah had heard Patricia say she probably wouldn't retire so soon if she could stomach the boss. It was a shame she felt forced to give up a job she loved so much.

Patricia was all humility and tears as she spoke about her service tenure. She talked of missing her co-workers, especially those she'd worked very closely with. Her comments about her experiences on the job, the good and the bad, were gracious and honest. All in all, she was proud of her employment record at *L.A. Press,* proud to be a part of one of the most prominent and flourishing newspapers in the state of California.

Upon mentioning her desire to get in a lot of traveling, reading, sunning on the beach, while enjoying the freedom of spontaneity for the first time ever, she received applause, cheers and a few shrill whistles. Before retaking her seat, she thanked her co-workers for all they'd done to help make her job easier, calling out many of them by name. A standing ovation and another round of applause broke out as Patricia left the podium and reclaimed her seat. Smiling, she wiped the sentimental tears from her eyes.

Kaye Sparks, the administrative assistant to March, came to the podium next, announcing that dinner would now be served. She then humbly voiced the invocation.

Chancellor leaned into Laylah. "I'm glad we're about to eat. I thought I'd have to take you outside and devour you before the meat and potatoes showed up."

Laylah laughed. "You can save me for dessert. How about that?"

"You'll get no argument here, babe. You always satisfy my sweet tooth."

The sudden look of sadness on Chancellor's face caused her to shudder. She wondered if he was missing Chandler right now. Probably so. She wished she could tell him she had a lead on his twin, but getting more information first was best. Although she was having a great time, Laylah couldn't wait until this dinner was over.

How to slip away from Chancellor was her next dilemma, but she had to see Byron tonight. Her curiosity wouldn't let her wait until tomorrow morning. She'd think of something to tell him. She could always use the "duty calls" excuse—and she really wouldn't be lying since she had vowed to help find his brother, unbeknownst to him.

Chapter 13

Chancellor and Laylah were beaming all over by the time they left the ballroom, their joy darn near uncontainable. The couple had had a delightful time dancing and conversing amicably with her co-workers and other associates. Once the engagement was announced by Kaye Sparks, a lively but heartfelt toast had been made on their behalf.

Much to Laylah's surprise, Chancellor had reserved a lavish suite for them in the same first-class hotel where the dinner had been held. This sudden turn of events would make it hard for her to slip away from him to see Byron, but she was thrilled over the hotel stay. She had toyed with the idea of going ahead and telling Chancellor what she'd learned about Chandler, but this annoying niggling not to do so just yet won out.

White chocolate–dipped strawberries and vintage Moë champagne, ordered by Chancellor especially for his bride-to be, had been enjoyed by the couple before they'd settled into the

Jacuzzi tub for a relaxing bath. Bathing together was a lot of fun, but fatigue soon took them over. Right after they took turns thoroughly drying each other off, they fell into bed. He had also presented her with a sexy nightgown in siren-red lace.

Feeling guilty for slipping out of the hotel on a soundly sleeping Chancellor, Laylah was seated in Byron's office down at the L.A. county jail. Listening to what he had to say about Chandler wasn't easy. It would upset him to know Chandler had been jailed for a couple of weeks, though he'd been looking for him a lot longer than that.

Chandler's arrest for stealing food and snack items from a convenience store and also for public drunkenness would probably be an embarrassment to the prestigious Kingston name. However, Laylah was sure Chancellor would be too happy to see his loving brother to worry about any of that. A day had yet to pass that he hadn't talked about his twin brother and how much he missed him.

Laylah laced her fingers together. "Can you please get me in to see Chandler?"

"Probably during normal visiting hours."

"Come on. You can't do better than that? I'm here right now."

Byron frowned. "I'll see what I can do, but I can't make any promises."

She nodded. "I appreciate any extra effort you can give to this matter."

"Sit tight, Laylah. Hopefully I won't be gone too long."

While she watched after Byron, she silently prayed that he could pull all the right strings. Talking to Chandler before saying anything about it to Chancellor was important to her for lots of reasons. For one, she wanted to see if he remembered her. Because Chancellor was so worried that Chandler might be suffering from mental illness, she wanted to see for herself if there were any outward signs. If he in fact suffered from mental deficiencies, he didn't belong in jail. A psychiatric hospital would best serve him.

Byron had agreed with Laylah on that point, believing, too, that mental-health issues existed in Chandler. He also thought they should be dealt with in a psychiatric setting. He'd only spent a short time with Chandler, but he'd told Laylah he'd seen significant signs that coincided with intermittent psychotic episodes.

Laylah couldn't help wondering if Chandler's problems could be dealt with by medication. Refusing to think anything but positive thoughts, she recalled Chancellor's long-ago statement about doing just that. On one hand she couldn't wait to see her fiancé's face once he was reunited with his brother, yet she also felt apprehensive about it. Seeing Chandler behind bars would no doubt hurt Chancellor something awful.

As Byron strolled toward Laylah, he gave her the thumbs-up sign. "Fifteen minutes. That's the best I can do."

"Would've been happy with five," she responded. "Can I see him now?"

"Right now. The guard is expecting us. They'll take us to a communication room."

"Will there be glass between us?"

"No. He's not a violent offender."

In less than ten minutes Laylah was seated at a metal table with Chandler sitting right across from her. Byron and another police officer were also in the room as a safety precaution.

"Hi, Chandler. Do you remember me?"

His sweet smile was so engaging. "You're the compassionate lady from the homeless shelter. How could I ever forget you? But what are you doing here?"

"I heard you were in here so I came to visit you. Is that okay?"

He shrugged. "Yeah, but you really don't know me. I also did something wrong. I broke the law. Do you know what I did?"

Laylah smiled softly. "I do. Do you know why you did it?"

"I was simply hungry when I took the food, but I knew it was wrong. The other charge is false. I wasn't drunk. My thoughts sometimes get real fuzzy. It comes on all of a sudden. That's when I don't feel in control. On occasion I stumble around while trying to get my bearings. I also forget so many of the things that happen to me from time to time. Do you know what *is* happening to me?"

Sympathy for his plight shone brightly in her eyes. "I don't. But I think I know someone who might be able to help you find out." She handed him the snapshot of Chancellor she'd taken out of her purse. "That's the person I'm talking about."

Tears rushed to Chandler's eyes. "You know Chance, too?"

"He came to the shelter looking for you. Do you want him to come see you?"

"Not like this." Chandler lowered his head in shame. "I don't want to embarrass my brother. That's why I haven't tried to contact him. I don't like hurting him."

"He won't be embarrassed or hurt. He's desperately looking for you. Can I please bring him here to see you? He'll definitely want to get you help for the fuzzy episodes you mentioned. Getting you out of here and into a program where you can get the proper help is what's needed right now." It concerned her that he acted so childlike, so fearful.

Chandler wiped the tears from his eyes. "I want to see Chance. I really do. Please tell him to come here. I *do* need him. Do you really think he'll come?"

"I know he will. No doubt in my mind."

Byron tapped his watch so Laylah could see her time was running out.

As much as Laylah hated to leave Chandler, she knew she'd been privileged to get in to see him, period. Reaching across the table, she took his hand and squeezed it. "Chance will be here during normal visiting hours." She looked over at Byron. "Do the afternoon visiting hours start at one o'clock?"

He nodded. "One o'clock."

Laylah got to her feet. "Look for Chance around that same time."

"Will you come back, too?"

"I don't know. I think your brother might want to spend time alone with you, but I *will* see you again. I promise. I could never forget you either."

"Are you in love with Chance?" he asked as she turned to walk away.

"We're getting married. And we need to get you out of here and get you all better so you can be our best man. Chance would love that."

"Me, too," Chandler responded, fresh tears spilling from his eyes.

Whether it was appropriate or not, Laylah gave Chandler a warm, reassuring hug before leaving the room with Byron.

Once out of earshot of others, she asked Byron what he thought Chandler's chances were of being released.

"He can probably get out on his own recognizance. He's never asked to be released. A good lawyer can make all this go away or possibly get it busted down to a misdemeanor. I believe he pleaded not guilty to the public-drunkenness charge."

Byron went on to say that as many times as he'd seen the Kingston twins' pictures in newspapers and magazines he never would've associated Chandler as one of the duo. He looked so different from his photographs, a lot more unkempt, with much longer hair. At any rate, Byron had only gotten involved in checking the system for Chandler's name when Laylah had asked him to help her out.

Back in his office, Byron clued in Laylah on the latest developments in the Ashley Roberson case. Renee Matthews had finally been indicted by the grand jury and charged with child endangerment. While the natural father was supposed to have gained sole custody of the little girl, his past drug history had been brought into question. Ashley had been turned over to her maternal grandparents, A. J. and Clara Matthews, where she would reside until her parents were able to responsibly live up to their parental duties.

Laylah and Byron also discussed the case of the illegal aliens who had been brought into the country illegally and held against their will. A half-dozen men were indicted on charges of human trafficking, kidnapping and extortion, including the leader of the ring. More charges were expected to be filed against him, the same man who was also in the United States illegally. That anyone would sell his own race into bondage made Laylah sick to her stomach. She knew the story all too well.

Laylah left the building after Byron walked her up to the front exit doors. She was excited and could hardly wait to get to the hotel to tell Chancellor she'd found Chandler. She could imagine the surprised look on his face. God had answered their prayers.

Chancellor was in the shower when Laylah walked into the room. All the way there she had wished she'd left him a note so he wouldn't worry about where she'd gotten off to. Unfortunately, she hadn't thought about it beforehand.

Laylah slipped out of the more professional-style attire she'd worn to the jail and quickly pulled on a pair of beige jeans and a beige-and-yellow striped halter top. She was just zipping up her denims when Chancellor came out of the bathroom. Rushing over to him, she warmly hugged him, then took his hand and guided him over to the bed, where they sat down and faced each other.

"Lady, where've you been? Do you always disappear like this? I was worried."

"I've been down at the county jail." He looked thoroughly puzzled. "One of the detectives down there is a valuable source for me. After I gave him information on Chandler, he did a state-wide system check on his name. Your twin brother is downtown in the L.A. county jail."

Chancellor couldn't believe his ears. He actually stuck his finger inside his ear and turned it a couple of times, as if he were ridding it of wax buildup. "You found my brother? Please tell me you're not just pulling my leg."

"I'm not. I saw him, too. He remembered me from the shelter. More importantly, he knows who he is and he remembers you. I showed him a picture of you, instantaneous tears. He misses you as much as you miss him, but he's ashamed of his wrong-doing."

Chancellor appeared dumbfounded, awestruck. "What did he do?"

Laylah told Chancellor the two charges leveled against Chandler.

"Public drunkenness? No way. Chandler doesn't get drunk. He's very careful in that area. My brother is not a thief either. If he stole food, it must've come during a time when he wasn't himself. Also, he had to have been hungry."

"He *was* hungry. He admitted that much to me. He feels horrible about it and is obviously suffering from deep depression. He knows something odd is happening to him, but he doesn't know what it is. He looks scared to me and acts almost childlike."

Chancellor looked terribly anxious. "When can I see him? *Can* I see him?"

"The next visiting time is one o'clock this afternoon. He'll be waiting for you. I promised Chandler you'd come to see him then."

"A promise I darn well intend to keep." Chancellor kissed Laylah hard on the mouth. "Thank you so much. I know my comments are totally inadequate—and so is my gratitude—but it's all I have right now. I'll thank you properly when the shock wears off."

This petite woman never ceased to amaze him. Every man should have a woman just like her in his corner. He still found the incredibly good news hard to believe, but he knew full well all of it was true. He felt like bawling like a newborn baby. Knowing it could start a chain reaction had him fighting back his tears.

Laylah copied Chandler's inmate number and cell number from the sheet of paper Byron had given her. She also wrote down the address of the jail and Byron's name, phone number and extension. "When you get there ask to see Detective Byron Gates to cut down on the red tape. He'll get you in quicker than you'd manage on your own."

"What? You're not coming with me? I need you there with me, Laylah."

"I'm there." The pleading look in his eyes had gotten to her. "I've got a little work to do yet, so come to the office and get me when you're ready." She looked at the clock. "To give ourselves plenty of time to arrive at the jail and to also register for the visit, we should leave my office at noon, no later than twelve-fifteen."

As she turned to walk away, he whirled her around and brought her into his arms. He looked deeply into her eyes. "Don't know what I'd do without you. Thanks for coming through for me and Chandler. I couldn't have done this alone."

Laylah thought Chancellor would've eventually gotten it done all by his lonesome. He was quite resourceful. Her lover had been operating on pure fear, which had nearly paralyzed him. The two brothers would be reunited in a couple of hours. That was all that mattered to her.

Once Laylah logged on to her computer, she pulled up her story and continued to type it out. She was pretty sure Chancellor's and Chandler's part would have a happy ending. The image of them seeing each other again for the first time was a powerful one.

As Laylah's hands flitted rapidly across the keys, she decided to put into her story the visit from Lavonne, wondering if Chancellor had made up his mind to see her or not. If she asked her where Chandler was, he could say he was out of the country. The Kingston twins traveled all over the world, often, according to the documents she'd read.

After Laylah typed in the details of Lavonne's visit and Chandler's arrest, she saved the pages on a CD and then transferred it to her computer at work via e-mail. She also printed out the pages to read back to herself later on. The ring of the telephone came before she could retrieve the papers from the printer. It was Brandon. "Hey, big brother, what do you need?"

"Baby sister, I'm in trouble. You recall what we discussed when you came here?"

"When we talked L word?"

"Exactly! I can't say I'm in love with Sierra for sure, but I'm crazy over missing her. I can't get her off my mind. I still can't believe she dumped me. Any suggestions on how this brother can get back into good graces with a sister?"

"Go to her and tell her you want to continue seeing her. If you don't, you'll never know where the relationship could've gone. Be sincere. If she senses that you're trying to get her back so you can dump her later on just to save your ego, you're history. She won't give you another chance. And only go to her if you seriously want to work things out. Hope I've been helpful. Got to run."

"But, Laylah, I need more advice."

"Don't have time right now. I'll call you this evening. Think about what I said."

Without waiting for his return response, she disconnected.

Brandon would figure it all out, she thought. She didn't know Sierra well enough to get all up in the middle of her personal business, but she loved her brother and wanted to be there for him. Chancellor called out to her just as she was about to shut down the computer. She finished closing up shop and ran to his side.

One o'clock hadn't come soon enough for Chancellor. He had nearly worn a hole in Laylah's carpet, hawkeyeing the clock every second. Laylah had been unsuccessful in calming him down. Nothing she said or did had had any effect on him. He'd been beyond hyper and she'd realized she had to let him work the energy off in his own way.

The reunion between the two brothers was heart-wrenching. They had cried in each other's arms, hugging each other fiercely, while voicing how good it was to be together again. Her tears had fallen, too. She couldn't remember a time she'd done so much bawling. She would have to be a marble statue not to feel everything they felt.

With their heads bent lowly together, the two brothers talked softly about what had landed Chandler in jail. The incarcerated twin once again maintained his innocence on the drunkenness charges. Chancellor believed every word of what Chandler had to say.

Chandler had the courage to tell his twin about the strange things that had been happening to him recently and those that had occurred as far back as a year or so, which he'd likened to out-of-body experiences. Chancellor assured him he understood. He even dared to bring up the idea of Chandler having a psychiatric evaluation, promising to be there with him through every step. At this point, Chandler was open to whatever might get him back to his old self. He was scared out of his wits of remaining in jail long-term.

Laylah was content to sit back and let the two men hash out strategy. She couldn't help but notice how patient Chancellor was with Chandler, pretty much the same way he was with her. Rather than a brother-to-brother relationship, it was almost like a father-son liaison. She admired her fiancé for his willingness to hear out his brother while keeping an open mind. Not once had Chancellor displayed a judgmental attitude toward Chandler.

Chancellor toyed with the idea of telling his brother about Lavonne wanting to see them, but after much thought he believed his brother had enough on his plate for the moment. Their mother had waited thirty years to see them, so she could wait a little longer. Stabilizing Chandler's mental health was the only important issue right now.

Before Chancellor and Laylah left, he had called their trusted corporate lawyer to ask him to recommend and then make contact with the very best defense attorney money could acquire. Retaining a criminal-defense lawyer was a must if Chandler was to be released. Chancellor already had a great psychiatrist in mind to evaluate his twin's mental capabilities, as well as his deficiencies.

It had taken less than three hours for Chancellor's newly hired defense attorney, Layton Blount, to secure Chandler's release. Layton came highly recommended. He wasn't cheap but he was one of the most brilliant legal minds in the country.

Once Layton arrived at the courthouse, things had begun to

move and shake in rapid succession. Once he'd understood mental-health issues were involved here, he recommended to Chancellor that he allow him to call in a highly skilled psychiatrist, one he'd worked with on a number of prior mental health cases.

The psychiatrist wasn't the least bit worried over Chandler's criminal charges. As Byron had told Laylah earlier, these particular allegations could be handled with relative ease. If Chandler was released from jail, Chancellor was instructed to make an appointment for him to see the psychiatrist for a thorough evaluation.

Thinking about all the activities of the previous day had Laylah dizzy as she lay across her bed, both physically and mentally frazzled. Her brain felt as if it had been deep-fried. Eager to hear from Chancellor, she was anxious about how everything had turned out. Since the five o'clock hour had just ticked by, she figured court was already over. Whether Chancellor been able to secure Chandler's release was the question uppermost in her mind. She had prayed fervently that Chandler would walk out of jail on bond.

Over the phone earlier that morning, Byron had told Laylah that he still didn't see any reason why Chandler couldn't bail out. She sure hoped he was right. Byron felt that Chandler should not be in jail because he seemed to suffer from deep depression. His bond wasn't all that much for the not too serious crimes he'd committed.

Chandler's depression and state of mind were so bad. The result of hopelessness had kept him from reaching out to his brother and his friends. Chandler had pretty much withdrawn into himself. Byron had seen so many cases just like Chandler's go before the judge. Mental imbalance was an effective defense for those who suffered from it.

Bringing his brother home with him would make Chancellor the happiest man alive. His life had been inundated with finding his twin. Now that he had located him, she couldn't help wondering if things would change between her and him.

Would he still have time for her? God forbid that he should forget all about her because he'd become so preoccupied with nursing Chandler back to his old self. She wanted to give their relationship all it was worth, but it took two to make it work. She couldn't carry the load all by her lonesome. Chancellor also had to contribute his best.

Glad to have someone to talk to, Laylah reached for the phone. Seeing Brandon's name on the caller ID had caused her to sigh with relief. They hadn't talked since he'd called her about Sierra.

"Hey, baby sister, what are you up to?"

"Just stretched out on the bed doing a bunch of nothing, though I have a million things I should be doing. Actually, I was thinking of Chance. His twin went to court today. I don't know the outcome yet."

"Drats! That's one of the things I was calling about. I was hoping you'd already know the outcome. Not a word from Chance, huh?"

"Not one. I'm sure he'll call as soon as he can. Court should be over. I expect to hear from him any minute now, unless he runs into complications. The lawyer seems to think Chandler's chances for bonding out on his own recognizance are excellent. I guess we'll just have to wait and see." Laylah laughed nervously.

"*Wait and see.* That seems to be the name of the game. I've finally talked to Sierra, after calling and calling her place. It looks like we're going to try to work things out. She says she cares for me, but she has to know she's number one, the only one.'

"Good for her. That's how it should be. Are you up to the task?"

"Actually, I believe I am. I've never given all of me to any relationship. Although Sierra knew that about me up front, she's no longer willing to play the game."

"I'm really surprised at how well you're taking this. I'm glad you care about her. It's time you take women's feelings seriously. You'll be much happier that way."

"I plan to give this relationship my all. Sierra deserves that from me."

"I agree with you. It's time for you to settle down and learn how to treat a lady."

"Thanks for all your great advice. I'll keep you posted on our progress."

Laylah clued Brandon in on the outcome of little Ashley's fate, though both felt she'd have a more stable existence living with her grandparents. The young girl deserved loads of love and attention. Her mother had put her in danger instead of protecting her like she should have. "I don't want to see her mother go to jail, but there has to be some sort of penalty for putting her daughter directly in harm's way."

"I agree, though jail time is not the answer. Parenting classes and a lengthy probation, to include community service, might work better for Renee in this instance. I can't imagine how Ashley might feel if she's ever asked where her mother is. Kids are cruel enough as it is. I'd really hate to tell someone our mother was in jail."

"That's for sure." The call-waiting feature on Laylah's line beeped. "That might be Chance, Brandon. I'll call you later on. Keep the Kingston family in prayer."

"Will do. Love you, Laylah."

"Same here." Laylah clicked over to the other line. "It's Laylah."

"Hi, it's me. Chandler's out now. No bond. He got OR. Meet me at the house?"

"Sure. What time?"

"In about an hour or so. I need you, Laylah. I can hardly wait to see you. If I'm not there yet, Effie and Harold will let you in. I'll call and let them know you're coming."

"I can only imagine what you're feeling. See you in a while, love." She hung up the phone and made a mad dash for her closet. Seeing Chancellor was heavy on her mind.

Instead of ringing the chimes, Laylah backed away from the large double doors with the idea of taking a stroll around the lovely grounds. She had admitted being fearful of this entire situation with Chancellor, but she didn't want to let him down.

Chancellor had promised not to insist on her doing anything she didn't want to. But attending social and business functions with him was part of the package. People would expect his wife to stand by him and all his causes—business, social, political or otherwise. A wife was supposed to simply be there for her husband in all capacities.

Laylah could sure use a few words of advice here and now, yet she knew the final decisions were all hers. No one could make up her mind for her. Loving Chancellor and vice versa wasn't in question, yet their love was at stake. There were so many things she needed to consider, yet he'd told her love was the only thing he'd expect from her as his wife. It all sounded wonderful, but was any of it based on reality?

She decided she'd have to figure all this out later. Chancellor needed her. She guessed he was pretty happy to have his brother out of jail, but the fact that the case wasn't completely closed out had to be an emotional drain on him.

Comforting Chancellor was the only thing she desired to do right now. In consoling him, she'd find consolation, too. She always found sweet peace when he held her tenderly in his arms. This time would be no different.

With being there for him in mind, she rushed back to the front door, ready to save the day, ready to fight for their love with all her might.

Before Laylah could press her forefinger to the bell, the door flew wide open. Chancellor quickly swept her up into his arms, squeezing her tightly, softly sobbing against her hair. Dread filled her, yet she stood stock-still, wondering what in the world had happened since she'd last spoken with him over the phone.

As Chancellor rained kisses into her hair, the dreadful feelings went away. He finally let her feet touch the ground, holding her slightly away from him. "I'm so glad you're here." He hugged her fiercely, kissing her mouth tenderly. "You have no idea how much I want and need you, Miss Versailles. No idea!"

Laylah pushed her fingers through his hair. "I think I do, because I need and want you just as much. I love you, Chance." She threw herself back into his arms.

Chandler entered the foyer to see the warm, loving exchange between his twin and Laylah. He didn't need to examine them closely to see they were in love with each other. Happy for them as a couple, his bright smile was broad.

If Chandler couldn't have Laylah, he was thrilled that his older-by-seconds brother was the lucky victor. He'd also fallen into deep infatuation with Laylah when he'd first met her at the shelter, but she'd never know about it. His brother deserved a sweet angel of mercy more than he did. With the mental-health issues he now faced, he couldn't be strong for her. Chancellor could and would be her tower of strength.

Laylah rushed over to Chandler and gave him a warm hug. "Hello, Chandler. It's so nice to see you free and smiling. I'm happy you're back at home where you belong."

"Thanks. If it hadn't been for you, I might still be sitting in that musty jail cell. I'm glad you had the best hunting dogs out there tracking me down. Detective Gates told me how adamant you were about finding me. And find me, you did." He brought Laylah to him for another toasty hug. This time he included Chancellor in the circle of affection.

"So confident was Effie that Chandler was coming home, she fixed all of his favorites," Chancellor told Laylah. "We'd like you to stay and have dinner with us."

Laylah smiled her pleasure at Chancellor's invitation. "Since I'm already somewhat addicted to Mrs. Watson's cooking, I'll kindly accept your offer."

Chapter 14

The hard pounding and incessant ringing of her doorbell scared Laylah to death. She couldn't imagine what was happening, especially so early. Daylight had just stolen into the skies. Fear gripped her as she thought about Chancellor and Chandler. Perhaps something had happened to Chandler and her man was teetering on the edge.

After grabbing a robe and slipping into it, she slid her feet into a pair of flat slippers. Rushing out into the hallway, she ran up to the front of the house, wishing the bell would stop ringing. She already had a headache and all the noise wasn't helping any.

A quick look into the peephole revealed a distraught-looking Chancellor holding a crumpled newspaper in his hand. Laylah jerked off the locks and snatched the door back in one quick motion. "Darling, what's wrong? Please don't tell me something has happened to Chandler since I last saw you two?"

The vulnerable look in Laylah's eyes was nearly Chancellor's undoing, yet his anger was bigger than anything he could conquer at the moment. His rage nearly out of control, he thrust the newspaper against her chest. "Is this what your love for me is all about? Is this how you care about someone you profess to love? If so, I want no part of it or you. How could you do something as evil as this? You sure in the hell had me fooled."

Laylah's hands trembled as she tried to straighten out the wrinkled newspaper. When she finally got it into a readable form, the bold headlines nearly brought her to her knees. The huge color picture of the Kingston twins appeared to take up half the page.

Unveiling of the Kingston Twins, the Wealthy Entrepreneurs of Fitness First Health Spas: While Chancellor poses as a homeless man on the streets of Los Angeles, his twin brother, Chandler, is a guest of the L.A. county jail.

The sickness in Laylah's stomach threatened to erupt. As she continued reading the rest of the Kingston story, she recognized some of the writing as her own. Many other items had been added to what she'd written, all of them downright lies. Someone must've gotten a hold of the papers she'd written her story on, the ones she'd failed to shred because of a couple of interruptions.

Lavonne Kingston had been one of those interruptions. Either Kelly or Brandon, she couldn't recall which one, had also phoned her when she'd been working on the story. Besides those two sources, someone must've also tampered with her computer. She clearly recalled sending the story from her laptop at home to her work computer, yet she hadn't printed out the pages from her desktop. She knew that for a fact.

Laylah had no idea where the made-up portion of the story

about Chandler's arrest had come from. Nothing about his detainment had been made public, as far as she knew. The one charge against him had been handled through probation and community service and the drunkenness charge had been dropped. It couldn't be proven and Chandler had denied it vehemently. Chandler's release had also been done in a private manner, or so Laylah and Chancellor had thought.

Tears welling in her eyes, Laylah gave Chancellor a pleading look. "This is not what it looks like…."

"Then why don't you tell me exactly what it *is?*" he thundered.

Chancellor's harsh tone earned him a scathing, how-dare-you look from Laylah.

"Did you or did you not write this story?"

"I did write it, some of it, but it was supposed to be for my eyes only."

"You expect me to believe that? I should've bailed the minute you told me you were a reporter. I despise the lot of you. If you can't find any dirt on people, you just make up a believable scandal—and then you have the nerve to sensationalize it. Never thought you were capable of something as tawdry as this. Boy, did I peg you wrong!"

"Chance, stop it," Laylah screamed. "Stop it right now! You're not even trying to hear me. I didn't know this story would be printed. I only wrote it to help sort out my thoughts at the time. There was never any malicious intent on my part, nor did I write the entire story. Someone added a bunch of lies to what I wrote."

"Tell it to the judge when I sue you and this rag-style news-paper for all it's worth." With that said, Chancellor walked out, slamming the door hard behind him.

That Chancellor didn't believe one iota of her explanation

made Laylah feel as if both his feet had landed in the dead center of her midsection. The pain was excruciating. Crying wouldn't help matters either, but she failed to keep the stinging tears away. It was killing her spirit to witness Chancellor acting like anything but a man in love, let alone a man in love enough to ask to marry the woman of his supposedly undying affection. She had suddenly become his number-one enemy.

Was reconciliation even possible between them after all this? Marrying a man who didn't trust and believe in her just couldn't happen.

As Laylah dropped onto the sofa, she tried to figure out how the story had found its way into their newspaper and who had added to it. The first person who came to mind was March.

Although Laylah didn't want to believe March would go to these lengths to hurt her, he was the only person she could think of contemptible enough to release such sensitive information. The fact that it was her man and his brother who were targeted in the article was enough proof for Laylah to believe March just might be the culprit.

Why hadn't her co-workers warned her about this article? It wasn't as if they didn't know she was romantically involved with Chancellor.

And here Laylah had thought she was rid of March forever, especially after seeing how he and Amelia had been so lovey-dovey during the retirement dinner.

If March was truly responsible for this vulgar story, it was all about his ego. Her rejection of him was probably at the forefront of his decision to try to destroy her relationship with Chancellor.

Since Laylah and Chancellor had announced their engagement and upcoming nuptials to everyone in attendance at the retirement dinner, with Patricia's blessings, March had to know any

future attempts to win her over would be futile. If he was responsible for this story, he had definitely struck the last blow and had
had the last say.

However, Laylah had news for March Riverton. She was not
about to take this deviousness lying down. If it was the last thing
she ever did at *L.A. Press,* she would expose him for his complete
incompetence as editor in chief. She wasn't into paybacks, but
she was into stopping folks without any scruples whatsoever.

Time ticked off the clock at what seemed like an unusually
slow pace. Laylah thought Chancellor would've taken time to
calm down and then call her back and give her a chance to
explain by now. She thought it was unfair of him to have walked
out on her without giving her any say, any chance to defend the
charges. She didn't know what hurt her more: what Chancellor
obviously thought of her, or him walking out on her.

This wasn't about pride for Laylah. This was about fairness
and equality. He should've at least heard her out. He had jumped
to all the wrong conclusions. She hadn't written that article for
the newspaper nor had she taken it to them to run as a feature
story. There was no way she would've hurt him like this.

With crystal clarity Laylah recalled Chancellor saying he
didn't like reporters. Yes, there were a lot of irresponsible journalists; she just didn't happen to be one. She was both ethical
and fair, the kind of reporter who checked and rechecked her information. She didn't knowingly print lies or purposely write
stories to hurt an innocent party. The very idea of Chancellor
thinking she was anything like that hurt her badly.

Her hands were just itching to wrap around March's neck.
Strangling him was too kind an act for what he'd done to her.
He wasn't the only person she was mad at, though. Chancellor
should know her better than this. His low opinion of her stuck

in her craw. She'd love to stuff a big old fat crow down his throat when he realized how badly he had misjudged her.

Laylah felt like going after March in the same way Chancellor had come at her, but she knew that kind of behavior never solved anything. Although she had walked into his office without knocking, she hadn't expected to find Amelia darn near sprawled out in his lap. After all, this was a place of business. They made the obvious show of being caught in the act—patting down hair and straightening clothing.

Laylah posted her right hand on her hip. "You know why I'm here, don't you? Just in case you're not sure, I brought along a full-page clue." She tossed the vile newspaper article on his desk. "What gives you the right to do something as awful as this? *L.A. Press* is not a rag sheet, at least it wasn't until now."

Amelia picked up the paper, acting as if she were reading the headlines for the first time. A couple of minutes into reading the follow-up story, Laylah realized the young woman *hadn't* read the paper before now. The look she crucified March with was a good indication of how Amelia felt about what he'd done. She appeared to be really upset.

March threw up his hands. "What can I say? It's a great story and we're a newspaper. We print excellent stories. Compelling stories sell papers."

"This is scandalous, March, and you darn well know it," Laylah shouted. "Besides, you somehow stole this story from me—"

"Oh, so you're mad I printed it before you got a chance to. Is that it?"

"I never planned to run this story. This is personal for me and writing the story was my private way of dealing with it. You have no idea what you've done."

The office door opened and in stepped the vice president of

the newspaper, looking none too pleased. March tried to grab hold of the newspaper on his desk, but Frank Sanders was quicker. "Why try to hide it when you've already plastered it all over the entire city? Are you responsible for this intriguing story, Mr. Riverton?"

March didn't look as if he knew whether to own up to it or not. Since his boss had referred to the story as intriguing, March thought Mr. Sanders just might be okay with it. "I authorized the print run, sir." Besides, everyone in printing knew who ran the story.

"That's very unfortunate. The elder Kingstons have always owned stock in this newspaper. If they were alive, I don't think they'd be too pleased with us." Sanders looked right at Laylah. "Since you were with one of the Kingston twins at the retirement dinner, I'm sure you don't have anything to do with this travesty."

Laylah lowered her lashes for a brief moment. "I'm afraid I do."

Sanders looked surprised at Laylah's response.

"I wrote the story as a part of my personal journal, but I never planned it as a feature story because I'm in love with Chancellor Kingston. We had plans to marry. Someone found my notes on my desk and I believe they also tampered with my computer, or at least my e-mail. I sent the rest of my notes to my e-mail address here at the paper." She looked March dead in the eye. "I personally believe Mr. Riverton stole my notes and also tampered with my e-mail. I can't think of anyone else with motive."

"Well, we know for sure that Mr. Riverton authorized the print run." Mr. Sanders looked at both Laylah and Amelia. "If you young ladies will excuse us, Mr. Riverton and I have some important business to discuss. Thank you."

They wasted no time in vacating the room.

Outside the office, Amelia actually apologized to Laylah for what March had done, telling her she thought it was wrong of him. She thanked Amelia and then proceeded to her office, hoping Mr. Sanders would give March exactly what he deserved: his walking papers.

Laylah had barely sat down at her desk when Sanders popped his head in the doorway. "There's suddenly a vacancy for the editor in chief's position. I hope you'll apply. We've had our eye on you for some time now. Please don't disappoint us."

"I won't, Mr. Sanders," Laylah said, sounding like a bullfrog. "Thank you for the vote of confidence. I really appreciate it." Laylah's heart was ready to jump out of her chest.

Without further comment, Mr. Sanders smiled and winked at Laylah. He then went on his merry way, leaving a jumping-for-joy employee alone to celebrate a possible victory. As happy as she was about what might happen for her career-wise, her tears also fell over the deep sadness she felt. If only Chancellor knew how much she loved him…

To try to calm down, Laylah pulled out her trusty pen and paper. Writing a poem might help her get through this rough time. Before she began composing from her heart she prayed Chancellor would see how wrong he was and then come back to her. *Yes, she'd forgive him.* She had answered the question in her mind. She loved him.

Lost in reading over the poem she'd written earlier and planned to read later on in the evening, Laylah nearly jumped out of her skin when her doorbell rang. Hoping it was Chancellor, she couldn't get to the foyer fast enough.

Another unexpected visit from Lavonne surprised Laylah yet again. That the lady knew where she resided was also quite bothersome; so much for living in a security-gated community. It looked as if nonresidents were able to waltz in and out of the complex at will. Laylah would make an issue of the problem at the next home owners' association meeting.

Despite Chancellor's foul mood, he cheered loudly as he hung up the phone. While he ran all through the house looking for Chandler, he couldn't wait to share the good news he'd just received. Upon finding his twin out on the terrace, he sat down at the table. "Everything has been thrown out. You're off probation and you no longer have to perform community service."

Chandler's eyes widened in disbelief. "Are you kidding me?"

Chancellor shook his head in the negative. "Not one bit. I just got off the phone with Dr. Courtier. The judge has accepted his psychiatric evaluation and all of his recommendations for your treatment. Since you've already agreed to let Dr. Courtier treat you, that's all you'll have to do to wipe the slate clean. Between the psychiatrist and Layton Blount, everything has been all worked out."

Chandler was beside himself with joy. He couldn't have been happier with his brother, who had stood by him through every single detail of the legal and mental-health issues. But it was Laylah who'd found him. Chandler wanted them all to celebrate.

"Get Laylah on the phone, man, and see if she'll join us for dinner tonight. I'm ready to celebrate somewhere in the city. If it wasn't for Laylah, I'd still be in jail."

Chancellor punched his right fist into the open palm of his left hand. "That can't happen, man, for lots of reasons."

"All I need to hear is one reason." Chandler sensed that something was wrong.

"We're no longer together. We won't be getting married."

Chandler looked as if he'd been hit hard in the midsection. "Sorry, but now I need more information. For starters, why is your engagement off?"

244   *Indiscriminate Attraction*

Chancellor took a seat and then launched right into what had occurred between Laylah and him. He didn't know anything, other than losing his brother and grandparents, could be so painful. Leaving Laylah the way he had was killing him slowly but definitely not softly. He could see that Chandler was also hurt. "I trusted her, man, with all my heart and soul. I just knew she was the one, the only one for me. I guess I was wrong."

"What you are is a damn fool, especially if you believe any of what you've just told me. Laylah would never do anything like that. I thought you knew her, man. You obviously don't know her at all."

"And you do?"

"I believe so. She's one of the most compassionate, courageous and kindest women I've ever met. When faced with something emotional, you have the tendency to rapidly jump to the wrong conclusions. I have to believe this case is no different. Why would she do this to the man she loves? What's her motivation?"

Chancellor scratched the center of his head. "She's a reporter, Chandler. Those people will sell their souls to the devil just to get a good story."

"What she strikes me as is a responsible journalist. How can you say you love her in one breath and mistrust who she is in the next? I think you're wrong about her. Dead wrong. Laylah's the best thing that ever happened to you. I think you need to go see her and make it right. Grovel. On your knees if you have to. Just win back her heart. Laylah truly loves you. Otherwise…" Chandler purposely didn't close out his sentence. He was positive Chancellor could finish his remarks for him.

Otherwise, I'd go after her beautiful heart all for myself—and I'd never let go.

Chancellor looked back and forth between Chandler and the telephone.

"Don't even think about doing something so important over the phone." Chandler stared hard at Chancellor, who looked terribly confused. "You haven't left yet?"

Chancellor got up from his seat and rushed around the table to hug his twin. He was the oldest, but Chandler was by far the wisest. It didn't surprise him that his brother had fallen for Laylah, too. Their taste in women had always been similar, but neither brother had ever gone after a woman who held the romantic interest of the other.

Chancellor somehow feared it just might've been different in this instance.

Chancellor's eyes filled with tears as he listened to a black male recite his poem. While he'd been getting dressed to go see Laylah, he'd remembered it was Friday night open mic. Sure that Chandler would enjoy the poetry readings, he'd invited him along.

As Laylah's name was called out as the next reader, Chancellor sucked in a deep breath. If he'd lost her, he didn't know how he'd ever face tomorrow. He had let his rage control him instead of controlling the situation by simply asking who'd written the story. Instead, he'd gone to her home, with both barrels blazing—pointed right at her head. He believed with certainty she loved him enough to forgive him. He also knew he didn't deserve it. If he could win back her heart, he'd gladly offer her a lifetime of groveling.

Chancellor had a hard time believing Lavonne was in the same room. He figured Laylah had invited her since she was seated with her co-workers. He had planned to see his mother eventually. Though he hadn't intended to meet with her so soon, he'd make his and Chandler's presence known. A meeting between them was inevitable.

Upon Laylah spotting a few of her colleagues, and Lavonne,

whom she'd invited to Bella's, she flashed her usual bright smile. "My poem is entitled 'I Remember.'

I remember when those strong, toasted-brown arms held my security tight, emanating their strength into my very being. Like bands of steel, they enveloped me in the prison of your fiery passion, a passion I had hoped would carry a life sentence.

I remember when the joy of our laughter transcended time as it drifted into uncharted space. It was then that we could feel one another's smallest of thoughts and touch the quaking emotions of our trembling hearts.

I remember the day we crashed into the end of the rainbow. Do you? I relive it often, soulfully. The dazzling kaleidoscope of colors captivated us. The gleam from the pot of gold outshone the brilliance of the sun, yet it couldn't touch the haloed feeling that entombed us. The universe was our very own playground. The moon and the stars were ours to command.

I remember how the exotic dew from your sun-kissed lips quenched the thirst of my burning, sexually overextended body. The intoxicating sweat from your granite physique kept me drunk with desire, turning my weightless mind over to the gentle command of your sweetly scented whispers.

I remember that even in the darkness of the bedroom we saw light, as it cast the shadows of our love onto the pastel-painted walls. The candle that flickered in the blackness was hardly a match for the illumination of truth we brought to one another's souls. Even the sun paled in comparison.

I remember when our hearts danced wildly to the rhythm of love.

I remember when we were one—spiritually, physically, emotionally.

I remember that it's night again. It's cold. Warmth is playing hide-and-seek, yet I'm no longer a participant in the game. The rainbow has disappeared, stripping my heart and soul of its dazzling color. The laughter that used to effervesce inside of me is not strong enough to reach the top of my throat, let alone transcend time and space. The rings of Saturn have been flushed from my eyes by the scalding acid rain of my tears. Those same tears scorch my cheeks as they uncontrollably gush forth.

I remember that we are now worlds apart, yet I don't understand why. I wouldn't understand even if you could explain it to me, though I doubt you can.

You are not here.

All alone, I am elsewhere.

Yet so vividly I remember.

Do you remember?

I remember!"

The applause was deafening as Laylah attempted to leave the stage. Goose bumps ran up and down her arms as tears fled from her eyes. She tried to move, but her feet seemed rooted to the spot. Then she saw him, the man she'd always remember, the one she'd never forget, the man she had spoken of in her poem, the man she'd love forever.

As Chancellor's tearful eyes locked in on her beautiful face, he wished he could kiss her hurt away, especially since he was no doubt responsible for it. He would wipe her tears away, now and forever. If only she'd forgive him and take him back...

Chancellor stepped up to the microphone. "I remember. I remember how much we love each other. I remember that there's no other woman in the world for me. I remember asking you to marry me. Although I vividly remember your answer to that question, I'd love for everyone present to hear it. Will you please let me spend the rest of my life apologizing to you for being such a fool earlier? I am here. You are no longer elsewhere. Do you remember? I remember. Will you still marry me, Laylah?"

Laylah ran over to Chancellor and threw her arms around his neck. "We have the rest of our lives to get it right. When we perfect it, I want to be right there by your side. Yes, Chancellor, I'll marry you!"

The happy couple sealed their engagement with a passionate kiss.

Deafening applause broke out again when Chandler joined his brother and future sister-in-law onstage, the three of them coming together for a group hug. When the ladies realized there was a duplicate of the groom-to-be, they went absolutely wild.

As folks continued to shout out their congratulations and wishes for happily ever after, Lavonne Kingston couldn't have been happier for both her sons. Laylah would be a wonderful wife and a great daughter-in-law. Perhaps the twins would give Lavonne the opportunity to one day become a great mother and mother-in-law, her heart's desire.

Chancellor, Laylah and Chandler joined her co-workers and Lavonne at their table, where a toast was quickly proposed to the happy, spirit-filled couple.

Chancellor touched his glass to Laylah's. "You are my greatest inspiration. I promise to love and cherish you. Forever and ever. I love you, Laylah Versailles."

Laylah smiled sweetly. "You will forever hold the keys to my heart, Chancellor Kingston. I have found in you all of my heart's desires. I love you, too."

Book #1 in

THE THREE MRS. FOSTERS

THIS TIME FOR GOOD

FAVORITE AUTHOR

CARMEN GREEN

About to lose her family business because of her late husband's polygamy, Alexandria accepts Hunter's help. But she's not letting any man run her life— not even one who sets her senses aflame.

"Ms. Green sweeps the reader away on the lush carpet of reality-grounded romantic fantasy."
—*Romantic Times BOOKreviews* on *Commitments*

Coming the first week of May wherever books are sold.

KIMANI ROMANCE™

www.kimanipress.com   KPCG0650508

her kind of *Man*

Favorite author

PAMELA YAYE

As a gawky teen, Makayla Stevens yearned for
Kenyon Blake. Now he's the uncle of one of her students,
and wants to get better acquainted with Makayla.
The reality is even hotter than her teenage fantasies.
But their involvement could damage her career…
and her peace of mind.

"Other People's Business…is a fun and lighthearted story…
an entertaining novel."
—*Romantic Times BOOKreviews* on
Pamela Yaye's debut novel

*Coming the first week of May
wherever books are sold.*

KIMANI™
ROMANCE

www.kimanipress.com

KPPY0670508

"Byrd proves once again that she's
a wonderful storyteller."
—*Romantic Times BOOKreviews*
on *The Beautiful Ones*

ACCLAIMED AUTHOR

ADRIANNE
byrd

controversy

Michael Adams is no murderer—even if she did
joke about killing her ex-husband after their nasty
divorce. Now she has to prove to investigating
detective Kyson Dekker that she's innocent.
Of course, it doesn't help that he's so distractingly
gorgeous that Michael can't think straight....

*Coming the first week of May
wherever books are sold.*

ARABESQUE®

www.kimanipress.com

KPAB1000508

*Overcoming the past to enjoy
the present can be difficult...*

YOLONDA TONETTE SANDERS

Secrets of a
Sinner

After years of doing whatever was necessary to survive,
Natalie Coleman finally feels her life is getting back on
track. Returning to the home she ran from years ago, she
confronts the painful events of her past. As old wounds
heal, Natalie realizes God has led her home to show her
that every sinner can be saved, every life redeemed.

"Need a little good news in your novels? Look no further."
—*Essence* on *Soul Matters*

Coming the first week of May wherever books are sold.

KPYTS1320508